At Frances's insistence there were to be no black ties. The service would be a celebration of Paul's life. A successful, happy, astonishingly trouble-free half century that had culminated in the most wonderful – not to say timely – party just a couple of weeks before his death. Thanks to that there were even two cases of champagne to get the wake off to a good start. Afterwards, they could move onto the Volnay he had taken such pleasure in choosing during their holiday in France earlier that summer. Paul would approve wholeheartedly. He always liked a good party.

Also by Amanda Brookfield

Alice Alone
A Cast of Smiles
Walls of Glass
A Summer Affair
The Godmother
Marriage Games
Single Lives

Amanda Brookfield gained a degree from Oxford before working at an advertising agency for several years. She wrote her first novel while living in Buenos Aires with her diplomat husband, and her second while in Washington, D.C. She has two young sons and now lives in London and divides her time between writing fiction and looking after her family.

The Lover

Amanda Brookfield

FLAME
Hodder & Stoughton

First published in Great Britain in 2000 by Hodder and Stoughton
First published in paperback in 2000 by Hodder and Stoughton
A division of Hodder Headline

A Flame Paperback

10 9 8 7 6 5 4 3

A CIP catalogue record for this title is available from the British
Library.

ISBN 0 340 71268 6

Printed and bound in Great Britain by
Clays Ltd, St Ives plc.

Hodder and Stoughton
A division of Hodder Headline
338 Euston Road
London NW1 3BH

For Brian and Joan

Chapter One

At Frances's insistence there were to be no black ties. The service would be a celebration of Paul's life. A successful, happy, astonishingly trouble-free half-century that had culminated in the most wonderful – not to say timely – party just a couple of weeks before his death. Thanks to that there were even two cases of champagne to get the wake off to a good start. Afterwards, they could move on to the Volnay he had taken such pleasure in choosing during their holiday in France earlier that summer. Paul would approve wholeheartedly. He always liked a good party.

The more Frances said such things, the easier it became. As well as being true, such platitudes acted as crutches to help her through each day and deterred people from asking how she felt. No amount of kindness on the part of the enquirer could make up for the fact that Frances had no coherent view on her feelings, let alone any concept of how to articulate them. To die of a heart attack on a tennis court was not an end anyone could have predicted, least of all for a man with a natural appetite for moderation, a man for whom the term close shave applied solely to the activity of his razor. In terms of recent health scares, Frances could recollect nothing beyond a bad cough that had clung on into the spring and an infected mosquito bite which had required a course of mild antibiotics. Being so suddenly deprived of him felt like waking up and finding a limb had been removed in the night. There was the shock of it, the feeling that he was still there, the pain of imagining he was.

While friends and family seemed to derive some measure of consolation from the fact that Paul had died while indulging in one of his favourite pastimes, it was an aspect of the situation which gave Frances herself little comfort. A part of her could not help thinking that there was something undignified, comical even, about dying in pursuit of a forehand. Though unable yet to say such things out loud, she could feel them pressing at the edges of her grief, confusing it. Just as her indifference to Paul's departure for the club that Sunday morning confused her, making her long to be able to lay claim to an inkling of a presentiment. The sheer mundanity of their behaviour during what turned out to be the last hours of their marriage made her almost ashamed. They had exchanged a kiss on the doorstep, but perfunctorily, without thought or tenderness. She couldn't even remember their exact last exchange of words. It was not only sad, but inadequate. It made her wish that humans could write the script for their own endings, so that they could be approached with grace and preparation, like wedding anniversaries and christenings.

Which was precisely why people had funerals, Frances reflected grimly, clenching her jaw as Felix stepped up behind the lectern, his fine, pale features flexed with the effort of managing his own emotions. To pay a public tribute to his father had been entirely his idea, his way, Frances supposed, of putting the seal of peace on what, recently anyway, had not always been the most harmonious of relationships. Daisy, more weepy than Frances herself, had been half appalled and half admiring of her younger brother's determination in the matter.

'I won't be able to talk to anyone, let alone proclaim anything moving or clever from the pulpit. I'm dreading it, seeing everybody, knowing that they're staring at you, feeling sorry for you, it's unspeakable.'

'It won't be so bad,' Frances murmured, stroking her daughter's cropped mop of bleached hair, 'people will be there to offer support, to show how much they liked and respected your father—'

'And to see how much you cry, and whether you're coping or cracking up. I know because I'm like that too – curious about other people's misery – we all are.' She seized a fresh tissue from the box which had taken up permanent residence on the kitchen table and left the room.

'Leave her,' growled Felix, seeing his mother push back her chair.

Frances had sunk back into her seat with a sigh. As with the glib responses she had been spouting for friends, some part of her was aware that she was merely going through the motions of offering comfort to her children. The truth was she felt too numb to offer anything. It took all her strength to walk through the course of each day, to open her eyes at dawn and maintain the pretence of being conscious and sane until an hour respectable enough to swallow one of the Valium tablets prescribed to her by Dr Leigham.

While Felix addressed the congregation, Frances clutched Daisy's bony hand, inwardly longing for some of the protective numbing gauze that helped her drift off to sleep each night. Although with his head of sandy fair hair and delicate features he had always looked much more like her, his voice was uncannily like his father's. Even the way his eyes flicked nervously between his script and the congregation reminded her of Paul, cautious but fundamentally confident, modest but ultimately sure of his place in the world. Although barely eighteen, Felix was just a couple of weeks from taking up a place at university. In many ways he already seemed much more mature than his twenty-year-old sister, who had dropped out of art college the year before in order to move to Paris with an art dealer boyfriend called Claude, to whom the family had barely been introduced. Frances swallowed hard in a vain attempt to dislodge a new lump blocking the back of her throat. Worrying about Daisy had been very much a shared burden, jointly taken up during the year their carefree, freckled twelve-year-old metamorphosed into a creature filled with enough self-revulsion to want to starve herself into

9

nonexistence. Without Paul she wasn't sure they would all have weathered the crisis as they did. He was always better at remaining calm, the one who stepped back and was rational, the weight of common sense that kept her rooted to the ground.

The image of Felix blurred. Frances's cheekbones and jaw were beginning to ache with the effort of not crying, of keeping her mouth still and closed. Inside she could feel a howling, a swelling of private sound pushing to get out. She tried to focus on the coffin, but could think only how small it looked, how absurd it was that Paul's impressive six-foot physique could fit inside. If Daisy's hand had not remained clenched round hers she would have slid to the edge of the pew and raced out of the church, and run till her heart burst. A celebration of life, indeed. Who had she been trying to fool?

Outside in the fresh September air, the urge to howl receded. As the coffin was lowered into the plot, an orderly rectangle dug into the large, well-groomed graveyard backing on to St Martin's church, Frances felt brave enough to glance along the semicircle of solemn faces on either side of her. Paul's younger brother, Thomas, was standing ashen-faced, the palms of both hands resting on the shoulders of his youngest son. The child looked as mournful as his father, but self-consciously so, as if determined to prove equal to the adult emotional demands of the occasion. Next to them, Thomas's wife, her eyes masked by stylish black sunglasses, fiddled nervously with a crumpled handkerchief. In the row behind was Frances's own sister Carol, who had kindly flown over from New York. In high black heels she towered above the other women, the picture of pallid composure, her arm linked authoritatively through their mother's. It was only at such times that not being a close family mattered, Frances reflected, casting around for a face that offered more reassurance and lighting upon Alistair and Libby Taverner, clustered together at the back with their four teenaged children. Their two families had met and become friendly ten years before, during the first few months after the

Copelands' move to the country. While Alistair and Paul had enjoyed manly bonding over the delights of trout fishing and a potent local brew of real ale, Frances's and Libby's fondness for one another had blossomed out of the more practical challenges of motherhood and school runs. Since the Taverners' ramshackle farmhouse was only a couple of miles away, on the other side of Leybourne, friendships amongst the children had flourished for a time as well, until divergent interests and activities took them down separate paths.

Sensing she was being watched, Libby glanced up and offered Frances a tight smile of encouragement.

'Ashes to ashes and dust to dust . . .'

Even their hermit of a neighbour had turned up, Frances observed, touched in spite of herself at the sight of Joseph Brackman hovering awkwardly in the background, his sallow, unkempt features shrouded under the protective hood of his green anorak. When she looked again he was already dodging through the gravestones back to the main path.

'You're doing so well,' murmured Libby, putting her arm across Frances's shoulders for the walk back to the cars. 'Are you sure you want people to come to the house? I mean if you're not up to it I could easily—'

'No, of course they must. Daisy and I have been up since dawn making sandwiches. Gave us something to do,' she added with an attempt at a brave smile. 'And there's all that champagne from the party. Paul would have wanted us to make merry . . .' Her voice tailed off, defeated by the sense that at last even the platitudes were running out of steam.

'It's an amazing turnout,' said Libby gently. 'You should be very proud. And Paul would have been proud of you, the way you're getting through it, all three of you.'

Frances turned to check on the progress of Daisy and Felix who were walking arm in arm behind. At the sight of them, tucked so closely together, looking sombre and adult, she felt such a twist of protective love and terror that she almost groaned out loud.

A few mourners had taken the precaution of bringing brollies, but there was no need. Where grey skies during the previous few days had led to rainy afternoons, on this occasion the sun broke through just as most of the congregation were manoeuvring their cars off the muddy grass verge opposite the church gate. It was late August at its most alluring, filled with the lush green legacy of a long wet summer, yet already heavy with the impending arrival of autumn. It would be dry enough to use the garden, Frances realised with some relief, staring glassy-eyed out of the window as the long black car provided by the undertakers cruised round the narrow country lanes, its engine purring like a predatory beast.

With so many guests it was impossible not to be reminded of the party. They had used the garden then too, decked the branches of the apple trees with multi-coloured lights and positioned flame torches to mark the edges of the path and the perimeter fence separating the bottom of the garden from the path down to the river. The area of grass nearest the fence had been so boggy that Paul had placed several rows of wooden planks by way of a false floor, to minimise the amount of dirt being trailed through the house and to preclude the possibility of lost or ruined party shoes. The river was so full that for the first time that either of them could remember, it was lapping right up to the edge of the path itself, only a few yards from the garden gate. The cellar, in spite of the expensive water protective treatment injected into its walls a couple of years before, had flooded again, so badly that all Paul's precious wine stocks had had to be moved upstairs to the spare bedroom.

A live jazz band, housed in a small marquee along with several round dining tables, had been one of the many memorable touches to the evening. The players performed tirelessly, providing a subdued serenade through supper and then raising the pace and volume once the furniture had been pushed back for dancing. Paul, an eager performer whenever the moment called, had led Frances by the tips of her fingers to the centre of the boarded floor, where he began jiving round her, much as he had at their wedding party twenty-one years before, ducking and swaying to the clapping encouragement of onlooking guests. Frances, moving as always with more reserve, had clapped too, happy for her husband to take the spotlight, happy to see him happy. It was his night. His swan-song, as it turned out.

Aided considerably by the necessity of distributing food, Frances managed to circulate amongst the mourners, accepting compliments about the service and offers of help. 'Anything we can do, anything at all . . .'

But what? she wanted to ask. What could anyone possibly do? When the impulse to voice such retorts out loud grew dangerously strong, she dumped her triangular, wholemeal, egg-and-cress offerings on the hall table next to Carol's huge, still unwrapped bouquet of lilies, and fled upstairs to the sanctity of the spare room. She was sitting on the bed, winding the tassled hem of the counterpane round her fingers and sadly contemplating the case of vintage port which Paul had been saving for Daisy's twenty-first, when Libby appeared in the doorway holding a mug of tea.

'Drink this. I've put in a spoonful of sugar, for energy. You'll faint if you're not careful.'

Frances dabbed at her eyes with the counterpane and accepted the drink gratefully. 'Forty-three doesn't feel old enough to be a widow . . .'

'It isn't. It's hateful and unfair.'

'I always thought seven years was a bit of a gap – I mean, I did wonder whether it would come to matter at some stage, whether Paul might go ga-ga like his mother somewhere in the run-up to eighty, while I, a mere sprightly seventy-year-old, would end up devoting the last few years of our married life to wiping dribbles from his chin and helping him shuffle to the loo . . .' She broke off to let out a laugh which somehow transformed itself to a sob. 'I just never thought . . .'

Libby squeezed her arm. 'None of us did. We're all in shock.'

'I mean, just at the party, just two weeks ago, I thought – so many times – how well he looked, how young and energetic for his age. And it wasn't just me – loads of people said things about how fit he was, joking about it . . .'

'Drink your tea,' murmured Libby, hoping she did not sound as at a loss as she felt inside. Paul Copeland had indeed been a model fifty-year-old, an amiable country solicitor who enjoyed the pleasures of life without taking them to excess. Libby's own husband, Alistair, a forty-four-year-old self-employed architect, had for years been under far more daily stress than ever seemed to afflict the Copelands. Whereas Paul's small practice had seemed impervious to the vagaries of the economy, Alistair was still reeling from the most recent recession. Without Libby's own enterprise, a gift shop on the outskirts of Hexford with a maddeningly fluctuating profit margin, and Charlie and Beth's music scholarships, they would long since have floundered in deep financial distress. Arrested by this particular train of thought she found herself blurting, 'Are you all right for money? I mean, don't they freeze everything for a while, probate and so on . . .'

'They do, but I'm fine. Heaps of the bloody stuff. We'd just transferred some savings for a down payment on converting the garage. Which I've cancelled now of course . . . all Alistair's lovely drawings . . .' Frances broke off to take a swig of tea, scowling at the sweetness, but swallowing like a dutiful child. 'From what I can gather I'll get some kind of lump sum and also Paul's pension – and we'd already put aside the money for Felix to go to university . . .' She managed a wry smile. 'From the point of view of being well-looked after, I couldn't have asked for more.'

Seeing that she was on the verge of tears again and wanting to distract her, Libby leant across to study the two pencil sketches of Daisy and Felix which hung above the bed. 'I love these. They ought to be downstairs instead of skulking up here where no one ever gets to appreciate them.'

Frances shook her head, muttering. 'The children would be embarrassed to have their mother's etchings of their formative years on public display. The sight of them always makes me feel guilty for somehow never having the time to get out my pencils and start on . . .'

The sentence hung incomplete between the two women, ensnared in the harsh truth of Frances's new circumstances. The days of Paul appearing home four days out of five in the hope of a bowl of homemade soup for lunch were over. There was no longer anybody to cook for each evening, no shirts with fiendish double cuffs to iron. Soon, there would not even be Felix, who preferred to wear his clothes as crumpled as possible, but who nevertheless made considerable demands on the fridge and washing machine. Adjusting to his impending absence was something Frances had been dreading anyway. She would even miss the muffled thump of his CD player, the one apparently vital accoutrement to the business of revising for A levels which had driven his father – for whom silence had always been a prerequisite for mental exertion of any kind – into paroxysms of anger. Remembering the rows earlier in the year, Frances flinched and shut her eyes. Thinking of the bad times felt too disloyal. 'I suppose I better go back downstairs,' she said, not moving.

Libby crossed to the window and stared out with a sigh. 'I think it might be going to rain after all.'

Frances left the bed and went to stand beside her. For a moment both women studied the sombre-clad groups arranged on the lawn below. The plea for no black ties had been largely ignored. Daisy's white-blonde head stood out like a beacon, as did Felix's bright red tie. They were talking to guests, but still standing next to each other in a show of mutual support.

'The children are being wonderful,' said Frances, biting her lip.

'How long is Daisy staying?'

'The rest of the week, I think. Her plans, as ever, are hazy. She says she wants me to go and stay with her and Claude, but I don't think she means it.' Frances stared at the subsiding mountain of old grass clippings, concealed from general view between the garden shed and the end fence. Cutting the lawn had been one of Paul's favourite weekend chores. His birthday present that year had been an expensive four-wheel mower, the size of a small tractor. For the ageing gardener, Frances had teased, watching him open the small wrapped parcel that contained the ignition keys. He had used it once, just before the party, steering it with all the glee of a small boy, leaning out at the corners as if the garden were a Formula I circuit instead of a one acre rectangle with a few trees.

'If Daisy's asked you, you should go.'

'Maybe.'

'And when's Felix off?'

'He starts in two weeks.'

'At least it's Sussex and not Edinburgh. It's only an hour away . . .'

'An hour and three quarters.'

'Well that's nothing,' concluded Libby brightly, as if a forty-three-year-old mother could expect to commute to her son's student digs every other day of the week in search of distraction and entertainment. 'And that children's charity you're always helping,' she continued, a little desperately now, 'no doubt they'll be making their usual heavy demands, they're always frantic after the summer, aren't they?'

'Oh yes, always.' Frances drained the last of her tea. 'Help me get rid of them all will you? I've had enough.'

Chapter Two

The moment the guests had gone, Frances wished she could summon them all back. Surrounding herself with Paul's friends felt suddenly like the surest testimony to his worth, to the fact that he had existed at all. The last to leave were Libby and Alistair, who had stayed on with all four children to help clear up.

'Call whenever you want,' said Libby, winding down the car window. 'Day or night. Promise me you will.'

'I promise,' Frances lied, knowing from the glimpses of despair she had suffered already that communication of any kind felt impossible and pointless, let alone dawn phone calls to sleep-deprived friends.

Soon after the Taverners' mud-spattered Volvo had disappeared from sight, Felix announced his intention to go on a walk, warning that he might be quite a while and no one was to worry. Daisy, looking spectral, the smudges of her mascara having merged into the dark circles under her eyes, complained of a headache and the need to lie down.

For something to do, feeling abandoned and blank with sadness, Frances dragged herself round the garden, touring Paul's treasured flower beds. They were still bulging with colour, but she walked with unseeing eyes, absently bending down to retrieve the occasional escaped paper napkin and forgotten wine glass. The tedium and exhaustion of grief were unexpected and like nothing she had ever known. When her father died ten years before, there had been as much relief as sadness. Watching the only member of her family to whom she had ever felt close succumb to the pain and indignities of prostate cancer had made her long for the end. While her mother, never one for indulging in emotions at the best of time, had responded to bereavement by joining another book club, redecorating the house and embarking on the first of many subsequent package holidays with widowed friends.

At the thought of her mother, Frances sighed. They had spoken a little after the funeral, but the truth was she had been thankful that Carol had been there to deflect most of the attention. They were much more alike, the pair of them, both filled with a frenetic energy which Frances neither shared nor trusted, suspecting its origins to lie with an urge to dodge life rather than look it squarely in the eye.

At the garden gate she stopped and stared down towards the River Ley, shrunk now to its original proportions, glinting silver through the trees in a last burst of afternoon sun. The land separating the end of their garden from the river bank was part of a public bridlepath. Next to it lay several acres of farmland which were usually given over to daffodils or rape seed, providing a vivid yellow backdrop to the sandstone of the house and the kaleidoscopic beauty of the garden. To have such an uncluttered view of the Kent countryside was a privilege, Frances knew, and one that had been a prime factor in their decision to purchase the house ten years before. With the children then eight and eleven it had also been an ideal time to move to the country, away from the prison of small gardens and schools that required negotiation with the South Circular. Paul had also been eager to move from the enormous, prestigious London practice in which he had mastered his trade into a more personal set-up where he would enjoy an easier ride up a shorter, less greasy pole. In fact, the only reservations about abandoning their three-bedroomed Edwardian house had come from Frances herself. Her parents lived in Chiswick and it was during the period that her father was very ill. While this provided an excuse for her reluctance, Frances had been aware that it in fact went much deeper. Weekend sorties to friends already ensconced in various rural cul-de-sacs within the commuter belt of the Home Counties had never convinced her that it was a lifestyle with which she would feel any natural affinity.

Contentment had come with time and a little determination. Early resolutions to keep a foothold in London, to pop up by train for social and cultural excursions, were soon put to one side; missing Clapham Common and the Barbican proving unhelpful emotions for a woman whose children loved screaming round muddy fields and whose husband fished and liked to cycle to the local tennis club.

Frances was wrested from her reverie by an icy sensation in her toes. She looked down to see her smart black shoes almost submerged in mud. She stood quite still, studying the soggy ground, aware that she was slowly, imperceptibly sinking into it. For a mad moment she found herself embracing the sensation, drawn to the notion that the world would obligingly swallow someone who had had enough of it; that she might sink without trace and avoid the black tunnel of readjustment stretching ahead.

A glimpse of Joseph Brackman's green anorak through the trees stirred her to her senses. Terrified at the prospect of having to make conversation, she quickly stepped out of sight, the earth squelching its reluctance to release her feet. Back inside the house, she found Daisy sitting at the kitchen table in front of a glass of wine, both hands busy with her tobacco pouch.

'Headache better?' Frances filled the kettle, more for something to do than because she felt like a drink.

'A bit.' Daisy pulled out a square of thin white paper and began deftly filling it with shreds of tobacco. There were faint yellow nicotine stains towards the ends of the index and third fingers of her right hand which Frances did not remember seeing before. She watched as Daisy sucked deeply on her creation, flattening one end of the paper between her lips. 'By the way, I've been meaning to tell you, I've got a job.'

'A job? But that's marvellous – you should have said something earlier.'

Daisy picked a fleck of tobacco off her lower lip. 'It's hardly been the right time. And it's only helping out in a gallery three days a week. It's a nice gallery though – a good one – lots of modern stuff. Claude says it's the perfect place for meeting people, for making contacts for my own work, setting up exhibitions and so on.'

Although Frances did her best both to sound and appear enthusiastic, she was hampered by her own state of mind and the fact that her daughter's future as an artist was something about which Daisy herself always sounded half convinced. Her decision the year before to leave college early had left both parents exasperated, particularly Paul. It had taken all Daisy's daddy's girl charm to win him round, to persuade him that Claude would be a far more effective nurturer and marketer of her talent than a second-rate art college. The move to Paris would prove the launch pad of her career, she had assured them excitedly, the place where everything would come together. Regarding the gaunt, pallid face of her daughter now across the table, her cheeks hollow with the effort of sucking the last thread of smoke from her cigarette, Frances was suddenly glad that Paul would be spared the disappointment of seeing Daisy's grand plans come to nothing. With both children she had always been the better compromiser, the one who could settle for less and not mind. 'Working in a gallery will be good language practice too,' she murmured, stirring her tea but feeling little inclination to drink it.

'And it'll mean I can help out with the rent and so on,' Daisy pressed on, 'get me away from being completely dependent on poor Claude. Not that he ever complains. He's incredibly generous.' She stubbed out her cigarette. 'I did tell you, didn't I, how very much he wanted to be here today? A last minute work thing blew up – an important deal that's going pear-shaped. He's desperately sorry about Dad and has been very sweet to me, very understanding . . .'

'I'm so glad.' Frances tipped her untouched mug of tea down the sink and began returning dry wine glasses to the cardboard box of thirty-six that they had hired from the off licence. She moved slowly, burdened by the sense that everything she said, every move she made, was being performed for the sake of it, that nothing derived from a genuine impulse towards action. Even breathing felt like a conscious act. It struck her then that grief, rather than being an emotion, was in fact an absence of the ability to feel, an absence of interest in the world or the self. Hard for anyone, let alone a woman who had never been particularly interested in herself anyway.

Felix walked fast, his shoulders hunched, his head bent so that he had nothing to contemplate except the trail of puddles at his feet. After only ten minutes or so he began to feel a blister forming on his little toe. The boots were his father's, not only two sizes too big but also damp from having been left forgotten next to the boot-scraper outside the back door. Wearing them felt like necessary pain. The same necessary pain that had driven him to stand up in front of scores of people in church and to speak, through gritted teeth, about things he felt too confused to feel. Respect, admiration, gratitude. Things any normal eighteen-year-old son should want to say about a parent.

Felix stopped at the humpback bridge over the river and checked his watch. After glancing round to make sure he was alone, he hopped over the lowest part of the bridge wall and scrambled down the steep incline towards the river. The water was moving so fast and furiously that for a moment he was almost afraid. Then, as his eyes accustomed themselves to the dim light under the bridge, he saw that the dry bank remained, less of it than usual, but still a good couple of yards in width.

The blanket was where he had left it, folded into a neat square and tucked into a gap between two loose bricks. He shook it out, picking off bits of moss and leaf still attached from the last time. The ceilinged arch of stone was so low that when upright he had to keep his shoulders stooped so as not to bang his head. It was a relief to get the thing spread on the ground so that he could sit down and stretch his back and legs. He pulled a flattened pack of cigarettes from the back pocket of his trousers, noticing as he did so that a slight drizzle had started up outside. It was falling like a curtain of grey mist, screening nearly all the light from outside in a way that made him feel both alone and yet wonderfully protected.

Ten minutes later, when Felix had started playing guessing games with the hands of his watch, there was a faint rustle overhead followed by the sound of someone slithering down the bank.

'Sal, I was getting worried.'

'So was I.' She stooped under the arch and dropped to her knees on the rug beside him. 'Dad said Sheba didn't need to be taken out and what about giving poor Mum a hand with clearing up and making supper and what did I want a walk for when it was about to rain anyway. Mum keeps bursting into tears and shoving Dad off when he tries to get near. Pete plugged himself back into his computer like it was any other weekend and Charlie shut himself and his oboe in his bedroom. The only good thing was Beth, who's been playing the angel ever since your dad died and who said of course I might want to go on a walk at a time like this and she'd help Mum with supper. Then she hugs Dad to shut him up, Sheba's allowed to stay in her basket and suddenly I'm free.'

Felix stalled this run-down on events in the Taverner family by putting both arms round Sally's waist and pressing his tongue between her lips. They embraced for several minutes, displaying a fervour which two months of expression had done nothing to diminish.

'You were brilliant this afternoon, brilliant.' Sally pulled back to study his face, running her nail-bitten fingers round the edge of his hairline. 'So brave and strong. When inside you must have felt like shit.'

Felix swallowed. 'It helped having you there, knowing you were on my side, that you understood.' They kissed again, but less frantically, subsiding sideways until they were stretched full length on the rug.

'Can we do it?' she murmured, pushing one of her skinny legs between his and moving her lips down to his neck. 'I mean, I'll understand if you don't want to . . .'

'You've got to be kidding,' he growled, pulling up her shirt and running his hands over the smooth flat of her belly. 'Like I could ever not want to do it with you.' Half tending to these new attentions, Sally reached out into a lower part of the wall and extracted a packet of prophylactics. 'Only two left,' she whispered in a giggle, 'we'll have to stock up on supplies.' She turned onto her back, closing her eyes. Felix slid her shirt off over her head and began running his tongue from her tummy button up between the still girlish, wide flat space between her breasts. Sally opened her eyes and kissed the sandy waves of hair tickling her chin. Taking hold of his ears, she then pulled hard, forcing his face to come level with hers. Felix gave a playful yelp of pain.

'Shh,' she scolded, laughing confidently, feeling more like twenty-five than fifteen, knowing that no one could hear them, with the drum of rain on the ground and the rush of water at their side.

Chapter Three

'I just thought you might want to come too. There's loads of space. If you change your mind at the last minute, it's no problem. We'll be going anyway. Apart from Pete who's off back to Bristol for the term and Beth who's going to stay the weekend with a friend. So it will just be Alistair, me and the two younger ones . . .' Seeing her husband trying to catch her eye, Libby waved him away furiously and turned her back. 'I just thought it might be nice for you to have a break, get away for a couple of days. The forecast isn't brilliant, but still it's in a lovely spot, right near some cliffs and a bit of rocky beach. Good for walking . . .' Alistair crossed the kitchen and bent his face round and under his wife's so that she could no longer ignore him. 'Leave her alone,' he mouthed.

Libby made a face and continued talking. She had only seen Frances once all week, on calling round with a mushroom quiche and some fruit a couple of days after the funeral. She had looked thin and grey-faced, literally drained of energy. Even her lovely long fair hair had somehow lost its brilliance, hanging in flat untidy clumps over her back and shoulders. Daisy had already returned to Paris and Felix was in Leybourne buying a few last minute things for the start of his first term. She was driving him to Sussex the following morning, Frances had explained, humbly accepting the quiche and offering Libby a cup of coffee. She made one herself, but barely touched it, picking at the cuticles on her nails instead. The next day Libby had telephoned to ask how Felix had settled in, only to find herself listening to Paul's voice on the answering machine. It gave her such a start that she burst into tears. If it were bad for her, stumbling across such poignant reminders, what must it be like for Frances, she had wondered, living with them surrounding her all the time?

Almost more depressing was that since Paul's death nothing had felt right in her own household either. While the children seemed bent upon discovering new ways of being hateful and awkward, Alistair was ploughing on with life as if no calamity had occurred at all. No one meeting him in the daily round would have had any inkling that one of their closest friends had dropped dead on a tennis court. In contrast, Libby found herself telling everybody: postmen, sales assistants, shop customers and anyone else prepared to listen. Talking about the tragedy was the only way she had discovered of making herself feel any better. As well as allowing her to elicit sympathy on Frances's behalf, scrutinising the facts from every angle somehow made them seem more acceptable. The more she tried to involve her husband in this process however, the more determined he appeared to withdraw, to act as if nothing had happened, as if there were nothing to talk about. To such an extent that Libby had even caught herself wondering whether in her own case the premature death of a spouse would be such a bad thing after all. To be capable of such meanness bothered her; Alistair had been the one and only love of her life, and beneath the daily tussle of surviving four children and a large mortgage, she was sure she still adored him very deeply. Losing touch with the adoration happened from time to time, but not usually when she felt so emotionally battered and in need of all the spousal support she could get.

The call to Frances inviting her to spend the weekend at a friend's cottage on the Isle of Wight had followed on from a largely unsatisfactory attempt to air some of these complicated

grievances. As well as being obviously irritated at the suggestion that his own version of mourning was not demonstrative
enough for his wife's more extravagant tastes, Alistair had
voiced the upsetting opinion that Libby's eagerness to be
supportive was dangerously close to pestering.

'Of course she won't want to come away for a jolly
weekend with us.'

'It needn't be jolly.'

'Oh, well in that case why are we bothering to go at all?'

'You know what I mean.'

'No, I'm not sure I do. You seem to think that Frances being
miserable under our scrutiny is better than allowing her to be
miserable on her own. Which is probably what she wants.'

'I don't think she knows what she wants.'

'I'm sure you're right and it's up to us to give her the space
to find out.'

'I'm going to call anyway, just to ask, just to show we
care . . .'

'She knows we care,' muttered Alistair, ramming dirty
dinner plates into the dishwasher and angrily sweeping aside
condiments and unused cutlery in order to create a space large
enough to accommodate a set of plans on a loft conversion in
Hythe.

'Thank you, Libby,' said Frances firmly, 'but it feels too
soon . . . to go anywhere. It's very sweet of you to ask.'

'But are you all right?' pressed Libby, feeling helpless and
wanting reassurance for her own sake. Across the room,
Alistair rolled his eyes at the ceiling. His wife turned back to
the sink and pointedly stuck a finger in her ear. 'I mean, of
course you're not all right, but are you . . . coping?'

Frances stared out of the sitting-room window. Three geese
were streaking across the sky. Black arrows on a white
board. Sharp, fast and focused. Watching them, she felt a
twist of envy at the obvious clarity of their destination, their
purposefulness. 'Coping . . . ? Yes, of course, keeping busy,
you know . . .' She looked round the sitting room. Old papers

lay strewn across the sofa, a blue sock of Felix's was poking out from under an armchair. Her tea mug from that morning was still sitting on the coffee table, gathering a fine head of white scum. Things she would normally have done without thinking she no longer wanted to do. The hours, the days, her life, had lost their structure. The lethargy afflicting her was so crushing that sometimes she had to remind herself to blink.

Libby put down the phone feeling unreassured but helpless. That Frances had reacted according to her husband's predictions did little to soften her feelings towards him.

'It'll take time,' he said quietly, adding after a moment's pause, 'especially for a woman like Frances.'

'What's that supposed to mean? "A woman like Frances".' Libby picked a bruised apple out of the fruit bowl and angrily plucked out the stalk.

Alistair sighed, sensing conflict, but too sure of the veracity of his opinions to be deterred from expressing them. 'A woman who so clearly needs a man, whose entire life has been dictated by nothing but the humdrum demands of her family.'

'She's always had other interests too, you know, like her drawing and helping out with those Feed The Children people . . .'

Alistair raised one eyebrow and made a pencil note of something in the top, right-hand corner of the piece of paper in front of him. His silence communicated what Libby knew but out of some perverse sense of loyalty was unwilling to acknowledge, that while never in all their years of acquaintance appearing idle or inactive, Frances Copeland had never actually done very much beyond the modest demands of her small family.

'I've only ever worked because we need the money.'

'No you haven't.' Alistair put down his pencil. 'You work because your instincts for survival as an individual have always driven you to seek fulfilment outside the blissful womb of domesticity which regularly threatens to throttle us. You've perfected your juggling act because it gives you satisfaction to do so, because you are the kind of woman who can happily exist within the stimuli of her own motivations, the kind of woman who, should she find herself bereaved, would have little trouble in picking up the pieces and carrying on. You don't need me, Libby. It's one of the things I find most attractive about you.'

Libby opened her mouth to speak but closed it round the apple instead, disarmed and exasperated.

'Frances needs a man,' he continued, 'someone not only to look after, but also to define her. Her best hope is to meet someone else and begin again. Which isn't to say that I don't feel enormous sympathy for her plight. I do.' He picked up his pencil and tested the sharpness of the lead with his fingertip. 'She is the very worst kind of person this could have happened to. And in case you have any doubt on the matter, I miss Paul enormously. He was a good man, a good friend.'

Having bitten into the bruise by mistake, Libby chewed and swallowed slowly. She hated her husband's calmness, his self-control, but admired him for it too. She was also secretly pleased at his image of her as so independent and capable. He had never said anything quite like that before, not in so many words. 'So Frances needs a new man,' she murmured, going to sit opposite him at the table and placing both elbows on top of his papers so he had to look at her.

'Actually, an old-fashioned one would suit her best,' Alistair replied, smiling to show that he detected the softening in her attitude and welcomed it. 'And of course, lots of support from her friends too. I know you want to help her, love.'

Libby reached forward and gently eased his glasses off his face. 'We could both do with an early night . . . it's been a hard week.'

'Hm . . .' He kissed the tip of her nose. 'And where are our brood exactly?'

Libby raised four fingers. 'Away, out, doing homework and

watching TV.' She folded his glasses and slipped them into their case, whispering, 'Even we independent types have need of our menfolk sometimes.' Taking hold of his tie she pulled him towards her side of the table. They kissed, with the slow unhurried pleasure of mutual familiarity. Later on in bed they were rougher and less tender. Perhaps because it was several weeks since they had last found the energy for sex. Perhaps because of some dim connection to the events of the previous week, the need to reassert themselves against the threat of their own mortality.

Frances meanwhile continued to sit staring at the telephone, puzzling over her longing for interruption from the outside world and the repellence she felt the moment any arrived. Even the television, the most obvious relief for her new solitude, seemed too abrasive a companion for the fragile emptiness of her mind. Not because murders and hospital dramas were in any way upsetting, but because their glib portrayals of emotional states and the subsequent menus of consequences seemed false, flat and irrelevant. As the days dragged by, it felt increasingly to Frances as if in real life there were no consequences, that she could continue to sit on the sofa forever, with nothing but dull, pointless willpower to trigger the necessity of doing anything else. Her only, some-what surprising release, was sleep. The exhaustion of misery was a new discovery, lately even precluding the necessity of Dr Leigham's little white pills.

Leaving the dirty coffee mug and the remains of the sand-wich she had half eaten by way of supper, Frances dragged herself into a standing position and headed for the stairs. Since she had not moved from the house all day there was no point in checking locks and bolts. Re-reading letters of condolence, one load of washing – on the half-load button – these were her sole achievements of fifteen hours. The washing had not even made it onto the line, though she had spent some considerable time staring at the rotary dryer, spinning useless and empty in the brisk autumn breeze. The thought of her underwear and two shirts, pegged alone outside had been too much to bear. She had stuffed them into the tumble dryer instead, guilty at the extravagance of closing the door on so light a load.

Chapter Four

Three weeks later Frances awoke, as she always did, to a split second of heavenly vacancy before the memory of her new circumstances came flooding in, each time as terrible as the last. Now that it was late September, the bedroom felt unpleasantly chilly in the mornings, a problem which raising the temperature on the thermostat seemed to have gone no way towards solving. The radiators, unused since the beginning of the summer, were lukewarm and full of gurgles. She would have to phone British Gas. The thought even of something so mundane, filled her with unreasonable dread.

Struggling to an upright position, she took a sip of water and turned on her bedside light. Although it was only six o'clock, she felt wide awake, tense at the prospect of another day alone. Next to her alarm clock was a list she had written the night before, a pitiful token gesture at injecting some sense of order into the blankness inside her head.

Visit grave
See vicar
Call lawyer
Buy food

Picking up a pen lying beside her water glass, she added, *Call British Gas*, before putting the list down again. Though it was pointless and exhausting she then allowed herself to cry, reaching for one of Paul's hankies, which she had taken to stowing in her bedside drawer.

Since the funeral she had only visited the graveside once and derived little solace from the experience. The flowers and wreaths had looked wind-battered and sad. Replacing them with a small arrangement of roses from the garden, had generated not comfort but a sense of futility. Instead of feeling closer to Paul she had felt, if anything, more removed. There was more intimacy to be had at home, in the faint aroma of after-shave on his dressing gown, in the loop of his handwriting on a letter or the flyleaf of a book. Not being an adherent to the notion of the life hereafter, Frances accepted that even this sense of proximity would inevitably fade with time, that it did not evince anything beyond the physical remains of what had once been a life.

The unwelcome sense of obligation with regard to Reverend Aldridge arose from his having made an impromptu house-visit the week before. During the course of a cup of tea and a stale Hobnob he had emitted gentle utterings about the omniscience of God's love and the existence of bereavement support groups. 'Help is all around you,' he had said, pressing her hand between his palms and peering at her kindly from under the shelf of grey bushy eyebrows.

'Thank you,' Frances had murmured, unable to prevent herself wondering whether the eyebrows grew vertically of their own accord, or were steered that way by their owner out of some misguided sense of vanity.

'You are welcome any time at the vicarage, or indeed at St Martin's. Please call round whenever you want. The Lord's house is for all travellers, whatever their origins or destination.'

You mean even if they don't believe in him, and never go to church except for funerals and weddings Frances had wanted to say, but didn't because it would have seemed ungrateful and unkind. The necessity of considering other people's feelings was one of the more irksome and unexpected aspects of her stricken state. As with Libby telephoning each day and the grocer in Leybourne High Street recounting the minutiae of his wife's battle against thrombosis, Frances felt bound to accept the reverend's consolation in the spirit in which it was so clearly intended. Spurred by such impulses, wanting only to be released from the immediate stress of the moment, she had declared, 'I will call round, I most certainly will,' and then looked at her watch with a cry of exclamation, as if the position of the hands on the dial still meant something to her.

Calling the lawyers was merely another prong in this strategy of survival and deception, the aim being in this instance to promote an impression of understanding and control, when in reality she felt very little of either. While transplanting his career to the countryside, Paul had retained a London firm of solicitors to act on the family's behalf. The man who had contacted Frances, both by letter and once by phone, was called Hugo Gerard. In the not too distant future a meeting would be required he explained, his voice resonating with the clipped intimidating confidence of the English public school, so that Frances could sign various documents relating to the will and a few other technical matters. He had described what the matters were, but Frances had lost concentration half-way through, distracted both by a lack of familiarity with the vocabulary and a sudden pressing, almost hysterical sense of unreality.

Picking up her list again, she wrote *LIBBY* in capital letters across the bottom of the piece of paper and then blew her nose. Coping with the attention of her closest friend was proving almost hardest of all. Since the invitation to the Isle of Wight she had backed off a bit – only telephoning as opposed to suggesting actual meetings – but still with enough frequency to make Frances feel uncomfortable. It seemed incredible that in the once normal, now distant world of their previous lives, whole weeks had slipped by quite naturally without them talking or seeing each other. Now she felt as if Libby were watching her, scrutinising every inflexion for signs of rallying or recovery. Not being able to deliver even a faltering start to such a process only made Frances long all the more to be left alone. But it made her feel bad too, because of Libby trying so hard and getting nothing in return. Sighing, Frances drew a large question mark next to Libby's name, which, after a little more doodling became a flower, linking up via a grapevine of stems and leaves to all the other items on her sorry list, until the words themselves were barely legible.

In recent days she had even started shying away from running the gauntlet of Leybourne high street for her groceries. Instead, she had taken to scurrying around the soothingly vast and impersonal aisles of the new Tesco super-market, whose opening had caused such a furore amongst the Leybourne retailers the year before. Her wants were so meagre that after watching them rattle around in the bottom of a trolley, she had switched to a handbasket instead. Standing in line at the express checkout, she stared at the queues of mothers and wives packing mountains of weekly shopping with a sense of wonder that she herself had once led a life along similar lines. Sometimes she wanted to shout at their gloomy faces, to warn them to enjoy what they had, because it wasn't safe and wouldn't last.

Even hearing from Daisy and Felix, who called regularly, was something Frances found hard. Not because she did not want to talk to them, but because she guessed that the frequency of their calls related to concern for her rather than any genuine impulse to discuss matters arising from their own lives. The idea of becoming a gloomy millstone of a mother filled her with horror. Interesting futures beckoned for both her offspring and she was desperate that each should feel free to march towards them. So when Felix suggested popping home for the weekend she put him off. And when Daisy put forward dates for a trip across the Channel she said she would be busy seeing Felix.

After propping her list against her alarm clock, Frances decided to eat up some of the long morning by going to the graveyard on foot instead of by car. The bridlepath along the bottom of the garden led eventually into the grid of back lanes running into the old part of Leybourne, where St Martin's medieval profile dominated the skyline. It was the most attractive end of the town, full of thatched cottages and timbered almshouses, the ancient nucleus of a community which had long since spreadeagled itself in a contrastingly ungainly fashion for several miles further down the road. On the far side of town a plot had recently been assigned for another hundred council homes, together with a large roundabout destined to forge a link with the main road to Hexford and the coast. The Taverners, whose converted farmhouse was only a few hundred yards from the proposed site, had been amongst the many local protesters at these plans. But the council were going ahead anyway, armed with government housing quotas and talk of splintering families needing roofs over their heads.

Frances walked quickly, clutching her newspaper bundle of garden flowers to her chest. The weather was cloudy, and damp enough to make the wisps of hair escaping from her headscarf twist into little curls. Slowed by the weight of the mud clogging the soles of her boots, and the need to step onto the grass verge in order to escape the puddle spray of passing cars, it took a good forty minutes to complete her journey. At the bottom of the lane leading up to the church, the heavy clang of the church door caused her to look up. Reverend Aldridge was striding down towards the roadside gate, a pair of white trainers poking somewhat incongruously from under the black hem of his cassock. Acting on reflexes she had no time to analyse, Frances quickly side-stepped behind a broad-bellied chestnut tree. She pressed herself hard against the cold damp bark, praying either that she had not been seen or that the vicar would have the grace to ignore the eccentricity of an unhinged widow. Hearing the light tap of his footsteps recede, she relaxed and opened her eyes. Strewn around her feet were scores of spiky green conker cases, many of them split, revealing glimpses of the polished mahogany inside. She stood on one with the ball of her foot, pressing hard until the conker popped out, rolling away under a cluster of wet leaves.

A moment later she remembered that the vicar was on her list, that the best, the only, way of getting people to leave her alone in the long term was to make them believe she was all right. Pulling back her shoulders and taking a deep breath she hurriedly emerged from her hiding place, only to find the road empty and the church gate swinging, its rusty hinges squeaking faintly in the stillness of the morning.

The mound of earth still looked fresh. The roses from her previous visit had collapsed over the edge of the metal vase. The few petals that remained were flattened with rain and trailing in the earth. Crouching down, Frances began briskly plucking out the dead stems and inserting the fresher offerings from the folds of her newspaper. Petals scattered like torn scraps of tissue. She tried to concentrate on feeling close to Paul, but could not think beyond the stiffness in her knees and the fact of his once imposing body rotting just a couple of metres beneath her feet, his finger and toenails growing unchecked in the silky lining of the coffin. The thought triggered an image as vivid as any she had experienced, of Paul sitting up in bed trimming his nails with a pair of staple-like clippers and then noisily, irritatingly, buffing them into neat semicircles with a metal nail file, scattering specks of white dust across the sheets.

Frances rammed the rest of the flowers into the metal vase, overcome with weary despair that grief could be triggered by such an enduring cause for annoyance. Feeling the familiar onrush of yet more tears, she dropped her face into her hands.

'There's nothing to be done.'

Frances remained on her knees in the sodden ground, shaking her head and waving the owner of the voice away. Glimpsing green anorak out of the corner of her eye, she waved even harder.

'Death is a bastard,' remarked Joseph Brackman, before turning and walking away.

When she was sure he had gone, Frances blew her nose and wiped her eyes with the back of her hands. Before rejoining the road, she checked up and down it, tightening the knot of her headscarf nervously. Once she got back onto the bridlepath, she found herself squinting in the direction of the red-tiled roof of the Brackmans' cottage, poking out from amongst a clump of trees in the stretch of land beyond the river. It had once been a railway station and in the area surrounding it there still lay half buried sections of old line and rusting pieces of machinery. Local gossip had it that the house was as dilapidated as the track it had once served, that the council rented it out for a pittance to the penurious Brackmans in order to save themselves the bother of expense and renovation.

A couple of years after their move from London Frances discovered that Daisy and Felix had been sneaking over the footbridge that led towards the old railway in order to play spying games round the threadbare hedges marking the boundary of the Brackmans' garden. In the pocket of her daughter's dungarees she had found a notebook inscribed with the words, *Watching witches*, which contained a few disjointed jottings about the comings and goings of Mrs Brackman. She had scolded both children severely, trying to impress upon them the importance of respecting other lives, no matter how strange. While in her heart she sympathised with their fascination, nursing her own apprehensions about a man who elected to live with his mother until middle age, a man who wore open-toed sandals in winter and who kept his face permanently hidden in the lee of an anorak hood.

Having longed to get home, Frances found herself hesitating with the front-door key, dreading the emptiness awaiting her inside. As she pushed the door open her eye was caught by something in the milk-bottle rack. Bending down she saw that it was a jar of homemade jam, with a small square of checked cloth for a lid, and a label saying, *'98 Brackman*. Frances picked it up with a groan of reluctance, resenting the sense of obligation such an unwarranted gift placed upon her. In a bid to bury such feelings, she hurried into the kitchen and threw the offending item into the rubbish bin. The only person ever to eat jam had been Paul, she reminded herself; Daisy was too weight conscious and Felix preferred peanut butter. A few moments later however, overcome with shame at her own mean-spiritedness, she was scrabbling desperately among the food scraps and soggy tea bags in order to fish it out again. Cursing under her breath, she wiped the glass clean and wedged the jar at the very back of the larder shelf, between an unopened bag of flour and some gravy powder which she never used but could not bring herself to throw away.

Chilled from her walk and disinclined to do battle either with the half-hearted performance of the central heating system or the maze of answering machines representing British Gas, Frances ran herself a bath. She lay in the water for a long time, staring at the pale curves and dips of her body, feeling suddenly overwhelmed by a sense of physical isolation. The cold tap was dripping slightly as it always did; she watched each silver dribble of water form and fall, heard the sound of each small splash echo through the silence. She remembered Paul's large, comforting hands, the dry warmth of them on her skin. The frequency with which they had made love had dwindled over the years, but not the tenderness. Sinking lower into the water, Frances hugged herself, too desolate suddenly to cry, missing not sex, but the memory of being held, of feeling her husband's broad arms around her, moving with the rise and fall of her breath.

At the sound of the doorbell her first instinct was to slip deeper into the water. When it rang a second time she put her fingers in her ears and closed her eyes. The prospect of stumbling to the door in a wet dressing gown was inconceivable. Coping widows did not seek mid-morning solace in hot baths. After a couple more minutes however, weary curiosity got the better of her. Wrapping herself in a towel, she tiptoed into her bedroom, approaching the window from a side angle, sliding along the wall like a thief. The drive was empty. The only signs of life were tyremarks in the gravel and the branches of the trees bucking in the wind. Stepping into full view, Frances stood looking out for a long time, hugging herself against the cold air, feeling somehow disappointed and yet bewildered at being so.

Chapter Five

Sally folded Felix's letter in half and slipped it into the pocket of her jacket next to the dog lead. In an attempt to justify her recent rekindling of commitment to the ancient family pet (Sheba had reached the age where she could go for days without the necessity of anything more strenuous than a stroll round the garden), Sally had lately enquired whether she might receive payment for domestic chores. Both parents had eyed each other in surprise, so clearly torn between snorting in amazement and offering some goofy form of encouragement that Sally had nearly laughed out loud at their pathetic transparency. They had settled upon two pounds per every hour of labour. Sweat-shop terms by any standards, but worth it, both for the extra cash and the freedom it gave for sloping out of the house after school without being subjected to interrogation.

It had been so muddy on Sally's previous visit to the bridge that on this occasion she took the precaution of smuggling out two black rubbish sacks from the cupboard under the kitchen sink. After tearing them open, she spread them out as an undersheet for Felix's tartan rug. The dampness still seeped in, but only round the edges and in the odd unprotected patch in the middle. It was still a comfort to lie on it, to bury her nose in the bristly wool and imagine she could still smell Felix's skin and the faintly acrid aroma of the opaque liquid they produced between them.

Banned from curling up on such hallowed property, Sheba retreated to a dryish spot near the wall, whimpering feebly to herself. Ignoring her charge, Sally took the letter out of her pocket and pressed it flat. It was only the second one she had received. Two letters in four weeks. A starvation diet of comfort.

> *Dear Sal,*
>
> *How are you doing? Sorry I haven't written for a while but life is incredibly busy. The work load is really building up now – three essays this week – and there's this terrible scrum for books. I never seem to make it to the library in time (never was much good at rushing anywhere!) and so end up waiting till other people have finished. Can't really buy them as there are so many and they're all so expensive . . .*

Sally had to resist the temptation to skim the next paragraph. There would be nuggets of affection, there always were. Just never enough of them.

> *Jerry, the guy in the room next to me turns out to be not such a geek after all. As he's reading the same subject we're going to get this sharing deal going over books, which should be quite useful. It's his birthday tomorrow and he's having a sort of party in the dive they call a bar in the basement of our block. He's invited me, but I might not bother to turn up. I do rugby training tomorrow afternoon and usually go for a couple of pints afterwards . . .*

Sally skim-read these details with a sinking heart. Telling herself that parties and drinking were a normal part of student life did not prevent her feeling threatened. By the end of the paragraph it seemed a serious miracle that he had bothered writing to her at all.

> *Of course all this would be a hell of a lot nicer if you could be here to share some of it with me. God, I miss your . . .'* An adjective had been scratched out and replaced by *fit*. Sally tried hard to see what his first choice had been. It looked like *brilliant* but she couldn't be sure. She frowned, continuing to read more

slowly now, savouring every word. '. . . *body. How is our secret space? Still warm and dry? When you go there do you think of me and all the things we did? Sometimes I still can't believe it, that you were right there all those years and yet it was only twelve weeks, four days and fifteen hours ago that we actually got it together. God, I wish you were here right this second, just to hold. The thought of it is turning me on so much I can hardly write . . .*'

Sally rolled over onto her back, kicking her legs in the air with yelps of joy that made Sheba prick her ears with suspicion. 'He loves me, you old pooch. He loves me to bits.'

'I guess I'd better stop before I get myself in a worse state than I am already. If you can get to a telephone on Saturday night – let's say six o'clock – I'll be waiting at this number – 01458 356798 – for fifteen minutes.

Hope you are surviving.

Love Felix.

At the sight of the last two words Sally could not help feeling a little deflated. He could have said, *All my love*, or, *lots of love* at the very least. Just the single *love* sounded muted somehow, especially since she had ended her last communication, *tons of love forever*. She re-read the best paragraph to reassure herself and then reached for some cigarettes and matches wedged into a gap in the wall. The matchbox was so damp that when she tried to strike it the whole thing caved in, spilling matchsticks all over the rug. Giving up, Sally pulled herself into a cross-legged position and stared out at the arch of countryside framed by the bridge over her head. A slice of white wintry sky was already yielding its insipid light to the pull of dusk, robbing the fields of their verdure and leaving only brown and grey. The river water, swollen to the tips of its banks, looked black and forbidding. Feeling disheartened, Sally shifted her gaze to the pair of weeping willows on the bend of the river, their branches sweeping the surface of the water with the grace of dancers' arms. Once, on a warm August evening, Felix had pulled her behind the trailing curtains of leaves and kissed her up against one of the trunks, pushing so hard that she could feel the ridges of bark pressing into her back. Remembering the sweet perfection of the moment, Sally experienced a wave of despair that it should already feel so distant and unreachable, lost in the long shadow cast by the milestone of Paul Copeland's sudden death and the hateful necessity of Felix leaving home.

Sighing deeply, she carefully folded away the rug and bits of plastic bag and tugged at Sheba who had fallen asleep. Having checked for the sound of approaching cars, she led the way out of the hideout and up the bank to the roadside. On reaching the tarmac, her eye was caught by a figure moving on the opposite side of the river behind the willow trees. Worried at the possibility of having been seen emerging from under the bridge, Sally paused to see who it was. It took her a moment or two to recognise Mrs Brackman, not because of the failing light or yards separating them, but because the old lady looked so different from Sally's last glimpse of her in Leybourne high street the year before. Instead of the neat Mrs Pepperpot bun, her hair hung in a loose, wild cloud around her face. Although it was cold, she wore what looked like a nightie and slipper-like shoes. Sally could see the veins in her calves, gnarled and twisting like the roots of an old tree. Her first instinct was to run. But something about the obvious distraction of the old woman got the better of her.

'Mrs Brackman, are you all right?' She walked briskly over the bridge, waving with her free hand.

For a moment the old lady looked panic stricken. She turned in little circles, examining the ground and sky to establish the whereabouts of the voice.

'I'm over here.' Sally waved again, but with less conviction.

On spotting her finally, Mrs Brackman waved both arms and beamed. 'I'm going home,' she called. 'Am I late?' she added anxiously, the smile dissolving.

Sally was just pondering how to respond, when Joseph Brackman appeared at a jog from round the bend in the river.

At the sight of him, his mother began hurrying in the direction of the road, leaving the path and wading through the long grass covering the steep bank up to where Sally stood. She came to a halt at the bottom of the slope, staring morosely at the clumps of brambles and bracken blocking her way.

'Am I late?' she said again, more urgently this time, piercing Sally's gaze with her black eyes.

'No, you're fine. Not late at all.'

By the time her son joined her she had become dazed and submissive. When he took her arm she began nodding and then seemed to try to bend down to search in the grass for something, plucking at the long stems with her veiny hands.

'Thank you,' Joseph Brackman called up to Sally, trying to steer his mother back towards the path.

'But I didn't do anything,' muttered Sally, thinking suddenly what a pitiful pair they looked, shuffling along the riverside in the gathering dark. 'Can I help at all?'

'No. We're fine.' He raised one arm but did not look back.

When Sally got home her mother remarked that she had been a long time.

'I met the Brackmans.'

'The Brackmans?'

'The old lady looked really sad and weird, like she'd gone wandering and forgotten to get dressed. He had come looking for her. He didn't have a hat on and you could see this massive scar across his forehead. It's utterly repulsive. By the way, do I get money job by job or at the end of the week?'

Libby laughed, relieved after several tense weeks, to see some small evidence of natural cheeriness return to her youngest daughter. Beth was a much easier proposition as a teenager, not nearly so moody and sharing her uncertainties instead of bottling them inside. There had been an independence about Sally right from the start, a blessing for a mother of four young children, but less easy to accommodate now that she was growing up. Sometimes Libby wondered if it was all her fault, whether Sally's wilfulness and introversion arose not from her allotment of genes so much as from having been sandwiched in the middle of her siblings. She had barely established a niche for herself before her younger brother stormed into the world, edging her out with his hollering and charm, for many months reducing the entire family to a state of exhausted exasperation.

'I'll keep a tally and pay you every Friday, like a salary. How does that sound? So long as you don't always choose the ironing pile over your homework. Talking of which . . .' Libby looked pointedly at the kitchen clock.

'I'm going, I'm going.' Sally retrieved her satchel and disappeared up to her room. Having locked the door, she lit two joss sticks and embarked on a long letter to Felix, telling him, among other things, that Mrs Brackman might know of their hideout, but it didn't matter because she was clearly mad.

Chapter Six

—◦◦◦◦—

When Libby marked the eight-week anniversary of Paul's death with an invitation to the cinema, Frances felt compelled to accept. Not simply because she knew she could not avoid friends forever, but because trying to appear capable of normal activities was a less daunting prospect than owning up to the fact that she appeared to have lost not only a husband, but her own personality. Almost two months on and the blankness of grief was, if anything, worse. Apathy continued to grip her like a disease. There was nothing she wished to do, no one she wanted to meet. Her doodled list of people to contact was long since covered in the ring stains from mugs of tea she did not drink. The radiators were still lukewarm and bubbling with air, the lawyers still waiting for her to confirm a date for their meeting, the vicar still unvisited. If the phone rang, she could not always bring herself to answer it. Sometimes Frances truly believed that her only motive for managing anything was the thread of guilt running through the lethargy, the self-disgust at how she was allowing all the props of everyday life to crumble away.

In spite of Libby's kind offers to pick her up, Frances had insisted she would drive to the Taverners' and go on with them from there. Apart from anything else, she was increasingly anxious to keep prying eyes away from the creeping chaos invading her home. Worse than house dust and kitchen grime was the state of the garden, where the plants seemed to sprawl with the surly look of creatures who knew no fear of chastisement. Frances had reached the point where she hardly dared to venture outside, dreading the way the long grass would close round her shoes and the trailing branches snag in her clothes. All that remained of Paul's grass clippings was a shrivelled pile of brown sludge, a spot he would have long since cleared for one of his beloved bonfires. The previous year he had completed all his pruning in time for Guy Fawkes. The Taverners had come, with three of the children and a large box of fireworks. Frances had grilled sausages and chicken drumsticks while Paul poured drinks and conducted a muted argument with Felix as to who would be in charge of the pyrotechnics. You're treating him like a child, she had wanted to say, but didn't, because of the guests and the certain knowledge that criticism made her husband dig his heels in. To compound matters, Paul saw fit to intervene when Felix reached for a second bottle of beer, declaring loudly that preparation for mock A levels would not be improved by a headache. Even the memory of it made Frances's face burn on her son's behalf. Annoyed and frustrated, she had busied herself with the ice-cream scoop, avoiding Paul's eye as he tried to ensnare her support. A bad evening. But, looking back, Frances found herself missing the friction. She realised now that such tensions had helped to define her, had given her something to push against and feel alive.

Backing the car out of the garage she suddenly noticed that some ivy had somehow wormed its way through a crack in the wall. A robust trailing green stem was snaking its way down towards a shelf of old paint pots. Leaving the engine running she leapt out of the car and seized the stem, tugging downwards, winding it round and round her hand till her fingers hurt. When it snapped at last, she looked up to see the small green stub she had created, bobbing insolently and vigorously at the entrance to the crack, in no way incapacitated from making a second descent. A sense of powerlessness flooded through her; so overwhelming, so draining, that it was several minutes before she staggered back to the car, groping for the steering wheel and seat like a blind woman.

In spite of careful screening beforehand, Libby was dismayed to find that her selection from the wide range of films on offer at the Hexford multiplex contained several deaths and one funeral. Even within the safe confines of romantic comedy in which these scenarios were enacted, she found herself cringing in the dark on Frances's behalf, wondering whether to have a stab at some lighthearted comment or to leave her alone. That Frances did feel mildly uncomfortable arose simply from the fact of being part of a threesome. She hadn't sat in a cinema as an appendage to a couple since her early teens, when Carol bribed her to act as camouflage for an unpromising liaison with a creature with long limp hair and guitars tattooed onto his forearms. Frances had hunched all her thirteen-year-old self-consciousness down into her seat, seeking solace in an enormous box of popcorn, chewing noisily in a show of nonchalance for the rustling intimacies taking place alongside.

'I thought it was rather fun,' declared Libby, as they walked towards the restaurant, the edge of defiance in her tone bearing testimony both to her concerns about Frances and marital tensions arising from a prolonged altercation with a new layout in Hexford's intricate one-way system.

'Great fun,' murmured Frances, whose own general unease had not been alleviated by the in-car sniping following their departure from the cinema. It was painfully apparent that Alistair's participation in the evening was under sufferance. The fatigue-gullies under his eyes looked particularly ragged and there was one moment in the film when she was sure Libby had nudged him awake.

'Look, we don't have to eat,' she ventured, 'I mean, I'm not saying I don't want to, but it is very late and you must be tired . . .'

'Of course we must eat. I'm starving and so's Alistair, which is why he's being so grumpy.'

As a precaution against treading on the toes of happier times, Libby had jettisoned all tried and trusted late dinner haunts in favour of a Chinese restaurant on the outskirts of Hexford called The Green Garden. When they eventually located both the restaurant and a parking slot she had made a deliberate point of hanging back to walk with Frances, leaving her husband to stride on ahead alone.

'A lot of fun,' repeated Libby determinedly, eyeing Frances's bent head over the top of her menu and gloomily thinking that the funeral of the father-in-law had indeed been a shade too close for comfort. Under the reddish gleam of the Chinese lanterns she was struck in the same instant by the quiet, yet striking quality of her friend's looks. If anything, suffering seemed to have lent a new edge to Frances's appearance. Even the pallor of her face suited her, giving an almost translucent look to her skin. She had lost weight too, drawing attention to the fine structure of her cheek-bones and the roundness of her eyes. Her hair, freshly washed for the evening, looked thick and shining. She had swept it back off her face into a loose ponytail that complemented the dense layering of colour – honey, brown and an almost lemony fairness that would take many years to reveal any evidence of grey. In spite of her friend's unenviable circumstances, this last observation caused Libby, who had already given up the battle to hide the steely streaks in her own mousy brown hair, to release a small sigh of injustice at so glaringly an uneven a distribution of natural assets between women of equal age.

'It was a clever plot,' announced Frances, aware that her silence was failing Libby and wanting to make up for it. 'Just the right balance of comedy and seriousness. I like films that do that – pull you in opposite directions . . .' she tailed off, not preoccupied with morose thoughts about death or burying loved ones, as her companions feared, but the comic way in which the seventy-year-old wife of the father-in-law had thrown herself into being single again: Salsa lessons, mini skirts and cordon bleu. Safely distant from Frances's own circumstances, it had made her smile in the dark and wonder whether she had judged her own mother too harshly after all.

'All I want is egg fried rice and duck in plum sauce,' announced Alistair, closing his menu.

'But we're all going to share each other's food,' began Libby.

'I don't want anyone else's food. I want duck in plum sauce.'

'But Alistair,' persisted Libby wearily, 'that's the whole point of Chinese, everybody trying bits of everything, and anyway, perhaps Frances wants plain rice – I'm not mad about the fried kind myself, as you know—'

'Well, you girls order plain rice then.' Alistair offered a tight smile across the table.

'I'll eat anything,' responded Frances hastily. 'Any rice and . . .' She picked a number at random from the long list of main courses, 'number twenty six, prawns with ginger and spring onion.'

'So how are you?' blurted Libby earnestly, once the atmosphere at the table had been lightened by the arrival of a bottle of wine.

'So-so . . . keeping busy, you know . . .' Frances took a sip from her glass, wondering what the Taverners' reaction would have been if she had confessed to the squalor and slothdom that was invading her life, the contradictory longing and abhorrence of company, her leaden sensibilities, her utter idleness.

'Too busy to see me, that's for sure – it's been weeks. I've felt positively rejected, haven't I Alistair?' She cast a quick look at her husband who delivered a grave nod of agreement. 'So tell us what you've been up to – that charity of yours, did you say?'

'Yes . . . mostly paperwork . . .' faltered Frances, inwardly justifying the lie by thinking that the letter formally withdrawing her services had at least involved paper.

'You always say they're frantic in the run-up to Christmas—'

'God, Christmas,' groaned Alistair, whose concentration had drifted somewhat from the theme of the conversation, 'what a hideous thought.'

'We'd love you and the children to spend it with us,' put in Libby, 'no need to answer now, but think about it, won't you?'

Frances nodded, her heart twisting at the thought of going through the rituals without Paul's determined enthusiasm to back them all up. 'That's very kind, Libby – kind of both of you – I will think about it, I promise . . .' She broke off at the arrival of their food, delivered by an oriental doll of a waitress with black button eyes and a thick curtain of blue-jet hair.

Unsure whether the dishes were oversalted or whether it was just her mood, Frances had to make a conscious effort to eat with relish. Absorbed thus in managing her own emotions, it was something of a shock to look up and see Libby dabbing fiercely at her eyes with her napkin. 'Sorry . . . sorry,' she gasped, 'everything's just so hateful at the moment . . . I can't help wanting to cheer you up even though I know it's point-less, but that's just me, wanting to cheer everybody up, even Alistair when he's being foul, like tonight –'

Alistair, clearly torn between indignation and the responsi-bility of offering sympathy, withdrew the arm he had laid across his wife's back and then replaced it, giving Frances a shrug of helpless apology.

'– and like Sally who's being utterly impossible . . .'

As Libby weepily continued to spill out her grievances, Frances was tempted to reach across her plate of oily prawns and give her a hug of gratitude. It was such a wonderful relief not to be the prime focus of concern, to see glimpses of troubles from some aspect other than her own. She squeezed Libby's arm instead and handed her a glass of water. 'You poor thing . . . so much on your plate and trying to sort me out too. I know I've been making it hard for you. It's hard for me, harder than I could ever have imagined, but the last thing I want is to bring you down with me. You're right, you can't cheer me up, so please stop trying. Although I'm deeply grateful, I do think I need to work things out on my own. In fact, I think a big part of my problem – as well as missing Paul of course – is that I have never had to work things out on my own in my life before. I let Paul run things, which was what I wanted, but now I'm paying the price. And don't worry about Sally. Remember all the trouble we had with Daisy during her early teens? But she came through in one piece . . . well, with an almost normal appetite and a couple of A levels anyway. Claude might not be the creature either Paul or I would have chosen as a lifelong partner, but she's at least making her own way, her own decisions. You just had an abnormally easy ride with Beth. And the boys are a piece of cake, but then I think boys are, generally. They blow hot and cold, but at least you know where you are. Felix didn't talk to us for six days once, communicated entirely with hand signals. In the end we had to admire his tenacity . . .' She broke off, aware that Libby was smiling instead of crying and that she had just delivered more uninterrupted sentences than she had managed in over two months.

The rest of the meal was easier and the drive back to Leybourne managed in companionable silence. They said their farewells with renewed and relaxed fondness, hugging in the beams of light cast from the Taverners' sitting-room windows.

'See what I mean?' muttered Libby, as Frances groped in her bag for her car keys. She pointed out the figure of her youngest daughter, framed in the window, curled up in an armchair in front of the television. 'The deal was bed by ten. Any normal child would be scrambling for the stairs, at least pretending they had obeyed orders.' She looked at her watch. 'Midnight, and God knows what trash she's watching. You'd better talk to her Alistair. I'll only shout and make it worse.'

They stood side by side on the doorstep while Frances backed out of the drive, both waving and watching her departure with such vigilance that Frances found herself feeling an unforgivable stab of empathy for the tribulations of their wayward third child. It was only as the lights of the farmhouse receded in her rear-view mirror, that the old fearful emptiness returned. She drove slowly, thinking of the contrasting darkness of her own home, devoid now of any emotions other than those she alone brought into it.

Chapter Seven

⸺◦◦◦⸺

The next morning Frances woke early as usual. Outside a raucous chorus of birds was celebrating the recent arrival of the sun. Pulling one of the pillows from Paul's side of the bed over her head, she closed her eyes, settling down to the interminable wait for the hands of the alarm clock to edge towards a time when it would not feel too cranky to have breakfast. The unutterable tedium of grief was not something people talked about, she reflected grimly, pressing the pillow so closely to her face that with each breath she sucked in a mouthful of linen. In spite of counting to a hundred, when she next looked at the clock it was still only five forty-five. Hurling off the duvet, she tugged on a pair of warm socks and her dressing gown, resolving for once, more out of angry boredom than anything else, to go with the flow of these new and inconvenient biorhythms and see where they led.

By the time the postman arrived Frances had not only eaten a bowl of cereal and drunk two cups of tea, but also trawled around the house with a rubbish sack, emptying waste paper bins and gathering several weeks' worth of half-read newspapers. It was only in the doorway of Paul's study, a cramped attic room where he had often retreated at weekends, that her step faltered. A visible film of dust covered the screen of his computer and the neat stacks of journals lining the lowest of the bookshelves. On the wall hung a picture of Paul as a student, balancing on a stone wall with a bottle of champagne in one hand and his mortarboard in the other. His hair was long and unruly, the set of the mouth determined, even in a smile. Though the picture showed him supposedly in the act of losing his balance, it had always been clear to Frances that he was playing for the camera, that behind the feint of falling he was sure-footed and in control. They had met several years after Paul's university days, in a crowded Soho bar at the birthday drinks of a mutual friend. Cautiously, fearful of the pain it would cause, Frances allowed her mind to travel back towards the memory, summoning the physical props of the occasion, the seventies' juke box, the mist of cigarette smoke, the spilt drink that led to their introduction – details rehearsed so many times to each other and to friends over the intervening years. Digging her fingers into the thin plastic of the bag, bracing herself for sadness, it was something of a shock to find instead the physical images dissolve, leaving only the kernel of the memory, the instant certainty of her feelings, the joy, the relief, of having stumbled upon someone who could offer her the security and love she craved.

Dropping the bag, Frances reached out and ran the tip of one finger across the computer screen, tracing two diagonal paths through the dust. A cross, or maybe a kiss? She squinted at the screen, lingering over the question as if it mattered beyond the garbled logic inside her own head. Before leaving the room she arranged the periodicals on Paul's desk into tidy piles, not yet having the heart to add them to the collection of debris in her bag, but aware that another miniature cog in the process of her recovery had edged into place.

Back downstairs there was a small heap of mail on the doormat which Frances took with her into the kitchen. Before sitting down she prepared toast and instant coffee, making a performance of setting the table, feeling suddenly as if life alone was a new private drama in which she had to learn to play her part. She opened the letters between mouthfuls, tearing up an offer of a new credit card and even managing a wry shake of the head at a health care scheme promising Paul and his loved ones longevity and peace of mind. Third in the pile was a hotel brochure advertising weekend breaks for anglers on the edge of a Scottish loch, with a telephone directory of luxury leisure facilities for the diversion of loved ones not so smitten with the notion of spending all day hunched over a fishing rod. Frances found herself scrutinising the leaflet, wondering whether it was unsolicited or something Paul had ordered specially. For a bank holiday break maybe, or their wedding anniversary. Their twenty-second, it would have been. With the see-saw state of her emotions, having no prospect of an answer to so simple a thing suddenly seemed to matter very deeply. It made her that see Paul's sudden death had cut off the script not only of his own life, but of hers too.

Aware that the fragile resolve with which she had managed to start the day was in danger of slipping away, Frances hastily turned her attentions to the next letter, a thick white envelope with a London postmark. Hugo Gerard, clearly tired of waiting for the promised initiative from his client, had written to suggest a time and a place in London for the sorting out of Paul's legal affairs.

'. . . *if you are unable to make the appointment time suggested, I would be grateful if you could let me know, either in writing or by telephone, as soon as possible.*

In the meantime, please allow me to reiterate my deepest condolences on the sad occasion and consequences of your recent bereavement.

I remain yours . . .'

The last envelope in the pile had clearly been delivered by hand. There was no address, only the words *Frances Copeland*, written in spidery sloping letters. Inside, on what appeared to be the back portion of an old Christmas card, was written, *'Come to lunch today, Joseph Brackman.'* It read more like a summons than an invitation, and with no let out, not even a telephone number, to facilitate refusal. Frances stared at it for several minutes, remembering the jam on the morning of their encounter in the graveyard and feeling again all the injustice of such unsolicited intrusions into the private wasteland of her life. Tearing the card firmly in two, she dropped it onto her plate, amongst the dry discarded remains of her toast. When the phone rang a moment later, she glanced nervously over her shoulder, like a child fearful of being caught doing wrong.

'Mum, it's only me, Daisy. Just calling to see how you were.'

'I'm fine.'

'Really . . . ? Oh . . . well, that's good. Look – I know I'm coming home for Christmas and so on – but I was wondering – that is Claude and I were wondering – when you would like to come and stay. I mean it doesn't have to be a weekend or anything. I'm only working part-time after all.'

'And how is the new job?'

'Very good, thanks. Look, why don't you come next week?'

Frances hesitated, struggling against the knot of resistance already tightening inside, not understanding its origins beyond an irrational surge of reluctance to leave the safe familiarity of her home.

'Daisy, that's sweet of you, but I'm really not sure whether I . . .'

'Please?' There was a sharpness in her daughter's tone.

'Well, certainly not next week . . .'

'The one after? Or maybe the one after that? Which would be . . . let me see now, the first week in December.'

'The first week in December,' echoed Frances, feeling browbeaten and weak. She heard the riffle of papers, as her daughter flicked through a calendar or diary.

'Week commencing the fifth. That looks fine. Come on Monday and stay till Friday. OK? Let me know flight details and so on nearer the time. Or take the Eurostar, it's really not bad at all. Do you want me to send you some stuff about it?'

'No, no, I can manage. I'll let you know, darling, nearer the time.' Frances put the phone down slowly, frowning at the realisation that the outside world was lapping at her door like the swell of an irresistible flood.

★

'We're having soup. Chicken and avocado. I made it this morning. It has to be prepared at the last minute otherwise the green of the avocado fades. A good colour, I think. A citron brilliance to it, like the skin of a lime. You must drink something. How about nettle wine? My mother makes it, or used to. Still plenty left.' Joseph seized a green glass bottle from a cardboard box and began pulling at the cork with his teeth.

Frances had not yet taken her coat off, but was hovering near the side door by which they had entered, as if entertaining the very real possibility of escaping back out of it. She had not meant to come. She had decided positively against coming, so positively that rather than play curtain-twitching games with the view of the Brackmans' cottage, its red roof tiles catching the light of the first sun they had had in days, she had resolved to go out in the car. But at twelve fifteen, just as she was closing the front door behind her, Joseph Brackman had appeared in the driveway.

'Thought I'd walk you down,' he said, turning and leading the way out of the gate as if there were no question as to whether she would follow.

'I'm afraid . . . it's awfully kind of you . . . but . . .' Frances had to trot to catch him up. If he heard any of her feeble protestations he gave no indication of it.

'A fine day. A fine day for a walk,' was all he said, not even turning to acknowledge her arrival at his side. 'We'll go by the road. The river path is still water-logged. Nearly lost my boots this morning'

They continued in silence for a few minutes, Joseph apparently studying the skyline while Frances tried to disguise her reluctance with a purposeful stride. A couple of hours at the most and she would be home, she reassured herself. A small endurance test, that was all. Be polite, but cool. Afterwards she could spin any number of lies to avoid repeating the experiment, say she was too busy, that she was commuting regularly to Paris, considering leaving the country for good, any story would do.

They left the road and took the overgrown path which had once formed the main approach to Leybourne station. Up ahead a raised section of rusting track protruded from a small hill, sticking over one end like a diving board over an empty pool. The path continued through the hill itself, via a crude, low-arched tunnel edged with dank, grey-brick walls. Inside the air felt moist and chilled.

'Walk near the edges, it's drier there,' commanded Joseph, continuing to make his own way down the sludge in the middle.

It was a relief to emerge into the sunshine on the other side, to see the moth-eaten hedge exactly as she remembered it from her excursions to retrieve the children from their spying games a decade before. But the garden on the other side of the hedge was a revelation. Once a brambled wilderness, it had been transformed into an immaculate layout of lawn, bordered with shrubs and broken by a cobbled path that snaked its way up to the front door. In the far corner was a miniature rectangle of a vegetable garden, organised into weedless tidy rows by sticks and bits of string.

'But this is lovely,' Frances had exclaimed, admiration for a moment driving out all her apprehensions.

'I like being outdoors. So does Ma.' He led the way round to the side of the cottage and kicked off his boots before pushing open the door for her to step inside. The kitchen was dark and unbelievably cramped, every available surface piled high with an assortment of jars, papers and saucepans. In the midst of the chaos sat a small, weathered kitchen table, set with three bowls and three spoons.

It was only after having successfully extracted the cork with his mouth that her host removed his hat. Not the hood of his anorak this time but a dark brown cap. Frances gave an involuntary flinch at the sight of the thick pink scar which had so impressed Sally, bulging high on his forehead near his hairline.

'A set-to with a barbed-wire fence in the summer when I was full of this stuff,' he said with a dark laugh, tapping first the scar and then the wine bottle. 'Doctors say it will fade with time. Offered me plastic surgery, but I couldn't be bothered with the fuss.' While he spoke he poured out a glass of a greenish liquid, flecked with bits, like fish food. 'Would you like me to put my cap back on?'

'Of course not . . . I'm sorry I didn't mean to stare.' Frances wrenched her eyes away from the twist of flesh, inwardly cursing the ineptitude which had sent her scurrying after Joseph Brackman instead of making the getaway she had originally intended. He handed her the glass before turning his attention to a large, grime-encrusted black oven wedged between a cracked porcelain sink and an oak dresser, so laden with things that the shelves sagged in the middle. Using a flimsy grey cloth, he extracted a tray of brown rolls, each twisted into monstrous shapes and heaving with heat. He tipped them onto a plate in the middle of the table and motioned at her to sit down. Frances obeyed at once, taking a sip of her drink, which was faintly fizzy but not unpleasant. When she looked up she found Mrs Brackman glowering suspiciously at her from the doorway leading to the rest of the cottage.

'Thank you so much for the jam,' Frances blurted, remembering the gift with a flush of guilt.

The old lady worked her jaw, looking anxiously at her son for some explanation.

'You know Frances Copeland, Mother, don't you, from the house up the lane? Lunch is ready.'

'Am I late?'

'No, no, not late.' He put a bowl of soup down and pulled back a chair. The old woman began to eat immediately, messily spooning soup to her lips and making loud smacking noises between mouthfuls. Frances, faintly appalled but determined not to appear so, waited until Joseph had sat down before embarking on her own portion. A silence descended on the table, bringing with it, for Frances at least, a vivid sense of unreality, as if she had slipped into a parallel world.

'This is very kind of you,' she began, nodding appreciatively at the soup which was delicious, but very rich.

'Is she staying long?' Mrs Brackman pointed at Frances with her spoon, flinging a shower of green specks over the table.

'Frances has come for lunch, Mother,' Joseph repeated, adding in a quieter voice to Frances, 'She has lost touch with the past, can only live in the present moment. It makes the world very threatening.'

'Oh dear, how . . .' Frances's sympathy was interrupted by the screech of Mrs Brackman's chair legs on the stone-tiled floor.

'It's time,' she announced, tottering from the room, taking some bread with her but leaving her soup barely touched.

Joseph leapt up and followed her out of the room. 'She likes to watch the *One o'clock News*,' he explained, returning a few minutes later. 'Mainly because of that Mr Stourton. She's got a real soft spot for him. Here, butter for your bread.' He passed Frances an unwrapped half pound before resuming his seat at the table and continuing in the same tone of voice, 'I know you did not want to come. Of course you did not want to come. Sometimes you have to go through the motion of things to remind yourself how to do them. Sometimes you have to pretend to do something and then suddenly, half-way through, you find yourself really doing it. I find that with writing poetry. I fear it, and yet I must do it. There is nothing that scares an idea away so much as the sense that it is being stalked.'

'So you write poetry, how interesting.'

He let out a sharp laugh. 'Like now, you see. You are pretending to be interested, but you're not really, not properly. You are a polite lady.' He pointed his knife at her accusingly and then smiled, revealing an impressive set of large yellowing teeth. His hair which had been pinned to his scalp from wearing the cap, had gradually loosened, exposing unevenly cut layers of brown streaked with grey. The front portion was so long that it flopped right into his eyebrows, hiding most of the scar. He was younger than Frances had always imagined, maybe even still in his forties, but aged by self-neglect.

'I am interested,' she said faintly.

'Sometimes I do translations too. To pay bills.'

'Really? Into what language?' she enquired, trying desperately after his comments to strike a note of genuine enthusiasm.

'Russian mostly. More soup.' It was a statement rather than a question. Frances watched helplessly as he ladled three generous spoonfuls into her bowl. 'At least you never had to mourn your husband when he was alive,' he remarked suddenly. 'At least you lost him as he was.'

'Whatever do you mean?' She dropped her spoon with a clatter of metal against china, the indignation blazing out of her, her sensibilities cringing at such unwarranted trespassing on such private ground.

He looked crestfallen. 'No, I didn't mean . . . I was just thinking of my mother. I miss her already, you see. She's gone from me. Alzheimer's,' he added quickly, seeing the look of enquiry on her face. 'It has drained her life of meaning. Disconnected objects, nonsense, she lives a nightmare. The nightmare.'

'Joseph, I'm so sorry, I . . .'

'Coffee now I think.' He quickly stood up and began clumsily stacking the bowls, leaving the spoons between them and pushing them to the furthest end of the table. 'And sweets.' He seized an enormous glass jar off one of the top dresser shelves, toppling a stack of papers and several other odd items to the ground. 'Sugar makes my mother happy,' he declared, kicking the papers out of his way and placing the jar next to Frances. 'Like a child. Her teeth are rotten, but at eighty it doesn't matter, does it?' He grinned, his whole face creasing to reveal a fleeting glimpse of the more endearing boy version of the man. 'I'm glad you came to lunch Frances. I know you did not want to. I see your sadness.' He pressed the palm of his hand to the left side of his chest. 'I feel it here.'

'Thank you . . .' she faltered, touched, but acutely embarrassed and desperate suddenly to get home.

The heaviness of the soup stayed with her long into the afternoon. But so did a curious sense of satisfaction. She felt different, better. As if the lunch, for all its weirdness, had broken another small link in the chain of empty lassitude which had been binding her. She put on a half load of washing and then sat down with the sitting-room telephone in her lap. She told Hugo Gerard she would come to London when his letter suggested. She phoned Libby and fixed a date for lunch. She even phoned British Gas, hanging on through a maze of computer responses until a very amenable woman with a thick Yorkshire accent promised to send an engineer round the following day.

Chapter Eight

Libby was so entertained that Frances almost regretted telling her.

'Feted by the recluse of Leybourne, Christ, you poor thing. But how terribly brave of you to go. Sally mentioned bumping into the pair of them the other afternoon when she was dragging Sheba round the countryside. She said the old woman looked quite batty and he had some hideous wound on his face . . .' Frances opened her mouth to explain the entanglement with barbed wire, but Libby was in full flow. 'Heavens, I've just had the most dreadful thought.' She slapped her hand over her mouth. 'You don't suppose he fancies his chances, do you? I mean, as far as he's concerned, you are a widow of substance . . .' She quickly checked herself, scanning Frances's face for any indication that she had overstepped the mark.

But Frances laughed easily. 'Don't be ridiculous. It wasn't remotely like that. He was being neighbourly, like the vicar, trying in his own way to help. Besides, the poor man is chained to a sick mother, I think he genuinely wanted some company. He writes poetry and translates Russian for a living. He's nicer than I thought, but still utterly strange. There wasn't the remotest suggestion of anything untoward.'

Libby patted her hand. 'I'm sure there wasn't.'

It was the end of the week after Frances's encounter with the Brackmans and the two women were sitting having a sandwich lunch in the tea house opposite Libby's gift shop, an overcrowded Aladdin's cave of an emporium in the well-to-do northern suburbs of Hexford. Through the windows beside them, already frosted with festive drifts of polystyrene snow, pedestrians were walking with heads grimly bent against the horizontal cut of the November wind. As usual, cars were crawling down both sides of the high street, impeded by jay walkers and several sets of traffic lights. In spite of the numbers of people in the street, business was poor, as it had been throughout the dismally wet summer and autumn, adding fuel to Libby's theory that the type of goods in which she traded were about states of mind rather than levels of financial solvency. If things did not pick up in the run-up to Christmas, she was going to have to have a serious re-think about the future. All she had sold that morning were two flashing pens and a couple of mugs.

'I hope you don't mind my saying this,' Libby continued, 'and obviously it's far too soon for anything yet, but I do hope that one day you might find someone else. I just mean,' she surged on, seeing the rush of colour to Frances's cheeks, 'that Alistair and I will be the first to support you should anyone else ever appear on the horizon. You know we were both very fond of Paul, but it simply would not be right for you to soldier on alone forever.' She posted a final mouthful of sandwich in her mouth and dusted the breadcrumbs from her fingertips, thoroughly enjoying the relief of being able to talk almost naturally again. Recognising Frances's suggestion of lunch as something of a milestone, she was determined to make the most of it, to prove that the roots of their friendship remained intact. 'We just would love to see you happy again,' she added with a sigh, patting her lips by way of an apology for talking with her mouth full.

'Well, thank you, Libby.' Frances paused, picking her words carefully. 'I must confess that I too hope that one day . . .' She was prevented from completing the sentence by an involuntary sob.

Libby, appalled and remorseful, quickly began thrusting paper napkins across the table. 'Oh Frances, I'm sorry, what was I thinking – bringing up such a subject when – God, what a fool I am – saying the first thing that comes into my head . . .'

Frances shook her head in protest, partly because of the inconvenience of crying and partly because she felt unequal to the task of explaining that what had triggered her outburst was not sadness so much as guilt, for having already arrived at the point where she felt able to discuss such things. Occasionally, in recent days, she had even caught a part of herself longing to be back under the safe crushing blanket of early grief. There had been a simplicity to it which she missed. Eleven weeks on there was still an inner emptiness to each day, a self-conscious sense of being acutely alone, but within that a renewed interest in the outside world was definitely beginning to assert itself. She had started watching television again and reading the papers. She had even bought a novel, a thriller about a murderer who cup up the body parts of his victims and posted them to relatives with boxes of Turkish Delight.

'So have you seen Joseph Brackman since?' enquired Libby gently, once Frances had recovered herself.

'No,' she replied firmly, 'nor do I intend to. I know he meant well, but it wasn't exactly the most relaxed lunch engagement I've known.'

Libby raised her index finger and gave a knowing tap to the side of her nose. 'Just you watch your step, my dear, that's all. Don't go letting him get any ideas . . .'

Frances pretended to look offended. 'Only a minute ago you were saying you'd support me if I fell for someone else.'

'And so I would,' she retorted, her grey eyes full of merriment once more, 'just so long as it's not a dishevelled, penniless poet with a history of insanity in the family.' Their laughter was interrupted by a bleeping from Libby's handbag. 'Dramas back at base, no doubt,' she muttered, rummaging for her mobile and craning her neck out of the tea-shop window, as if whatever problems her young assistant was encountering might be visible from across the street. 'Jenny, I'm on my way . . .' she began, before breaking off abruptly, the colour draining from her face.

Aware from Libby's altered expression that graver matters than stocktaking or recalcitrant tills were at stake, Frances discreetly signalled to the waitress for the bill.

'What's happened?' she asked the moment Libby lowered the phone.

'It's Sal. Not in school. She has a load of free periods in the morning so no one realised. That was the head asking if she was ill. I suppose she could have gone home, the little . . . Christ what is that child playing at now? I tell you, I've had just about all I can take.' She punched the digit pad on her mobile and embarked on a fraught rundown on the situation with Alistair.

'I'll keep an eye on Jenny in the shop if you like,' ventured Frances when she had finished.

'Oh, would you Frances? Thanks so much. The poor girl is pitifully scatty, quite incapable of doing more than one thing at once . . . God, do you think I should call the police?'

'Go home first. She may just have slipped out early. It's not time to worry yet,' Frances soothed, appearing calmer than she felt for Libby's sake, while aware that some subterranean part of her was relishing the long forgotten luxury of being useful.

It was already getting dark when Sally got on the train. Forty minutes to Hexford, then a twenty-minute bus ride back to Leybourne. She closed her eyes in dread at the thought. At Felix's insistence she had phoned and left a message on the answer machine at home. But there would be recriminations and hysteria nonetheless, for playing truant, for causing worry, for not being the kind of daughter they wanted. Sally slung her shoulder bag onto the luggage rack and slumped down in a seat next to the window. These days she felt increasingly as if her life had been reduced to a grisly game of charades, that all the things which mattered most to her had to be stapled inside for fear of causing panic amongst grown-ups. Not just about Felix, but everything else as well. Like the still undiscussed reality that she was going to flunk most of her GCSEs. Like the fact that she wanted to give up the violin, drama club and all the other petty activities into which she had been duped out of some misguided notion that she could emulate the effortless star qualities of her big sister. Whenever she dared to confront her parents about such things they had a cunning way of appearing to acquiesce, while at the same time making out that giving up on anything would constitute an admission of defeat from which the entire family might never recover.

Sally dug her little finger into a cigarette burn in the navy blue velour of her train seat and sighed heavily. Her grand day out had not gone according to plan. She had been so hyped up about skipping school that it was really only after she had located Felix's hall of residence that the potential for disappointment dawned. She had only the vaguest idea of how Felix spent his time, a blurred concept of lecture halls and libraries and things called seminars, which sounded like discussion groups with a fancy name. She hadn't realised how spread out the university was, that to outsiders there was no obvious focal point for anything. After the minor triumph of locating Felix's hall of residence, an ugly grey tower of a building with a flat black roof, she was brought to an abrupt halt by a security panel of numbers for releasing the lock on the door. She was staring at it, feeling deflated and hopeless when, to her utter astonishment and delight, Felix himself appeared, scurrying down the pavement towards her.

'But Sal . . . what the hell?'

'Surprise,' she shrieked, going onto the tips of her trainers and flinging her arms round his neck. 'I couldn't bear another day of not seeing you.'

He hugged her briefly, breaking off for an anxious look at his watch. 'I wish you'd told me. In fact it's incredible you found me, I only came back because I forgot my file. I'm bloody late actually.' He ran both his hands back through his hair, which had grown rather long, flopping over his ears in a way that Sally couldn't help thinking looked a bit affected.

'Surely you could skip whatever it is, just this once.' She had to trot to keep up with him as he punched in the door code and set off up the staircase, taking two steps at a time. 'I'm skipping the whole bloody day.'

'Are you?' He paused for a moment, genuinely impressed, before the enormity of what she had said sank in. 'What on earth did you tell everybody?'

Sally shook her head happily. 'Nothing. I just came. Why, what would you like me to have told them?' she added slyly, knowing that she was trespassing on sensitive ground. They had agreed not to make their relationship public knowledge until she had turned sixteen. Not just because of the sex side of things, but because of apprehension at the thought of laying themselves open to the general mirth and curiosity of their respective families. It was an argument about which Felix had always felt far more strongly than her. Indeed, a part of Sally would have loved to proclaim her feelings through a megaphone from the top of St Martin's spire.

Felix's room was stuffy and very untidy. A partition separated a bed and basin from a walled desk unit and a couple of muddy orange chairs. There were papers and clothes everywhere, strewn around empty biscuit packets and dirty mugs. Felix, cursing loudly, eventually found what he was looking for.

'It's a tutorial. I've got to read out this essay. I simply can't miss it. I'll be back as soon as I can. An hour and a bit, no more.' He kissed her on the mouth. 'See you soon.'

'Felix . . .'

He stopped half-way through the door, looking so Sally could not help noticing, impatient.

'Are you glad I came?'

'Of course, Sal.' He ran back and kissed her again. 'I'll show you just how glad when I get back . . . that is if you've got any . . .'

She patted her bag sheepishly. 'I collected remaining supplies from the bridge.'

The time passed slowly. Sally smoked five of the packet of ten Marlboro Lights she had bought at the station and browsed through the mess, looking for clues, though for what exactly she wasn't sure. Pinned to a small cork board in front of the desk unit were several invitations to parties, but also a small passport photograph of the pair of them, taken on a wet afternoon in Hexford when they had sneaked off to the cinema to see *Titanic*. Although tiny, no more than a pinpoint in the room, the sight of it cheered her enormously, as did the memory of larking in the supermarket photo booth, adopting silly poses and getting so hysterical that a man in uniform had asked them to move along.

It was a good hour and a half before Felix burst back in looking windswept and businesslike. 'I've got until half past two,' he announced, unzipping his flies and beginning to peel off his jeans. 'There's a lecture on Keynes – miles away – but I've got to go – bloody economics is so much harder than I was expecting, if it wasn't for Jerry next door—' He stopped, bare-legged, one sock in hand, aware suddenly that she had not moved from the desk chair. 'Do you want to make love?'

'Of course,' Sally whispered, slowly slipping her arms out of her sweatshirt, wishing they were somewhere else other than a poky room in the middle of a world she did not understand and in which she could play no part.

The bed was soft and squeaky and narrow. Sally found herself longing for the hard ground under the bridge, the tingle of the outside air on her bare skin. It took some effort to wrest her thoughts to the present, to remind herself that she was with the man she loved, committing a reckless act of her own making. Afterwards there was barely time to talk. Felix produced half a loaf of sliced bread and near empty tub of peanut butter. They ate quickly, spending most of the time discussing which train she could catch and whether she should call home. He seemed worried she might confess where she had been and made her promise to say she had spent the time window shopping in Hexford. 'And next time, tell me you're coming,' he pleaded, 'then we can sort out a day when I have more free time.' Sally had trekked back to the station feeling more suffused than ever by all the doubts she had so hoped her adventure might banish.

Her eventual homecoming was predictably grim: a muted reception of real anger, led not by her mother whose repertoire of noisy explosions Sally would have found almost reassuring, but by her jaw-clenched father. They were disappointed, he said, bitterly disappointed in her selfishness, her foolhardiness, her complete disregard for the feelings of others. There followed silence, bucketfuls of it, even from her siblings, who eyed her with a sort of admiring horror, scuttling past her as if she had contracted some infectious disease. Where she had gone was barely questioned. Following Felix's advice, she said she had been to Hexford, cruising shopping malls and the waterfront, seeking time and space to be herself.

'Next time try the garden,' her father had growled. 'And for the next month you can do extra chores for free.'

Sally had retreated to her room more miserable than she could ever remember being in her life. For once, not even the thought of Felix cheered her up. The long-imagined fantasy of thrilling him with a whirlwind visit had fizzled into the most unsatisfactory of realities. He hadn't seemed pleased, at least not in the way she had hoped. Before turning out the light she reached for the tatty bear who had shared her bed since baby-hood, burying her face in the familiar smell of its balding fur. On hearing a soft knock at her door, she hurriedly slipped it under her pillow and closed her eyes, maintaining the pretence of sleep, while her mother tiptoed into the room and out again. Only after the door had closed, cutting out the wedge of landing light, did she pull the bear back into her arms, dreaming of what she had wished instead of what had been.

Chapter Nine

It was with considerable trepidation that Frances boarded the train for London. The necessity of half a day away from home filled her with as much terror as the prospect of being closeted with Hugo Gerard and his colleagues discussing matters she only half understood. In the three months since Paul's death her only excursion beyond the safe proximity of Hexford had been the run to Sussex with Felix, which had barely involved leaving the car. To prevent her own emotions getting the better of her, she had hurriedly helped him empty the car and then pooh-poohed the notion of a cup of tea before embarking on the journey home.

Staring out of the train window, Frances's feelings of widowly isolation returned with a vengeance, reminding her of grief's accompanying sentence of dislocation, the way it condemned its victims to a sense of alienation from ordinary living. She found herself studying the faces of other passengers, wondering if their apparent integration into the world was genuine or merely the inference of an envious imagination. Outside, the verdure of the Home Counties, still homely in the grey light of an overcast December morning, gradually lost out to patches of urban development until every glimpse of green came in the orderly form of gardens or school playing fields.

'The world is eating itself up,' Paul had announced cheerfully, pulling her into the crook of his arm as they stared at the same view a year or so before. 'Soon we'll have wondered why we bothered to leave London.' The memory of the remark, made on a rare visit to his brother and the even rarer circumstance of her persuading him to go by rail instead of suffering on the M25, was so vivid that Frances glanced to her right, half expecting to find Paul sitting there. Sensing unwelcome scrutiny, her actual neighbour, a smartly dressed woman with a ginger beehive hair-do, sniffed dismissively and gave a protective tug to the edge of her magazine.

As well as bringing little respite to her mood, the sight of Battersea through the smeary panes of the train window made Frances wonder why she had ever wanted to remain in London. She glimpsed a street where she had once lived alone, during the brief period of her late teens before meeting Paul. She stared hard at the grimy terraced houses, trying to remember what she had been like, in what direction her hopes had been heading before the perhaps too easy definition provided by an early marriage and motherhood. The thought prompted the realisation that she had for years allowed her personality to be defined by outside events and other people. Alone she was afloat, not knowing who to be, how to be.

'Mrs Copeland. Thank you so much for coming. Do take a seat. Coffee? We even do biscuits. So good of you to come. A smooth journey, I hope? I commute from Wiltshire myself. Quite a grind, but it's always worth going home when you get there. Sugar? Milk?'

Frances shook her head to both, accepting the cup of black coffee gratefully. On getting out at Victoria her mood had lifted, slipping away with astonishing ease, as her moods seemed to these days, leaving her feeling relieved and faintly bemused. Instead of plunging down amongst the stream of people heading for the Underground, she had walked across the forecourt, past the taxi rank towards the buses. She took a bench seat on the lower deck, next to a smiling grey-haired woman, who smelt of mothballs. 'Turned out nice anyway,' the woman said, nodding at the view through the window behind them, 'I knew it would.' Frances had smiled back, acknowledging this reference to the sudden emergence of the sun with a nod of her own.

'I'm sorry, I know we should probably have done all this weeks ago,' she faltered, feeling faintly shabby in the leathered opulence of Hugo Gerard's office. He was wearing a charcoal-grey suit and what looked like a pure silk blue tie and shirt. A perfect triangle of matching blue protruded from his jacket breast pocket. 'I'm sorry I've been . . .'

'No need to apologise Mrs Copeland, no need at all. This won't take long – all very straightforward. You've seen your late husband's will –' he picked up a sheaf of documents from his desk '– everything goes to you apart from a small portfolio of shares and three thousand pounds for each of your children upon their reaching the age of twenty-five.' He paused and took off his glasses. 'Daisy and Felix, isn't it?'

'Yes . . .'

He put his glasses back on and swept on smoothly, passing Frances so many pieces of paper for scrutiny or signature that by the time she remembered her coffee it had gone quite cold. 'There's only one small unresolved matter Mrs Copeland, and that's the whereabouts of a missing share certificate. If you look at the list of your husband's shareholdings' – he pointed to the documents in her lap – 'you'll see I've marked the offending article with an asterisk. Perhaps you could let me know if it turns up at home, otherwise I—'

'It's just bloody maddening,' Frances burst out, 'to have . . . loose ends . . . I want – I keep trying – to accept – to close – a picture of the past, of how things were, only I can't because things like this –' she hit the paper with the back of her hand, sending half the pile floating to the ground, 'get in the way.' She was aware of the lawyer staring at her open mouthed. To be angry felt good suddenly, better than wailing and weeping. 'I'm sorry if it shocks you Mr Gerard, but a part of me is furious at –' she pushed the rest of the papers to the floor – 'all of this, so much muddle and mess because Paul bloody well had to go and die before any of us were ready for it. It might sound mad, but a part of me can't help thinking how *inconsiderate* it was of him . . .' She stopped abruptly, slapping her hand to her mouth, as if only becoming fully conscious of what she was saying. 'Sorry,' she gasped, 'you must think me quite dreadful . . .'

'Not at all,' he replied quietly, moving swiftly to Frances's feet and beginning to retrieve the papers into a tidy pile. 'I should be utterly enraged if Laetitia were to expire now, leaving me in the soup with school runs and nannies and what on earth to buy all my relations at Christmas. My entire existence would fall apart.' He continued to pick up the papers while he talked, unable to prevent himself observing as he did so that his client was in possession of a very fine pair of legs, shown off to excellent effect in a pair of sheer black tights, or possibly stockings. Guilty at being capable of such an observation at such a time, Hugo made a big to-do of stacking the documents back into a tidy rectangle. 'In fact there is no muddle or mess at all. Everything is in perfect order. Apart from carrying out your husband's behests to godchildren and so forth, you have nothing more to do. Your mortgage is paid off, thanks to the insurance policy attached to your endowment, you have an income, through dividends and your husband's excellent pension arrangements. In short there is nothing for you to worry about at all, Mrs Copeland, at least not on the practical side,' he concluded quickly.

'Thank you. You have been very kind. And I'm sure Laetitia will keep going for decades yet,' she added, wanting to convey some of her gratitude at his response to her outburst. She nodded at a photograph of a petite brunette with two small children in school uniform sitting on each knee. 'They look lovely.'

After taking a taxi back to Victoria, Frances bought a newspaper and a tuna salad sandwich and hurried onto the train long before it was due to pull out of the station. She was back on her front door-step by three o'clock. After making a mug of tea, she took a pad of paper into the sitting room and began to write to Daisy, fearful that if she resorted to the telephone her daughter would talk her round.

> *Darling,*
> *Don't be angry, but I just feel I'm not up to coming to stay in Paris next week after all. I'm such poor company you really wouldn't want me around. Christmas is so soon anyway, so I'll see you then. The Taverners have kindly invited us to theirs for the day. Granny is going to New York as usual.*
> *Lots of love, Mum.*

Frances folded the letter in half and slipped it into an envelope. As she ran her tongue along the flap her gaze drifted to the view of the garden through the french windows. The afternoon was already closing down, billows of grey cloud shuttering the last of the daylight from the sky. Something looked different, she realised, getting up slowly, squinting to see properly in the failing light. The grass had been cut. All the leaves which had gathered in drifts round the edges of the patio and along the path had gone. As she approached the windows she became aware of a faint smell of burning. Fumbling for the keys which were kept hidden in a pot on the mantelpiece, she hurriedly let herself out. 'Hello,' she called, striding to the bottom of the garden and peering over the fence. When there was no reply, she raced across to the garden shed. A mountain of bright green grass had been tipped up against the fence, covering the muddy mulch left from the end of the summer. A small fire was burning leaves in the metal brazier, sending spirals of thick smoke up towards the darkening sky.

'Hello?' called Frances again, more softly, knowing already that she was quite alone.

Chapter Ten

———=>o●o<=———

Felix stared disconsolately at the cars streaming round the roundabout, wondering whether to cut his losses and hop on a bus to the station after all. It was the first time he had tried to hitch anywhere, drawn to the idea as much for economy's sake as the appeal of being free and adult enough to do such things at will. The day, although cold, was radiant with sunshine, the sky flecked with clouds no bigger than seagulls. Wondering whether teeming grey rain might have worked more to his advantage, he trudged to the entrance of the lay-by and slung his rucksack to the ground. It was a spot which Jerry, who hitched everywhere – whether his destination was Scotland or a local pub – had particularly recommended. The roundabout fed all the main routes east and the lay-by, so he assured Felix, usually housed an excellent hamburger van. There was no sign of it that morning however, much to the dismay of Felix's stomach, which had recovered sufficiently from the excesses of the Christmas rugby dinner the night before to relish the idea of a greasy meal. The greasier the better, he thought longingly, wishing he had felt up to more than the can of 7Up which had constituted breakfast.

Sitting on his rucksack at the entrance to the lay-by, he began to go over the letters of his makeshift sign, pressing so hard that the tip of his Biro kept puncturing the surface of the cardboard. He had got as far as doubling the thickness of the *HEX* of *HEXFORD* when an old grey Ford turned in past him, a bicycle attached somewhat lopsidedly to a rack on its rear end. A man wearing faded jeans and a weather-beaten leather jacket got out of the car. Raising one arm in greeting, he went to fiddle with the various bits of string responsible for the security of the bicycle.

'You're in luck, I was only stopping because I was afraid this thing was going to cause a motorway pile-up.' He patted the upended wheels. 'In fact it's as safe as houses. I'm not going as far as Hexford – I turn off towards Farley – but that will still get you well over half-way. Are you coming then?' He jangled his keys. 'The car is pretty full, but I'm sure we can wedge that rucksack on the floor behind the passenger seat. A student from down the road, by any chance?' he added, pulling open the car door and inviting Felix to stow his bag inside.

'Yes.'

'Studying . . . ?'

'Politics and Economics – first year.'

The man held out his hand. 'I teach at the same establishment I'm afraid. Not in your field though. You could call me a ninth-year art historian – stayed on to do a thesis and never quite left.'

'Pleased to meet you,' replied Felix, a little put out at finding himself reunited with a member of the institution from which he had been only too happy to celebrate his departure.

'Are you enjoying it then? The course and so on?' His companion accelerated back into the main flow of traffic, settling into such an outrageously high speed that Felix began to consider the possibility of enjoying the journey after all. 'Let me see now, politics . . . that would bring you into the world of George Englefield and that lot. He's supposed to be rather good, as is the infamous Joanna Cathargy. Both of them getting almost too important to teach these days – spend their time on lecture tours in America. They pay better on the other side of the Atlantic,' he added dryly.

'No, I don't get taught by either of them, and to be honest

I'm not mad about the course either,' Felix confessed, drawn in spite of himself to be honest. At a guess the man was in his mid to late twenties. With his casual clothes and relaxed air, he looked rather as Felix had hoped his own tutors might look. His hair was thick and dark, cut so short that it stuck up in spikes around his crown, and matched by heavy eyebrows that moved when he smiled. His eyes were deep set and strikingly brown. Kind eyes, Felix decided, thinking wistfully of the grey-faced unsympathetic creatures manning his own faculty and adding, 'The politics is OK, I guess, if a little uninspired, we're just ploughing through ancient history at the moment, but the economics is dire. I had no idea so much maths would be involved. It was by far my worst subject at A level,' he conceded ruefully.

'Seen anything you'd rather be doing? Switching courses is naturally discouraged' – he lowered his voice in a show of mock gravitas – 'but by no means unheard of. Those prepared to tough it out usually get their way in the end. My best finalist last year began life as a geologist.'

'I hadn't really thought about it to be honest . . .'

'I should have a look around, see if there's anything else you fancy. My name's Daniel, by the way. Daniel Groves.'

'Mine's Felix. And thanks for the advice.'

'No problem.'

They continued driving in silence for a few minutes, both screwing up their eyes at the sun, which was shining directly into their faces and showing up all the smears on the windscreen.

'Got any wild plans for the next four weeks then?'

Felix had been lost in a sudden confusion of excitement and apprehension about Sally. Since her impromptu visit, their exchange of letters had been neither as frequent nor as effusive. It felt as if they had taken a wrong turn and he wasn't sure how to put it right. Caught a little off guard, he stammered, 'Me? Er . . . not really . . . in fact, I'm rather dreading going home. My father died in the summer and my mother is still pretty cut up about it.'

'That's bad luck,' said Daniel quietly. 'What did he die of?'

'Heart attack. Playing tennis.'

'Always knew it was a sodding dangerous game.' The moment the words were out Daniel feared he had gone too far. It was a relief to see his passenger smile cautiously and then laugh out loud. Daniel laughed too, thinking all the while that the boy looked pretty cut up himself, his face all eyes and his mouth tight as if he had got out of the habit of laughing. It made him glad he had done him a good turn. It was unusual for him to take pity on a student. By the end of term he had normally had quite enough of them and of the university scene in general.

'Play any sports then?'

'Rugby. Scrum half.'

'Lucky sod. Used to play myself until a bad concussion a few years back. I run now, which is dull but does the job. The bike's mainly for convenience,' he explained, glancing at its image which was blocking most of the rear-view mirror. 'Saves me a fortune in parking tickets.'

Sport continued to provide a conversational refuge until Daniel pulled into the forecourt of a small service area, explaining that it was the best stop-off point before the turn-off to Farley. 'Good luck, mate,' he said, offering his hand for a farewell shake. 'See you around sometime.'

After thanking him warmly, Felix slipped into the Happy Eater, going first to the toilets where he slapped water on his face and combed his hair before ordering a full English breakfast. He was just debating whether to ask for a second round of toast and coffee when a woman sitting at the table next to his pointed a long pink nail at the cardboard sign propped on his rucksack and said, 'I'm going that way. I'll give you a ride if you like.' She was clearly well into her forties. Her skin had the heavy weathered look of overexposure to the sun. Her hair was long, heavily bleached, and flounced a little theatrically round one side of her neck. 'Don't look so alarmed, I don't bite, you know.'

'I'm not . . .' faltered Felix, 'I mean I'm very grateful, a ride would be great.'

'Spirit of goodwill and all that,' she drawled, reaching for her handbag and casting him a sly smile as she set off in the direction of the Ladies' toilets. 'Back in a tick.'

It was the sort of opportunity eighteen-year-old men were supposed to dream about, Felix reminded himself, quickly settling his bill and gathering up his things. When the woman returned he could see that she had brushed her hair and attended to her lips, which looked pink and faintly gooey.

'Shall we go then?' she said, pulling the fake fur collar of her overcoat up round her ears, and leading the way out to the car park.

Chapter Eleven

————◇◇◇————

It took until mid-morning for Libby to remember why she hated Christmas Day. Misjudging the present wrapping the night before meant she hadn't got to bed until past one o'clock. By which time Alistair, full of festive punch from a works drinks do, was snoring so ferociously it had taken her another hour to fall asleep. The queue for an empty bathroom the next morning had resulted in her abandoning plans – already postponed from the evening before – to wash her hair and style it into something a little more spectacular than the asymmetric mess which she presented to the world on every other day of the year. Tugging on her apron to protect her outfit, a paisley, wine-coloured dress which she had worn the year before and to every meagre social engagement in the interim, Libby felt washed out, irritable and unattractive. Frequent and increasingly worried ministering to the turkey had raised the temperature of the kitchen to such furnace proportions that she resorted to opening every window in the room, even the warped stiff one above the fridge. She had just finished when Alistair, back from the eleven o'clock family service with Beth and the two boys, burst in beating his hands against the cold and singing the Gloria chorus from 'Ding Dong Merrily on High'. At the sight of the windows he gave a theatrical shiver and began reaching for the latches to close them all again.

'Alistair—' Libby had meant to explain about being hot, but at the sight of the trail of muddy brown footprints leading from behind her husband's feet across the kitchen floor and out along the hall carpet, she emitted a shrill scream instead. 'Bloody hell. I've only just put the mop and hoover away. The turkey is refusing to cook and won't be ready till teatime at the earliest. I'd opened the windows because I am expiring with heat and if you don't know why, take over the sodding cooking and find out.' She slung the oven gloves at him and marched towards the door.

Alistair managed to catch her by one arm. 'Happy Christmas, sweetheart. A day of joy, remember? A day for relaxing in the bosom of your family –' he lowered his voice, 'a day for saying bollocks to the turkey and all who sail in it.'

Libby relaxed a little, dropping her head onto his shoulder.

'Our children certainly appear to be getting into the festive spirit. Three volunteers for church has got to be a record. I'm sorry Sally clearly saw fit to avoid the kitchen, but I did catch her humming "O Come All Ye Faithful" when she thought she was safely out of earshot. And so what if we eat lunch at teatime? It's only Jack and the Copelands, hardly a critical audience. Poor Frances is just glad to have somewhere to be other than home and Jack would be happy with bread and soup.'

'Your brother adores his food,' she corrected him, 'he eats four times more than anyone else and is one of the best cooks I know . . .'

They were interrupted by the sound of the doorbell. Alistair kissed her forehead. 'I'll lay the table and then start despatching drinks. Beginning with you, my love. A large gin, doctor's orders.'

Felix and Frances stood clutching parcels on the doorstep, their breath coming out in little clouds. Daisy had rung the day before to explain that she would not be able to make it over the Channel for Christmas after all, due to some ill-defined, last-minute demands on the part of Claude's family. She had been very apologetic, but also faintly aloof, promising to make up with a telephone call to the Taverners' house on Christmas Day.

As Libby was beckoning her guests inside, the sound of a roaring engine heralded the arrival of Alistair's brother, in a sleek black vehicle with glinting silver wheels and a sun roof. The three of them turned to watch as he hoisted his portly frame out from behind the cubicle of a driving seat and bellowed cheery greetings across the drive.

'I've brought the Stilton, stinking and divine.' He waved a white parcel, the size of a small wheel, 'the higher the better, don't you think? The children are getting cheques – I gave up on presents long ago.'

Although Frances had met Jack on several previous occasions, she still found herself marvelling at the differences between the two brothers: one so quietly spoken, the other larger than life, with the kind of noisy cheerfulness that was as hard to ignore as a gale-force wind. He was wearing a green velvet bow tie and Father Christmas socks, which had been pointed out and waggled at them long before his arrival on the doorstep.

'Dearest Lysbeth, thank you for taking me in.' He kissed her on both cheeks, slapped Felix on the back and then gallantly seized Frances by the hand, kissing her knuckles, his beard prickling her skin.

In spite of Libby's culinary concerns, the lunch was a splendid affair. Seated in the middle between Jack and Charlie, the eldest Taverner boy, Frances was given little opportunity to indulge in surges of nostalgia. The only fraught moment came when Alistair raised his glass for a toast to absent friends. A hush descended in an instant, intensified by the almost tangible ripple of guilt that accompanied it. For managing to have a good time, Frances supposed, glancing across the table at Felix, who seemed to have developed an intense fascination for a stray Brussels sprout. 'And here's to the future,' she announced firmly, a little thrilled at her own composure, her ability to release them all from the moment. As she delivered the comment, she chinked glasses with Jack. Everyone else followed suit, an edge of relief to their tender murmurs of acquiescence.

With the teenagers delegated to clear up, the adult party retreated into the sitting room where the floor was still awash with wrapping paper from the morning. Frances bent to gather up an armful, but Libby stopped her, gaily kicking a clear path through to the sofa and flopping down with a sigh. Frances stuffed what she had picked up into an empty box and sat down next to her.

'That was perfectly lovely, thank you Libby. Felix and I would have been utterly downcast at home.'

'Shame Daisy couldn't come.'

Frances made a face. 'Everything's always last minute with her. She lives in a state of perpetual chaos. I wish now I'd gone to see her.' She hesitated. 'But it still feels . . . hard to leave home.'

'Of course it does.' Libby patted her hand. 'I think you're doing marvellously. Grief is like convalescing, it takes time.'

They sat in silence for a few minutes until Frances, wary of becoming morose, made a deliberate bid to switch the subject to woes other than her own. 'Sorry to hear about Jenny, leaving you in the lurch with the shop like that. I did suspect from a couple of exchanges we had on the day of that drama with Sally, that certain dissatisfactions were brewing. I should have warned you, but hoped it might blow over. From what I could gather she's got all sorts of boyfriend trouble too, which can't have helped.'

'The trouble is I can't afford to pay a wage decent enough to attract anyone who's any good.' Libby picked at a stray shred of wrapping paper, rolling it into a ball between her thumb and forefinger. 'December's been better, but still down on last year.' She flicked her pellet of paper across the room, aiming it at Alistair who was sitting in an armchair next to the fireplace, but managing to hit Jack instead, who was sprawled on the carpet like an overfed Roman, piercing dates from a box with a cocktail stick.

'Got me,' he groaned, writhing as if he had been struck by a bullet, until a brotherly kick in the ribs alerted him to the fact that it was his turn to make a move on the chess board Libby had given Alistair for Christmas; a set of marble carved men in pink and blue and grey, with hollow sombre faces and flowing robes.

'What about if I were to step into Jenny's shoes?' ventured Frances, broaching a matter which she had already given some considerable thought.

'Oh Frances, thank you but no, I couldn't possibly expect—'

'Let me finish, will you? I don't want money, I mean obviously you should give me a bit, but I've realised that I need an . . . occupation, so that I can start thinking about something other than the fact that I'm on my own. I've begun to realise that one of the reasons the last four months have been so terribly hard is because of the extent of my dependence on Paul. I mean, obviously I miss him because I loved him,' she faltered, 'but there's more to it than that. It's like I've forgotten who I am, who I was . . . when I went to London the other day I felt so pathetically inept, like a tiny, useless nonentity who had let her world shrink to a pin-head. I saw a street where I used to live and I couldn't even remember what I was like without Paul . . .'

'Nonsense,' declared Libby stoutly, wanting to cover up for the fact that she agreed with every word. 'You've just devoted yourself to your family, instead of neglecting them madly like the rest of us. And you've put in countless hours for that children's charity shop. And what about your lovely drawing—'

'Libby please stop. Those things are nothing. I have been doing nothing.' Frances smiled to show that such confessions were not intended as a reprimand. 'I suppose it's one of life's lovely little ironic twists that I've felt even less inclined towards philanthropy or creativity since I found myself drowning in the time with which to take up such pursuits. I tried the other day, to draw . . .' She broke off, pained at the memory. 'It was hopeless. No, what I want is something to get me out of the house.'

'Are you sure this isn't the wine talking, that you won't regret this in the morning?' Libby, aware of the throb of having drunk too much at the back of her own head, noticed suddenly that Frances's eyes were faintly bloodshot. The meal hadn't finished until five thirty by which time they had broken into the third bottle.

'Promise.' Frances smiled reassuringly. 'I mean every word.' They were interrupted by the sound of the telephone ringing followed by Beth shouting, 'It's Daisy.'

Frances carefully set her glass down on the lamp table next to her and stepped over Jack's legs to get to the door.

Beth was standing in the hall holding out the receiver. 'She wants to talk to Felix as well, but he's disappeared – probably on Pete's computer eradicating goblins. I'll root him out and send him down.'

'Thank you Beth.' Frances took the telephone and sat down on the hall chair, noting as she did so that soggy snowflakes the size of large breadcrumbs were beginning to drift against the hall window, collapsing on contact with the glass. Taking a deep breath she put the receiver to her ear. 'Happy Christmas, darling. We've missed you.'

Daisy slowly replaced the telephone and picked up the hand mirror lying next to it. The bruise on her cheekbone was flowering exotically, unfurling into her eye socket with petals of crimson and dusky blue.

Talking to her mother was like treading on eggshells, trying to read her mood between sentences, wanting to say appropriate things but in a way that sounded natural and which revealed none of the new troubles festering in her own life. Telling herself she had no right to expect motherly intuition or sympathy at such a time, did not prevent Daisy from hoping for some sign of it all the same. She had spoken to Felix too, but only briefly. He sounded somewhat preoccupied, speaking so quietly she had missed some of the words. He was in the middle of a computer game he said, and evidently keen to get back to it. By the end of both conversations Daisy had the strong impression of the three of them floating away from each other, like the slow-motion scatter of splinters after a crash.

Behind her, she was dimly aware of Claude entering the room. A few seconds later he was at her side, gently taking the mirror and laying it face-down on the table. Cupping her cheeks between his hands he began to kiss her face, beginning with her hairline and forehead and working downwards, lingering tenderly round her eyes, licking the tears spilling through her closed lashes.

'*Ma petite . . . pauvre.*' His mouth was on her neck, brushing her skin with kisses between words.

Daisy took his head in her palms, trying feebly to push him away, fighting the urge to luxuriate in this penitence, to sink into the sheer relief of it. It was so good to be wanted for forgiveness, to be cherished again. It took a conscious effort to check herself, to force her mind back to the horror of the previous morning, the shouting, the accusations, the slow steady spiral towards the release of violence, coming so fast and so furiously that there had been no time even to raise her hands to protect herself. Thinking back, Daisy even found herself struggling to recall the pain, the rag-doll weakness which had overcome her under the hammer of his fists. Already it was receding, drowning in the pleasure of this new submission, on his knees now at her feet, begging to be forgiven like a doting child. Slowly she relaxed her hands, letting her fingers run through the silky strands of his hair to the soft vulnerable spot in the nape of his neck. He dropped his head to her chest with a groan, tightening his arms around her waist, biting her skin gently through her clothes.

★

After putting down the phone, Frances remained in the hall for a few moments, suddenly furious at her daughter, for sounding so punishingly remote, for the way her last-minute absence had caused an unnecessary shadow over what was always going to be a difficult day. It was hard enough, she reflected grimly, clinching her hands into fists. Daisy should have made the effort to come. She felt so let down suddenly that she had to lean against the hall table to steady herself.

'All well out here?' offered Libby brightly, popping her head round the doorway from the sitting room.

Frances quickly straightened herself, brushing at invisible creases in her skirt.

'Come back and join the party. We've just had an open ballot on whether to move on to a pot of tea or uncork another bottle. The bottle won hands down. The children are all entertaining themselves somewhere and Jack's threatening to play the piano. He and Alistair do a couple of party pieces – quite well sometimes, particularly if they're full of wine.'

Chapter Twelve

Sally hovered in the doorway of Pete's bedroom boring her eyes into the back of Felix's head until he turned round. She could see that both her brothers were deeply engrossed in the computer and that their guest had been relegated to the role of observer. Beth was listening to CDs in her bedroom and the adults were getting drunk. Uncle Jack had started singing, which was always a sure sign.

The two boys barely noticed as Felix slipped out of the room. Taking his hand, Sally led the way up to the top floor which housed her own small bedroom and the much larger bed-sitting room belonging to Charlie. At the top of the stairs Felix stopped and shook his head. 'I really don't think . . .'

'Not in my room silly. In here.' She tapped on a low door set into the wall, leading to the eaves space that passed for an attic. 'No one would ever think of looking in here.' They had barely seen each other since the start of the holidays, thwarted both by appalling weather and the challenging logistics of arranging secret meetings. Since Sally's day of truancy both parents had been horribly vigilant. A brief ten minutes under the bridge on a dark chilly evening, without the time even to make love, had provided little by way of emotional reassurance. 'And no one's even going to notice anyway,' continued Sally breathlessly, 'they're all busy getting pissed.' As if to prove her point, the muted sound of Uncle Jack's throaty tenor came drifting up from the ground floor. 'Come on.' She lifted the latch and slipped inside. After a moment's hesitation Felix followed, quietly pulling the door to behind him. As his eyes accustomed themselves to the dark, he was able to make out crates of books, old suitcases, a couple of chairs, a table lamp. The ceiling was sloping and low, forcing him to stoop even at its highest point.

'Over here,' hissed Sally, already deep into the room. 'Look what I've found.' She was tussling with a single mattress, which had been propped up against an old chest of drawers. 'Perfect, wouldn't you say?' she exclaimed, pushing it to the ground. Clouds of dust flew into her face, stinging her eyes and making her cough. Undaunted, she spread out her arms in triumph. She wanted Felix if anything worse than before. To lay claim to him. To prove to herself that nothing had changed, to overlay all her recent doubts and disappointments with fresh better times.

'Sal, I don't know . . .' Felix glanced anxiously over his shoulder. The edges of the door were illuminated in a bright yellow rectangle by the landing light outside. 'And I haven't got any you-know-whats . . .' He patted his pockets helplessly.

'It doesn't matter, I'm in the safe time. Oh come on Felix, please. It will be good, you know it will.'

At the sight of Sally peeling off her T-shirt with the exuberance of a swimmer preparing to dive into a pool, Felix forgot all his reservation. He even forgot the episode with the flirtatious blonde woman. Nothing had happened, but he had wanted it to, which felt almost as bad. He had fantasised about it every night since, imagining moves of unbearable eroticism, waking in the night with a longing of such physical desperation that he was almost afraid.

Sally's skin glowed like soft ivory in the dim light. Felix began picking his way through the bric-à-brac towards her, reaching one hand to her outstretched arms. From downstairs the quietness was suddenly broken by the muffled strum of the piano and the rise and fall of two throaty male voices.

★

When Libby began talking about her being welcome to stay the night Frances knew it was time to go home. Aware that she had drunk far too much to drive, she was on the point of calling a taxi when Jack boomed his desire to be of service.

'I've been on coffee for at least two hours, in case you soaks hadn't noticed.' He blew extravagantly at the palm of one hand. 'Would sail through a breathalyser with full marks. I won't hear of a refusal.'

Frances exchanged looks with Libby who shrugged and raised her eyebrows in a way that suggested approval. He looked and sounded sober enough, reflected Frances, suddenly too tired to argue and beginning to gather up her things.

There was a last minute flurry when no one could find Felix. 'I thought he was still in with Pete and Charlie,' explained Beth, 'but they're both in the den watching telly. He must be upstairs.' Libby led the way up to the first landing, with Frances following behind. When all rooms proved dark and empty they carried on to the next floor, calling his name. Casting a quizzical look over her shoulder, Libby knocked smartly on her youngest daughter's bedroom door.

'Sally?'

'Yes?' After a couple of moments, Sally duly appeared, her short brown hair looking more unkempt than usual, her green eyes glinting with innocence.

'You haven't seen Felix by any chance? Frances wants to go home and we seem to have mislaid him.'

'Try Charlie's room,' she replied idly, 'I thought I heard some movement in there a bit ago.'

He was asleep on Charlie's bed, curled into an S shape and clasping a pillow under one cheek. Both women checked themselves, each struck by the insouciant vulnerability of a sleeping child, even an eighteen-year-old child with straggly hair and dark shadows under his eyes. 'Let him stay,' whispered Libby, retreating to the door. 'Charlie will be quite happy on the sofa bed. He looks so peaceful and it's gone ten. We'll fill him with breakfast and post him back tomorrow morning, I promise.'

'Are you sure?' murmured Frances, aware that some selfish part of her was reluctant to return to the empty house alone, but knowing too that it would be unnecessary cruelty to wake Felix up for a ten-minute journey squashed in the narrow back seat of a freezing car.

Peering through a crack in her door behind them, Sally burned with satisfaction. It was not long since they had emerged from their hiding place. Felix, full of yawns, had taken up her suggestion of lying down on Charlie's bed. While Sally, tense with energy and a thrilling sense of her own daring, had retreated to her bedroom. After answering the door to her mother, she quickly changed her pants which were sticky with semen, and slipped downstairs to join her brothers in front of the television.

Having said her farewells, Frances followed Jack to his car, skidding slightly on the crazy paving leading down to the drive. Thanks to the drop in temperature which had accompanied nightfall, all that remained of the snow was a sheeny, treacherous film of ice.

'Fuck me, it's worse than I thought,' declared Jack cheerfully, as his wheels failed to get a grip on the smooth tarmac of the road and the car slid forwards diagonally for a few yards, like a horse straining to be given the run of an open space. Frances, wedged beside him, her teeth chattering, felt faintly alarmed. 'No self-respecting traffic cop will be out in this anyway,' he added, managing at the same time to steady the car into a more or less straight course. 'Give me directions, won't you? I know where you live theoretically, but these lanes all look the same in the dark.'

By the time they turned into Frances's drive, the car was snug with heat. 'Find your keys before you get out, or if you're anything like me you'll be hopping around on the doorstep for ages.'

Frances laughed, patting her coat pocket. 'I know exactly where they are – and thank you Jack, that was extremely kind—' She was prevented from completing the sentence by the unexpected clamping of her companion's mouth on hers. His beard was like a rough cloth, and his tongue so quick off the mark that it took several moments to eject it from her mouth.

'Really, Jack, I . . .' she gasped, pulling free and hurriedly wiping her lips with the back of her hand. 'I don't think . . .'

He looked unperturbed. 'Wrong call eh? Sorry. Couldn't resist it. Perhaps I need more coffee after all. No bad feelings, I hope?'

'I guess not,' muttered Frances, scrambling out of the car and hurrying into the house – no longer a bleak prospect, but a welcome haven. Once the door was closed behind her, she burst out laughing, clapping her hand to her mouth like a schoolgirl. Less exuberant thoughts followed the hysteria. Had Alistair and Libby invited Jack to stay with her in mind? Had they guessed what the drive home might result in, engineered it even? Though unlikely, the notion induced a more sombre frame of mind. A forty-three-year-old widow was vulnerable in so many respects, she reflected gloomily, remembering Libby's suspicions over Joseph Brackman and wondering if they could be true after all. Feeling suddenly wide awake, she poured herself a thumbful of whisky and retreated to the sitting room. She slumped down on the sofa and flicked on the television, aware that for the first time since Paul's death she was feeling not so much lonely for him as just plain lonely.

On the screen Meg Ryan was half-way through her celebrated and very public rendition of a feigned sexual climax. Frances flicked channels to find the same actress on top of the Empire State Building clasped in the arms of a grieving widower with a young son. Thinking of Jack's bushy mouth and the contrasting bumbling events of real life, Frances turned off the television with a humph of irritation. On the table in front of her were the papers, still unread from the day before, together with the bumper Christmas issue of the *Spectator*, one of Paul's regular subscriptions which she barely glanced at but still did not have the heart to cancel. On picking it up to glance at the cartoon on the cover, the back page fell open revealing a section of classified advertisements. Frances was on the point of closing it when her eye was caught by a black box containing the words: *Intelligent, sensitive man. Likes classical music, Italian food, reading and walking. Fifty years old, reasonable looks. Lives Surrey area. Affectionate and loyal. Seeks lady for companionship, hopefully developing into lasting relationship. Love of Italian food and sense of humour essential. Serious enquiries only please. Box number SLH98/1240.*

Whether it was the effects of alcohol, her mood or the fact that the context was Paul's favourite periodical, Frances found herself irresistibly drawn to the idea of the author of the advert. She pictured a tall, distinguished, grey-haired man with grey twinkling eyes and a kind smile. A doctor maybe, or a connoisseur of antiques. By the time she finished her whisky, she had read the notice several times. It was the only one of its kind on the page, all the other personal listings relating to singles magazines and people offering to do tax returns. In the bottom left-hand corner was another box containing a note of warning from the editors, to the effect that they would not be liable for any damage incurred or suffered as a result of readers accepting or offering any of the invitations printed above. Which was reasonable enough, reflected Frances, trying unsuccessfully to transpose the image of her grey-haired doctor into an axeman with sado-masochistic tendencies.

Telling herself that she was merely experimenting with what one might say in such circumstances, she fetched a pad of paper from the bureau behind the sofa and began to compose a reply. Instead of a proper letter she found herself writing what could have been a similar advert for her own circumstances: *Intelligent, sensitive, forty-three-year-old woman. Recently widowed and seeking male friendship . . .'* She paused, wondering whether to add 'love'. *Fair-haired, slim build. Lives*

Kent area. Loves Italian food and in possession of good – if slightly rusty – sense of humour. Not knowing about box numbers or how to get them and dimly fearful of the axe murderer scenario, Frances printed the number to Paul's fax machine at the bottom of the page. Aware that the whisky on top of so much wine was probably taking a serious toll on her senses, she nonetheless could not resist slipping the page into an envelope and hastily scrawling the box office number across the middle.

It was only a joke, she told herself, once she was upstairs preparing for bed, a curious diversion to round off a curious day. Whether she chose to post it in the sober light of morning would be quite another matter.

More used now to the empty half of the bed Frances had no qualms in lying diagonally across it, stretching into the space with her feet and burrowing her arms up under Paul's pillows, loving the icy cool of the empty space. Sleep came quickly, spurred on by wild imaginings about being guided from beyond the grave, about finding someone to provide the fresh focus which her life so badly needed.

Chapter Thirteen

The teasing presentiments of Frances's dreams received something of a rude awakening at the startling discovery that Felix, returning while she was still asleep the next morning, had seen fit to deposit her response to the *Spectator* advert, together with a couple of other letters on the hall table, in the post box at the bottom of the lane.

'I had some stamps,' he explained simply, unaware of the implications of his actions and not having analysed his motives beyond a vague urge to atone for his behaviour at the Taverners' the previous afternoon. 'I've also tidied up a bit downstairs.' He placed a cup of tea on the bedside table and glanced hopefully at his mother for signs of gratitude. But Frances was too busy digesting the news about the letter and the fact that she had managed to sleep until the unprecedented hour of eleven thirty in the morning. Disappointed, Felix walked over to the window and tugged at the curtains. 'I was going to polish my halo even further by doing something useful in the garden, but I see you've got it looking splendid all on your own.' In spite of his irritation, he chose his tone carefully. Injecting too much congratulation into the remark might have sounded condescending, or as if he fancied himself as some great authority on how his mother should occupy her time now she was alone. 'It looks great,' he added, clenching his jaw, inwardly feeling the strain of having to weigh every word. Being home was even worse than he had anticipated. After so many weeks away in a new environment, there were none of the usual daily points of contact, nothing to refer to that they had in common. Except for the absence of his father, of course, which felt both too raw and too obvious to mention.

'You mean the grass . . . ?'

'Among other things. You've really done a lot.'

Frances pulled on her dressing gown and hurriedly joined her son at the window. Seen from above, it was clear that the lawn-cutting of the previous week had formed the basis of subsequent, even more elaborate attentions. The edges of the bed had been strimmed back to their original strong clear lines, perfect frames for the heaps of dark freshly weeded soil. The plants had been freed of dead wood and trailing flower stems, presenting instead an array of brutal but flattering hair-cuts, ready to enjoy a fresh burst of growth in the spring.

'Bloody man,' hissed Frances, much to the bafflement of her son. Forgetting her tea she began tugging on clothes.

'What's up?'

'It's not me, it's Joseph Brackman – he's been doing the garden—'

'So, what's wrong with that?'

Frances looked up, exasperated. 'I haven't asked him to. He just sneaks up here and does it. Which is not . . . not . . .' She struggled to articulate what it was that she found so wrong. 'I think perhaps he's hoping for some money . . .' She broke off again, reluctant to explain the exact nature of her distrust at their neighbour's motives. Even if Libby's warnings proved exaggerated, she had no desire to feel any further obligation towards the man – not even as an employer of his gardening skills.

'I'm going to go down there and have a word with him.' She took her wallet out of her handbag and hurried out of the house, leaving Felix staring at the untouched tea and wondering why he had bothered.

Deciding to take the quick route, Frances let herself out

through the garden gate and headed towards the river, placing her feet on the highest clods of mud, still solid from the icy temperatures of the previous night. It was only when she reached the footbridge that she slowed her pace, realising that she was dizzy and hungover and that to complain about kindness was not the easiest of missions, especially not on a crisp Boxing Day morning. The footbridge, no more than two planks thrown from bank to bank years before, with a crude balustrade on one side, was flecked with patches of brilliant green moss. What was visible of the wood looked black and slippery. Feeling somehow warned off at the sight of it, Frances turned to head for home, only to be confronted by Joseph himself, appearing soundlessly from behind a clump of spiky trees. Unnerved, her complaint spilt out of her, with none of the tact or cordiality she had rehearsed inside her head.

'About my garden – I know it's you – I'd really rather you didn't.' She popped open her wallet and began waving ten-pound notes in the air. 'Let me see, it must be several hours' worth . . .'

He was wearing his brown cap again. The two thirds of his face revealed beneath it looked grey and impassive. 'Don't you recognise a gift when you see one?' he growled, looking not at her but over her shoulder at the river. There followed a few moments' silence while Frances tried to collect herself, to rearrange her anger to address this new and unexpected response. She grew aware of the sound of the water next to them, forcing its way through the reeds under the bridge with gentle slaps and hisses.

'I know you mean to be kind,' she began slowly, 'but I would hate to feel . . .'

'I don't want anything from you,' he interrupted, 'not even friendship, if you're not prepared to give it. That must be a gift too, or it is nothing.' He looked quickly away, squinting at the reflection of the sun on the water behind. 'You haven't seen my mother have you?'

'Your mother? No, I . . .'

'She must have wandered off last night or early this morning. I usually hear her, but I'd been drinking.' He smiled ruefully, causing Frances to feel a sudden leap of pity at the thought of the grim realities of Christmas Day for such an isolated, eccentric pair.

'Would you like me to help look?' Ashamed now of her outburst, she was eager to make amends. 'Heavens, but it was freezing last night—'

'Don't worry. I'm heading home now anyway. I expect she's there. She usually gets herself back in the end – habit or instinct or something. Doesn't seem to feel the cold either. As reluctant to wear a coat as a child.' He stepped past her onto the footbridge.

'Joseph – look, I'm sorry,' she called. 'About the garden and so on, I feel such a fool.'

'No need. If you want anything done you have only to ask. I never had much time for your husband, to be honest, but he had an eye for beauty that's for sure, of the ordered kind, that is.' He touched the peak of his cap and stepped past her to the bridge, moving briskly, not bothering to steady himself on the side rail.

Back home Frances found Felix slumped in front of the television eating from a large bag of tortilla chips.

'I was going to cook some lunch.'

'Don't bother, I'm not hungry.'

'I'm not surprised.' Frances made a teasing lunge for the bag, but he jerked it out of reach with a grunt of irritation. 'I'll make a macaroni cheese – it won't take long—'

'Don't bother. I said I'm not hungry. I'm not a kid any more. I'll eat when I need to.' He flicked the television off and stamped upstairs to his bedroom, taking his snack with him. He knew he had hurt her, but didn't care. She barely seemed to notice him these days. It was like she had left the planet. He threw the remainder of the bag of chips into the bin and opened one of the text books he had been assigned to read in the holidays. Too preoccupied to concentrate, his eyes skimmed the words. Not missing his father did not prevent a baffling anger at the fact that he was no longer around. And even the Sally business, once so simple, had grown complicated. The day before, lying on the mattress in the attic after making love, she had wheedled so hard for reassurance, that he felt bullied. Feeling the same silent pressure behind her gaze over the mayhem of breakfast that morning he had deliberately ignored it, wolfing his cereal and saying a hearty farewell to the whole room. Yet looking back on the scene, remembering Sally's taut, sad face, he felt mean and regretful. Felix dropped his head onto his open book and closed his eyes, wistful suddenly for all the early tremulous uncertainty, when he had had to chisel away at Sally's fractious outer shell for signs of the softness inside.

Downstairs Frances set about making macaroni cheese, telling herself it would do for supper. Furious though she was at Felix's rudeness, she was determined not to make a big issue of it. It was a hard time for both of them, she reasoned, some conflicts were inevitable. Though tempted to bring up the subject of Paul on many occasions, she had mostly resisted, waiting for prompts from Felix himself. Knowing the delicate idiosyncrasies of her own grief, she felt she had little right to probe that of her son's. He would open up in time, she told herself, grating cheese so vigorously that yellow crumbs bounced off the plate. Maybe even over a nice meal that night. Feeling an old maternal stab of satisfaction at the sight of the heaped casserole dish, she carefully wrapped the remaining stump of cheddar in Cellophane and stowed it in the fridge.

But when Felix emerged from his room it was to tell her that he was catching the bus into Hexford to meet up with old schoolfriends. Dismayed, but not wanting to appear nagging, Frances waved him off with a show of nonchalance. She picked at the macaroni cheese alone, watching Harrison Ford seduce a girl young enough to be his granddaughter and wondering when, if ever, the pulse of normality might return to everyday life.

Chapter Fourteen

It was Sally who found Mrs Brackman. Or rather Sheba, rootling along the bank in the semi-darkness of late afternoon. She was floating face down, her straggly grey hair matted round the back of her neck, her white nightdress ballooning round her thin, veiny thighs. Sally recognised her at once, because of the hair and white nightie, and the purple roots of blood in the lower calves. Tugging at Sheba's lead, repulsed at the animal's eager curiosity, she allowed herself only one glance at the corpse before backing away. She moved slowly, taking big steps, her heels slipping in the soft mud.

Although the Brackmans' cottage was probably closer, Sally's instincts directed her back up to the road home. Darkness was falling fast and all was silent apart from the gentle scraping of Sheba's claws on the road. She walked as quickly as she could, soundless on her rubber soles, aware that in spite of her thin jacket and the increasing cold she was sweating. The gruesome image of her discovery floated alongside, adding such urgency to her stride that when she got to the phone box at the fork in the lane she almost passed it without stopping. Fingers trembling, she dialled not 999 but 192, in order to get the Brackman phone number. She dropped her ten-pence piece twice before managing to steer it into the slot. 'Your mother is . . . I'm sorry, but I've just seen her . . . in the river,' she stammered, when Joseph answered the phone.

'Under the old stone bridge next to Leybourne Lane. I'm so sorry.' Unable to manage any more she dropped the receiver and set off at a run for home.

At the sight of her family, ranged cosily round a three-dimensional counter game that somebody had given somebody the day before, Sally burst out crying and couldn't stop. It was several minutes before the cause of her hysteria was understood. There followed a flurry of telephone calls and soothing attentions. She was given a half inch of brandy and tucked up on the sofa like an invalid. When the sobs kept on coming, as irrepressible and persistent as hiccoughs, they explained it was shock and would ease with time. But Sally, shaking and shivering till her whole body ached, knew that it was more and worse; that finding Mrs Brackman's corpse in such a place at such a time had violated more than her peace of mind. The affair with Felix was over. Their coupling in the attic had sorted nothing. At breakfast he had looked not only sheepish, but ashamed. A little repulsed, even. She had gone to the bridge for comfort. Stumbling on old Mrs Brackman merely confirmed that there was none to be had, ever again about anything.

After an hour or so, Libby pressed her palm along her daughter's forehead and pronounced her ill. So ill that Dr Leigham was summoned from a family game of charades to administer reassurance and antibiotics. Sally, who knew that she was indeed sick, but on the inside where no medicines could reach her, submitted to each new development with a meekness that made her parents afraid. Deep inside some part of her relished being consigned to the role of patient, for the excuse it gave for withdrawal and passivity, for the way it allowed her father to bundle her in his arms and gently carry her to bed. 'Can't have you ill, little one, can we?' he murmured, nuzzling her hair with his nose, staggering a little under her weight at the turn in the stairs.

★

The old adage that other people's woes offered the best distraction from one's own was certainly proven in Frances's case during the course of the next few days. Sally ran such a high temperature that Libby refused to leave her side. No one was allowed to visit, not even Felix, who kindly offered to go round with a few cassettes and some music magazines. Instead of the promised gentle introduction to the challenging complexities of retailing, Frances ended up manning Libby's shop almost entirely on her own, with a telephone as the only lifeline for crises over Switch cards, the eccentricities of the till and guessing prices for the innumerable objects that had no tag.

Addressing the problem of helping Joseph Brackman, as Frances felt duty bound to do, was equally taxing. Having been at pains to keep him at arm's length, she was only too aware of the irony of finding herself on the doorstep of his cottage, thermos of soup and box of chocolates in hand, playing a role she had herself so recently despised. That it was the right course of action to take, however, she had little doubt. Not just because of the rules of common decency, but also because, with hindsight, she recognised the integral role played by the outside world in jolting her out of the black self-indulgence of her own unhappiness.

It took several knocks to summon Joseph to the door. He looked dazed with shock, chalky-faced, the scar a purple worm.

'I should have found her,' he murmured, over and over again, while Frances made tea and unscrewed the lid of the half bottle of brandy in her coat pocket.

'It wasn't your fault.'

'Hardly an Ophelia, but beautiful in her way, with the darkness and the silver moon. Hardly an Ophelia, but beautiful,' he repeated to himself, as if rehearsing refrains for the written page.

'It wasn't your fault,' Frances said again, handing him a drink and being vividly transported back to the early days of her own grief, when no consolations had any effect, and how she had needed to hear them all the same. Seeing the rawness of his emotions, the way he clumsily gulped the drink, she experienced a small stab of relief at how far she had moved on.

While less charitable members of the community murmured that Joseph Brackman's loss constituted perhaps the least harrowing of options from the spectrum of possibilities for human bereavement, Frances, after a couple of visits to the cottage, began to see that there was nothing easy about it at all. Not just because of the macabre circumstances of the old lady's death and Joseph's sense of guilt, but because of suddenly finding himself relieved of a role to which he had grown deeply accustomed. The millstone of a dependent mother had had its advantages, she realised, for the structure it imposed on his existence, for the pretext it gave for social isolation. While never openly addressing such issues himself, Joseph began to reveal an almost paranoic fear of being forced to exchange the cottage for one of the shoe-box flats on the new Leybourne estate. Frances reassured him on the matter as best she could, explaining that bureaucracies could take years to come up with such initiatives and that there were a hundred ways to resist them when they did.

In the midst of these dramas, Felix announced his intention to return early for the spring term. Ever since Christmas Day he had been so moody and irritable, so impervious to every effort at communication, that Frances was almost relieved to see him go. 'I don't know if he's missing his father or suffering under an avalanche of hormones,' she told Joseph, when she visited the cottage a couple of days after Mrs Brackman's funeral, resorting to the subject in a somewhat desperate bid to engage his interest. Recently he had seemed calmer, but in a tight, deeply controlled manner that lacked conviction. 'It has crossed my mind that my son's real reason for returning to Sussex so early could be a fermenting student love affair – mothers are always the last to know these things.'

Joseph, sitting nursing a mug of tea at his kitchen table, let out a dry laugh. 'The young Taverner girl won't like it if he is. The pair of them have been carrying on for months in nooks and crannies along the river.'

Astonished both at the lucidity and content of this response, Frances turned slowly from the sink where she had been working through a stack of dirty dishes. 'And which young Taverner girl would that be, Joseph?'

'The one that found Mother, poor creature . . . is she still running a fever?'

'She's much better, I believe,' Frances replied, shaking her head in wonder at having stumbled upon the cause of Felix's moodiness and debating what if anything to do about it. She returned her hands to the soapy water, pressing them palms down on the bottom of the old porcelain bowl, noting the thousands of hairline cracks criss-crossing its edges. While aware that she ought to disapprove, she felt instead a well of tenderness. She had met her own first serious boyfriend at fifteen. And Sally could do worse than Felix, who underneath his moods, was sensible and kind.

When she got back home, she reached for the phone with the intention of telling Libby, but changed her mind. Although Sally was well enough to cope with the now intermittent start to the school term and her own hours in the shop had been cut to a more reasonable three-day week, Libby was still fairly fraught. It would be unkind to burden her with further worries, Frances told herself, especially if the romance turned out to be over and done with, or merely the imaginings of a disturbed mind.

Still musing upon the possibilities, she wandered up to Paul's study with the intention of having a final, thorough look for the missing share certificate. Hugo Gerard had mentioned it again in a recent communication about dividends, his own tidy mind clearly still irritated by its disappearance. Kneeling down to pull open the bottom drawer of the filing cabinet, her eye was caught by several inches of paper hanging out of the back of the fax machine.

Dear Friend   *December 29*

Thank you for your reply. I would so like to meet you. It will be an ordeal I know, if you feel half the timidity I do. But some sixth sense tells me our apprehensions will slip away fast. And if they don't, no harm will have been done. Please call me to arrange a time. Since we have not exchanged photos, red roses in our lapels will have to do. My telephone number is: 01483 6539921. Call soon.

Yours hopefully,
James Harcourt

Frances gently tore the piece of paper from the machine and read it again, several times, her heart thumping inside her rib cage. After nervously checking for faxes in the days immediately after Felix's alarming good turn on Boxing Day morning and finding nothing, she had stopped bothering. With so much going on in the meantime it had taken little effort to put the matter to the back of her mind.

The fax had been sitting unattended for over a week, Frances realised now, glancing in horror at the date and then promptly telling herself that this was a sign that the whole enterprise was never meant to be, that James Harcourt would have long since followed up on other infinitely more promising replies. She screwed the paper into a ball with the intention of dropping it into the bin, only to find when she got back downstairs that it was still clasped in the palm of her hand.

Chapter Fifteen

At the sight of Felix's mother, half-way up a stepladder seeing to a display on a top shelf, Sally was tempted to turn and run out of the shop. But the little bell above the door had already announced her presence and Frances was smiling hello and asking how she was. Sally responded as politely as she could, observing in spite of her own preoccupations, that Mrs Copeland was looking better than she had ever seen her before. Stunning in fact. Her hair was pinned to the back of her head in a loose, sweeping bun, showing off delicate silver earrings and the fine strong line of her jaw. She was wearing make-up too, not much, but enough to enhance the greeny-brown of her eyes and the generous outline of her lips. 'You look nice,' she remarked shyly.

'Thank you Sally and so do you,' replied Frances a little briskly, stepping off the ladder and wiping a stray wisp of hair from her forehead with the back of her hand. Having endured quite a grilling from Libby, she was in no mood to confess her imminent blind date with James Harcourt to her daughter as well. 'You had everybody rather worried. It's lovely to see you looking so well again.' She beamed, feeling a stab of fondness for Felix and wishing she could come right out and ask the girl whether Joseph's claims about the pair of them were true.

Sally blushed, scowling at the compliment. She had been enduring similar remarks from teachers all day at school. That she looked healthier seemed to her to be a fact of the cruellest irony and one that arose from a new and frenzied appetite for food, confectionery in particular. Eating lifted her spirits, providing the only flimsy respite she had yet discovered for the misery still bubbling inside. While not officially splitting, she had barely glimpsed Felix before he scuttled back to university. It was the worst of all worlds, nothing resolved, but not much room for hope either. To make matters worse, her old skinny self was disappearing, drowning in a new, robustly fleshed profile that she barely recognised. Her once flat breasts were beginning to push into the creases of her bra, while her school skirt was so tight she had left the top button undone, hiding it under the hem of her jumper. Even her feet had grown. In fact the only reason she was in the shop was because of a promised expedition with her mother to go in search of new shoes.

Struck suddenly by how alike Felix and his mother were, Sally's blush deepened. They even had the same quizzical look in their eyebrows, like they were eager for a reason to smile. It was a relief to see her own mother emerging from the store room, winding a scarf round her neck and pulling on gloves.

'There you are.' Libby kissed Sally fondly on the forehead. 'Shall we go darling? Don't worry Frances, I'll be back to do the daily tally and lock up. Couldn't have you being late tonight, could we?' She grinned conspiratorially, making her new employee wish, for by no means the first time, that she had kept her date with James Harcourt to herself. Though Frances knew Libby meant well, there was something a little too eager about her attitude, as if she found the whole scenario entertaining. But she had been immensely supportive too, she reminded herself, remembering Libby's thoughtful eagerness to dispel any fears about such a bold move being in any way premature or disloyal.

By the time Libby returned to relieve her of her duties, Frances's apprehension about the approaching evening had turned to sheer terror. It was insanity. Unnecessary torture. Far better to return to the empty but familiar surroundings of her home, to kick off her shoes and drift through another evening alone. Lonely and dishevelled maybe, but in the bliss of un-demanding privacy. Attempting to re-do her lipstick in the rear-view mirror of the car, her hand trembled so much she had to give up, smoothing the colour out with the tip of her index finger instead. Putting on the inside light, she scrutinised the map for perhaps the tenth time, tracing the route down yellow and red lines to the small dark circle representing the town in which they had agreed to meet. Half-way between his home and hers, neutral territory, joked James Harcourt, his voice sounding – so she had thought at the time and reminded herself on many occasions since – pleasingly warm and rich. In the glove compartment of the car, its stem carefully wrapped in silver foil, sat a single red rose. She had bought it from the florists the day before, intending just to buy the one flower, but ending up shelling out almost ten pounds for a bunch of six instead. Not because she had wanted a vaseful for the hall table, but out of a momentary panic at the sheer osten-tatiousness of buying only one, dreading the look of enquiry it might prompt from the salesgirl.

The journey would take no more than thirty minutes, James Harcourt said, sounding full of manly authority. An authority she had missed, Frances realised with a lurch of her heart, meticulously taking down every one of his details about the route, which included numerous specific stretches of miles and yards and unmissable landmarks for turnings left and right. Their tryst was to be in a pub called the Dancing Bear. It served excellent food, James said and was informal without being noisy. Frances had ventured the reply that perhaps they should be meeting somewhere Italian. At which he had laughed, adding that he hoped there would be time for such treats later. Frances had laughed too, her heart pounding, half marvelling and half horrified at her daring. After she put the phone down, it had taken several minutes for her pulse to recede to its usual imperceptibility. Being alone had suddenly felt intolerable. As did the thought of surviving for any longer on a social diet of Libby and Joseph Brackman.

Sitting alone in the car however, waiting for the digital clock to creep round to six thirty, Frances felt very remote from such convictions. It was too early to set off, but there wasn't enough time to go home either. She switched on the radio and tried to concentrate on a derailed train in India and an emergency summit on the state of the world economy. There was a fresh peace drive in Northern Ireland and a toddler rescued from an icy lake by a family dog. With an enormous effort of will, she managed to listen to five minutes of the quiz show which followed the news before inserting the key in the ignition. It would not do to arrive early, to show any of the terror and desperation she felt inside. She would be cool and demure, she told herself, exiting from her parking slot at last. Once on the main road, she accelerated to a modest speed which she hoped would allow her to arrive five minutes after James Harcourt, all the while reminding herself not to shriek out loud if he had hairy ears or a bulbous wart on his nose.

This veneer of composure was soon shattered by a prolonged spell behind the mud-spattered bumper of an articulated truck. Usually wary of overtaking even a moped on dark country lanes, Frances found herself pulling out at the most reckless moments, and cursing viciously every time oncoming head-lights or a sudden bend forced her back into confinement. Just when she had convinced herself that James Harcourt must have dictated the same cross country route to the driver of the truck, it turned off, swinging out of sight like a ponderous dinosaur. It was already five to seven and she was barely half-way. With an open road at last, Frances drove like a creature possessed. She made up so much ground that on reaching the village before her destination, she was only twenty minutes behind schedule. To celebrate, she slowed to the prescribed speed limit and took a series of deep breaths. By the time she stopped at the last T-junction she had returned herself to a state of oxygenated serenity. Apart from a car already indicating its intention to turn into her road, the coast was clear. Seeing the car slow down Frances pulled out to turn across it. It was only then that she saw the cyclist, until that moment shielded from view on the far side of the approaching car. A split second later there was a terrible muffled thump, as the bicycle made contact with her bumper. With almost comic athleticism the cyclist flew several feet into the air before landing in the middle of the road, a frozen dark heap illuminated in the beam of her car headlights. Frances was so sure that she had killed him that she watched in disbelief as the man clambered to his feet and retrieved his bicycle. Realising suddenly that she was straddling the main road, she jerkily manoeuvred to the grass verge on the far side. The next thing she knew he was banging his fist on her back windscreen, yelling, 'Just you hang on a minute.'

'I was just parking,' she called, quickly getting out of the car and finding that her knees were shaking so much she had to lean against the bonnet to steady herself. 'Thank God you're all right. I just didn't see you – I mean suddenly you were there and flying through the air – I'm so sorry – thank God you're OK.' He was wearing a helmet, a dark jacket and jeans.

'It was my bloody right of way.' He undid the chin strap of his helmet, leaving it to flap against his cheek as he talked. 'And I'm not all right, I've hurt my ankle and the front wheel of my bike is buckled – Christ knows what that will cost – weren't you bloody well looking, or what?'

Frances felt close to tears. The shock was still with her, compounded by a mounting sense of helpless urgency. James Harcourt would be sitting at the bar looking at his watch, writing her off as a coward, or as someone incapable of punctuality – a trait he would not find endearing, she decided suddenly, a moment of lucidity briefly piercing the confusion inside her head. 'Look, I'm very late – on my way somewhere.'

'Well, sorry if I've inconvenienced you in any way.'

'No, I didn't mean . . . it was all my fault, I know. You were hidden by that car that was turning, I just didn't see you until it was too late and I'm sorry you're hurt and of course I'll pay for whatever damage has been done to your bicycle.' She rummaged in her bag for a pen and something to write on.

'Could do with a witness,' he muttered, glancing up as a van sped by, the car which had been the unwitting catalyst for their accident having long since disappeared. He limped over to where Frances stood, watching her write her name and address in silence, before suddenly blurting out, 'How do I know it's not false?'

'Because I'm not that kind of person,' Frances retorted, suddenly furious at the whole calamitous situation, at the vile inevitability of it. Of course she wasn't going to meet a handsome, kind stranger over a candlelit dinner for two. Life wasn't like that. Life was bumping into things in the dark and nearly murdering them. 'And I'd better take your details too.' She tore off a back page of her cheque book and handed him the pen. 'We can put the bike in the boot and your ankle probably ought to be looked at – I don't suppose there's a hospital with an emergency department near here is there?'

'I don't need a hospital, thank you. A lift home will do.'

Frances experienced a moment of hesitation. The way her evening was going it would be just her luck to have collided with a serial killer. But on seeing how he dragged his left leg on traipsing back to his bike all her guilt and sympathy returned. 'Oh dear, I am so sorry.' She tried to pick up one half of the bicycle but he swung it out of reach. She could see that the front wheel was badly bent. 'I'll pay to mend it of course,' she repeated weakly, watching him struggle to fold it into a position that would allow the lid of her boot to stay down, if not properly closed.

'If you could just take me home that would be great,' he muttered, easing himself into the passenger seat with a grimace of pain. He took off his helmet, revealing a young pale face and dark features. His eyes, she saw were dark brown and glowering with anger and discomfort. 'I'll get the bike seen to tomorrow.'

'Send me the bill, won't you?' she offered quickly, adding, 'Are you absolutely sure you don't need a doctor?'

'Just a hot bath, thanks. I live back that way.' He jerked his thumb over his shoulder.

'You'll have to direct me,' she murmured, 'I'm not familiar with this area.' After checking the road several times, she swung the car round in a U-turn. She drove steadily and with exaggerated care, not just because of the tremors of shock still pulsing through her kneecaps, but out of an awareness that every turn of the wheels increased the distance between her and the Dancing Bear. A distance that felt more than just miles, but of time and possibility too. Fate had clearly changed its mind, she reflected grimly, waving a mental farewell to James Harcourt and the whole harebrained idea of throwing herself at the mercy of strangers.

Chapter Sixteen

While the bath ran, Daniel poured himself a glass of wine. He sat sipping it on the edge, swirling his free hand in the hot water. He'd had collisions on his bike before but none at such speed or comprising so blatant a threat to his life. To be mashed by a car bumper at the tender age of twenty-six was not how he intended to make his exit from the world, even after a lousy term, an indifferent Christmas and with no obvious prospective mourners other than his immediate family. Vicky, his ex, would probably do a celebration jig on his grave, Daniel reflected gloomily, shuddering at the recollection of all the petty arguments over CDs and kitchen utensils which had helped to sour the previous year.

Having turned off the taps, he held out his left hand and studied it for signs of trembling, remembering not the moment of impact so much as the clench of his heart in the split second it had to brace itself for pain. There was no clear recollection of making contact with the car, only of the shock of his own weightlessness as he was catapulted across the road. What had nearly happened was in fact far more terrifying than the event itself, Daniel realised, easing off his T-shirt and levering himself into the hot water. Since arriving home, his left shoulder had started hurting, although the only obvious signs of bruising remained on his right knee and elbow. His sprained ankle did not even look swollen.

Dextrously using three toes to nudge the hot tap back onto full throttle, Daniel tipped his chin up until the water was lapping over his head up to his eyelids. With the benefit of hindsight he found it impossible not to acknowledge some culpability in the accident. Apart from his helmet, no aspect of his appearance or behaviour had been geared to further the cause of his own personal safety. He had been wearing dark clothes, without a single one of the numerous luminous accoutrements doggedly bestowed on him over the course of several years by his mother. As Vicky had warned him many times, the front light on his bike was so feeble it could be mistaken for a trick of the imagination. On spotting the woman's car waiting to turn onto the main road, it had even crossed Daniel's mind that he himself would not be so visible, that it might not be the most prudent of moments to accelerate past a vehicle slowing into his front wheel.

In a bid to fend off yet another detailed action replay of the collision, Daniel reached for the soap and began vigorously lathering his body. White and translucent bubbles streamed down from his armpits and through the dark hairs on his chest. He had been aggressive, he knew, even after the woman had offered to drop him home. Looking back he realised that this was not simply because of shock, but also because of the distinct – and somehow jarring – impression of her being in a hurry to get away; that even though his initial fear about her bolting had proved unjustified, a part of her would have liked to.

After submerging himself one last time, Daniel stood up and spent a few moments brushing water from his arms and body before stepping onto the bath mat. He reached for the towel on the back of the door, still faintly damp from his shower that morning, and hastily rubbed himself dry. He worked the towel like a saw across his back, cursing quietly at the ice-box temperature of the air. The bathroom was the only space in the cottage without a heater of any kind. In the sitting room there was an open fire, together with one of the large brick storage heaters which served the rest of the house. They were cumbersome but cheap, and quite effective once they got going. The lump sum left by his grandmother had all been swallowed up by the purchase of the property, leaving none spare for niceties like rewiring and radiators. On the whole, Daniel didn't mind. Having his own place was what mattered, especially since the income from his chosen career path would have precluded such a luxury for many years to come. Though most of his colleagues liked to hang around their university accommodation during the vacations, it had always been important to Daniel to have a bolt hole. Remembering suddenly that he was at the start of a six-month sabbatical, that his faculty was already in the thick of another term without him, he gave the towel a flourish of satisfaction. It was a breathing space for which he had fought hard and he was determined to put this inauspicious start behind him and enjoy every minute.

Thoroughly warm now, he knotted the towel firmly across his hips and rubbed a porthole in the steam on the basin mirror. Leaning forwards, he ran the palms of both hands over the dark bristles on his chin and cheeks, debating whether to shave, reminding himself that night shadow could be of no possible concern to men who slept alone. It was a relief not to have Vicky to worry about but it left a feeling of emptiness too. Beside him the green eyes of a printed replica of Botticelli's Venus peered through a thin veil of vapour, their demure gaze directed over his shoulder, as if too polite to confront his semi-nudity head on. Daniel picked up his razor and put it down again, spinning impatiently away from the basin and causing a sudden spasm of pain to shoot up through his ankle bone. Cursing volubly, he limped out onto the landing, supporting himself along the wall. Through the banisters he caught a glimpse of his injured bicycle, propped forlornly against a coat stand in the hall. There were bad scratches in the paintwork which he hadn't noticed before, as well as a curious lopsided look to the handlebars. Gritting his teeth, glad he had been so firm with the Copeland woman after all, Daniel proceeded gingerly towards his bedroom, making a mental note to call Joe at the garage in the morning and to tell him not to stint on the estimate for repairs.

'It obviously wasn't meant to be,' said Libby kindly, once Frances had completed her account of the disastrous events of the previous evening. 'Although I still think poor James Harcourt deserves some sort of explanation as to why you didn't—'

'I've told you, I tried a couple of times, but there was no reply, Frances insisted. 'The whole idea was insane anyway. I don't know what got into me. It's far too soon even to consider another relationship. Dreadful though it was, I even feel sort of grateful to that poor creature on the bicycle. When I got home last night – and again when I woke up this morning – I just felt so relieved, not only because I hadn't killed him, but because of having been saved the hideous embarrassment of a blind date. God only knows what I could have been letting myself in for. And the fact that James Harcourt hasn't made any obvious attempts to get in touch with me shows the feeling is almost certainly mutual. As you say, it just wasn't meant to be,' she concluded firmly. 'Now then, where did you say you wanted these?' She held up one of the wooden-framed pastel prints which had arrived amongst several boxes of stock that morning.

'I thought on the wall over there, above the decorative candles and jewellery boxes.'

'But it might look good in the window,' murmured Frances, casting a critical eye over the picture, a still life of asparagus and onion in smudgy pale water colours. 'I can just see it on one of the upper dresser shelves, maybe next to those kitchen jars in the shape of vegetables.'

Managing to suppress a pin-prick of pique that Frances's eye for arrangement was proving so patently superior to her own,

Libby clapped her hands in approval. 'Good idea. Do you mind giving the jars a dust first? I've had them for centuries. You ought to do some pictures of your own, you know,' she added, wanting to make up for the meanness in her heart. 'You could run up this sort of thing in no time.'

Frances laughed, flattered but uncertain. 'Your faith in my abilities as an artist never ceases to amaze me – but thank you, not just for saying that, but for everything, taking me on and so on. You've been marvellous Libby and I'm not sure I've told you.'

'Nonsense. You're invaluable. And I mean it about the pictures. If you ever want me to look at anything with a view to selling it I would be more than happy.' Feeling closer and better, both women turned to their tasks in a comfortable silence.

Still full of anxiety about James Harcourt, the sight of the flashing red light on her answering machine when she got in from work later that afternoon caused Frances's heart to skip a beat. But it was only Daisy, sounding chirpy and upbeat, insisting on a return call to have another go at arranging a date for a visit.

'Only if you're up to it obviously, Mum,' she said, when Frances came on the line. 'I'd hate to feel I was putting any pressure on you—'

'No no darling I've been feeling much better since Christmas, much more my old self,' Frances assured her, thinking the moment the words were out of James Harcourt and the fact that, while certainly much happier, her current existence bore very little relation to any of the routines with which her daughter associated her. 'I'm helping Libby in her shop now, but that's only three days a week so I could come from any Thursday to Sunday. Name the days that would suit you.'

They agreed on a long weekend in mid February. 'Third time lucky maybe,' murmured Daisy to herself as she put down the phone. The awfulness of Christmas felt wonderfully distant, almost like it was part of someone else's life. In the weeks since she and Claude had been if anything closer than ever before. They had gone back to making love almost every night, with an intensity that felt new and which confirmed Daisy's sneaking conviction that the explosion in December had been worthwhile. It had cleared the air, restored them to the alert generosity of the early days before familiarity began its stranglehold; before Claude's sudden and absurd fixation that she was having an affair with Marcel from the gallery. Eager to prevent such suspicions from ever souring their life again, Daisy had given up accepting invitations to lunch and was careful to inform her lover of any movements outside her usual routine. She had even stopped popping out of the flat for an afternoon walk for fear of missing his arrival home. Such sacrifices felt small in comparison to the rewards they reaped. Each day that passed Daisy grew surer that the horror of Christmas had really been about love, about Claude's terror of losing what they had.

Renewing her vigilance over the relationship somehow led to Daisy being more attentive over the domestic details of their life as well. Instead of succumbing to the lure of slobbishness to which she had always been prone, she began to make more of an effort over the flat, keeping it tidy and spotless as Claude liked, stacking daily debris into orderly piles and straightening the bedcovers before he got in from work. She even bought a cook book and tried a few new recipes, using her artistic skills to recreate the sumptuous pictures next to the instructions, arranging the colours and curling the garnishes to make each plate resemble a painting. Of painting itself, she did less and less. Working at the gallery was making her realise both the limitations of her own talent and the fact that she had skills in other areas. Customers liked the quaintness of her accent, the way she made suggestions without appearing pushy. One gentleman the other day had even asked for her by name. He had bought such an expensive work that Marcel had added a bonus envelope to her weekly pay packet. This modest success

had taken the edge off Daisy's desire to spend her free afternoons cooped up in the small attic room designated as her
studio. It had also helped her see that a measly square skylight
of a window, filtering what little illumination lay in the steely
Parisian winter sky, did nothing to enhance either her imagination or the bright ridges and ripples into which she liked to
work the oils.

Although inevitably wary of yet sharing such opinions with
Claude, a part of Daisy longed to tell her mother. The moment
their telephone conversation started however, she remembered the new distance between them. Their exchange of
comments felt like a negotiated instead of a natural process,
bearing testimony to the fact that they had not seen each other
for almost half a year. Understanding the reasons for this did
not prevent Daisy from minding very deeply. Prior to losing
her father, it would never have occurred to her that grief could
drive those affected further apart instead of pulling them
together; that it could make her go through all that she had
without telling a soul.

Chapter Seventeen

With the James Harcourt fiasco safely behind her, Frances was aware of another, hugely positive shift in her perspective. Looking back on the episode in the days immediately afterwards, she even felt as if she had been subconsciously propelling herself towards some sort of crisis, that the dramatic crash with the hapless cyclist had burst a bubble of insanity and restored another vital connection to real life. On work mornings she now threw herself out of bed with genuine eagerness, grateful for the easy focus it gave to the day. Back at home, instead of worrying about Joseph she began concentrating on restoring proper order to the domestic arena of her own life, applying herself to the long postponed chore of serious housework.

On the Friday morning of the week after the accident, Frances decided it was time to shift her rigorous cleaning programme to the kitchen. Kicking off her shoes and rolling up her sleeves, she set to work, humming quietly to herself and musing upon her circumstances with an objectivity which she would have once believed impossible. Wiping the mop across the patterned jigsaw of floor tiles, it occurred to her suddenly that getting over Paul was and would continue to be a haphazard process of many parts; not a linear thing at all, but a great hopeless zigzag. Every little thing she did was a part of it, she mused, turning her attentions to the oven, spraying the greasy interior liberally with white foam and then closing the door to stop the fumes stinging her eyes.

She had just tied her hair out of the way with an elastic band and filled the washing-up bowl in preparation for a final assault on the grill pan, when the doorbell rang. Annoyed to be interrupted at so critical a juncture in operations, she tugged her front door open with a sigh of impatience.

'Sorry to bother you.'

'Oh goodness, it's you,' Frances exclaimed, raising her hand to her mouth in surprise and then quickly dropping it in distaste at the realisation that she was still wearing rubber gloves.

'I hope you don't mind my coming in person. I was going to post the bill for damages, but then . . . well, to be frank, I felt I was rather . . . how shall I put it . . . abrasive on the night of our little fracas, and that perhaps I had not thanked you properly for ferrying me home. And it occurred to me that almost killing someone must be just as bad as almost being killed, in terms of the shock factor and so on. And I do have drawers full of fluorescent armbands and anklets which I never wear because I can't be bothered, because they look naff and are a pain to put on, especially if you're always late, which I tend to be. Sorry, this is obviously a bad time. I'll hand over my envelope and be gone. Not too bad a total, I think you'll find. There's a man at my local garage who's great for all this sort of thing, not one of your usual rip-off merchants by any means.' Daniel held out the envelope containing Joe's estimate of seventy-three pounds and forty-eight pence, but then hesitated at the sight of the pink gloves, each finger stained a gingery brown.

'Hang on a minute.' Frances fought to free her hands, her fingers sticking inside the rubber. Aware suddenly of her hair sprouting from its ugly brown rubber band and of her bare feet, she blushed, sure she must look like one of those women who had begun to let herself go and not even realised it.

'That's better.' She wrenched the rubber gloves off at last. 'And you're all right, are you? I felt so awful . . .'

'I'm fine.' He waited while she opened the envelope.

'That seems very reasonable, as you say. I'll write you a cheque now. Would you like to come in a moment?'

'That's very kind. I'll just lock my car.'

'There's no need,' she began, breaking off in dismay at the heaviness of the limp with which he dragged himself back to the dusty grey Ford parked in front of her garage, pulling the leg after him like some stoical war veteran. 'But you're in a dreadful way,' she gasped, 'tell me you've seen a doctor . . .'

He spun round with a gleeful laugh and trotted back to the doorstep. 'Just kidding. Couldn't resist it. I really am fine. In fact my shoulder hurts more than my ankle now.'

'That was extremely unkind,' Frances muttered, smiling in spite of herself as she pushed the door shut behind them and set off in search of her handbag. Having expected her visitor to stay hovering in the hallway, she was faintly bemused to find him following her into the kitchen and then the sitting room. 'I know it's somewhere round here. I used it for the milkman this morning. I'll just check upstairs. Hang on.' She raced up to the landing, taking two steps at a time, half expecting to hear the thud of his feet behind her. But when she returned, triumphantly waving her cheque book, he was studying a Christmas card, a late delivery from half forgotten friends in Canada, full of well wishes for Paul and the children.

'My friend Luca Signorelli,' he said, tapping the religious scene depicted on the front of the card. 'One of the more neglected geniuses of the Renaissance. I've just started a sabbatical with the aim of restoring the poor guy to his rightful status. Great at male musculature and virgins – I mean look at the expression on this one's face – clearly fed-up with breast feeding, not to mention all the pomp of having unwittingly given birth to the saviour of mankind. Like Patsy Kensit when she doesn't want to be photographed.' He chuckled quietly and returned the card to its place on the hall table.

'So you're writing a book about him?' enquired Frances, peering at the card with new eyes.

'No, nothing so grand. I've only got six months. It's more of an extended paper, one of those treatises that might elicit a few appreciative grunts from fellow academics but will set no fires alight in the rest of the world. An excuse to have a break more than anything.'

'Daniel Groves, wasn't it?' she asked, folding out her cheque book and beginning to write. 'I've rounded it up to eighty, I hope that's OK.' She blew on the wet ink and handed it to him.

'That's great, thanks.' He took the cheque, exclaiming, 'Wow, what immaculate writing – mine is hieroglyphics in comparison,' before slipping it into the back pocket of his jeans.

Frances laughed too, overwhelmed with fresh gratitude at not having killed such a personable young man. 'I'm just glad you're all right,' she murmured, opening the door and curling her toes into the pile of the carpet at the blast of cold air on her bare legs.

He didn't go at once, but hesitated, masking one hand across his mouth with a frown. 'Funny really . . . I mean, I wanted all this free time so badly and now that it's come I feel a little at a loss as to what to do with it. I keep putting Signorelli off, but not doing anything constructive instead.'

'I know the feeling.'

'Do you?' He looked genuinely interested.

Frances, aware of the damp January wind ventilating her hallway, shifted her weight uncomfortably. 'Oh you know, just that thing of being full of good New Year intentions and not getting to any of them.'

'Except scrubbing your oven.' His face broke into a grin. 'I noticed in the kitchen,' he explained, seeing the look of surprise on her face.

'Oh that.'

'You'll feel so virtuous you'll be able to laze for the rest of the day with a clear conscience.' He smiled and held out his hand. 'Nice to meet you in more pleasant circumstances.'

Frances quickly accepted the handshake, muttering similar pleasantries. 'And good luck with Signorelli,' she called as an afterthought, waiting half in and half out of the door until his car had disappeared up the road.

Daniel Groves was right, cleaning did generate a sense of virtue. But instead of using it as a pretext for slothdom, Frances found herself digging out her drawing board and box of pencils. Taking a stool from the kitchen and wrapping herself up warmly, she set up camp at the lowest point of the garden, where the river was a silver snake through the trees. In the foreground the ploughed mud of the field was still furred with frost, like gusts of icing sugar on a vast chocolate cake. Overhead the sun was no more than a flat white disc behind a screen of cloud, feeble but as distinct in outline as a large coin.

The slow, creeping realisation that she felt inspired, was like a warmth inside, compensating for the chill in her half-gloved fingers and assisting in the necessary stoicism of ignoring the aching numbness in her toes. What she drew wasn't very good. The trees were out of proportion and stiff, the river a lifeless band, the fields lumpy and dull. What mattered, Frances knew, was that sitting, icy on a stool with a pencil, was something she had chosen to do, something she had wanted to do, not to fill time, not for someone else, not out of any preconception about how it might be profitable to pass the day, but because an inner impulse had led her there. An impulse connected to a freedom she had not known – had chosen not to know – for years and years.

Packing away her things an hour later, she thought of James Harcourt and shook her head in wonder at how close she had come to doing the wrong thing. How naïve to imagine there could be anything like a simple replacement for Paul; that there could be any replacement at all. Having put the kettle on for tea, she whisked up an ancient favourite recipe for biscuits, liberally picking at the mixture as she went along. She ate two of the biscuits while they were still warm, sipping a second cup of tea and composing a letter to the friends in Canada.

'*Dear Paul died in the summer,*' she wrote, truly accepting it in her heart for the first time.

Chapter Eighteen

—————◆◇◆—————

England's performance in the West Indies made for poor accompaniment to the travails of Signorelli, especially when relayed through a shortwave radio with a tendency towards volume vacillation at crucial moments. When the team's batting collapse began to mirror Daniel's own sense of hopelessness over what had once seemed the simple task of combining scholarship with a genuine passion, he snapped shut the lid of his laptop and strode impatiently to the window. Gingerly he peered out at the half-hearted drizzle, which seemed to have gone on for days, wondering if he possessed the resolve to launch himself into it. Reaching his hands above his head, he rose up onto the balls of his feet and balanced for a few moments, stretching his back and testing the sensations in his left ankle. Though not exactly painful, it still felt very weak. It would have to be the bicycle, or nothing, he decided, returning to the flats of his feet and sighing heavily. Traipsing upstairs, he rummaged in several hopelessly over-stuffed drawers before eventually unearthing two yellow armbands and a vest with velcro tags that fastened round the waist.

Prior to setting off, he tested the brakes and the lights, which had been attended to in conjunction with the bicycle's other more obvious ailments. A scoot round the block, Daniel told himself, pedalling cautiously at first and then speeding up at the happy discovery that his bad ankle felt fine. After a few moments even the drizzle began to feel refreshing. He sailed past the post office and then instead of turning back down by the Coach and Horses, headed on out of Farley, down the pleasantly wide lane which had recently been treated to a fresh coat of tarmac. His wheels made a smooth whizzing sound on the wet ground.

One of the most striking features of Signorelli's religious vision is its lack of obvious personality; each virgin is a beauty in her own right . . .

After a few more miles, he realised he was heading towards his parents' house, more for a place to aim for than because he was feeling genuinely sociable. Christmas had been a sufficient reminder of their less than endearing foibles, his father preferring to appear stupid than admit to being deaf, his mother delivering her set of stock responses to every subject with such unwavering predictability that it often seemed pointless going through the motions of conversation. Even his amiable elder sister wasn't the same these days, tediously distracted by the demands of young infants and not seeming to mind that her oaf of a husband did nothing at all.

Acknowledging the fact that not even the blessing of exercise could make up for his disinclination to spend more time with close relatives, Daniel slipped into a lower gear and began to consider turning round. He was fond of his parents of course, having long since forgiven them for being ten years older than those of his peers. Somewhere along the line their existence had undoubtedly contributed to his continuing affiliation to a part of the world that had seen both his birth and most of his education. Apart from a year in Italy, the only serious opportunity to move beyond the cosy confines of southern England had been a promising vacancy at York a couple of years before. But by then Vicky was on the scene, at that stage a finalist biochemist with firm plans to stay on at Sussex for three years of research. With the sudden death of his maternal grandmother releasing sufficient funds to buy the cottage, Daniel had given up the York idea entirely, seriously believing that all the pieces of his life were falling into their allotted place. Remembering the slow process of disillusion-ment which had followed, the bitter taste of romantic disappointment, he hunched over the handlebars, pedalling so slowly that the bike almost teetered to a stop. After a series of brief unsatisfactory affairs with students and fellow graduates, Vicky, with her formidable intellect and statuesque blonde good looks, really had seemed the answer to his dreams. It took time to discover that it was a hard, mathematical, curiously childish cleverness, about winning arguments rather than understanding them, about being one-up instead of equal. Though the decision to split was mutual, the astonishment of friends and colleagues had contributed to Daniel's overall sense of failure. Trying to explain that beauty and brains were no defence against emotional immaturity sounded so much like sour grapes that he quickly gave up the effort. Instead, he slipped quietly from their social group, focusing his energies on work and his hopes on the prospect of a prolonged bout of solitude.

When the rain stopped, Frances took her fold-up stool and ventured outside, not to the bottom of the garden this time but to a corner of the front drive, where the hawthorn draped itself theatrically over the fence and a small troop of suicidal snowdrops had thrust themselves up through the grassy bank. She had not touched her sketchpad since the week before, not wanting to overtest the urge, to scare it away before she had produced anything worthwhile. In addition to which she had been busy, working in Libby's shop and continuing with her crusade of spring cleaning. She had progressed as far as the first landing, saving the top floor, where the dust was thickest, till last.

When the man on the bicycle entered her field of vision she barely looked up. And when he turned into the drive her first assumption was that he was some sort of special delivery postman.

'I thought you might want to witness the fruits of your cheque firsthand,' Daniel exclaimed, tugging off his helmet and running his fingers back through the wet slope of his fringe. 'And I needed to get some fresh air,' he added, in truth as much bemused by his presence in Frances's drive as Frances herself. Deciding to follow a sign to Leybourne had been an impulse thing, arising mostly from the fact that it made a more pleasing notional destination than his parents' bungalow in Rothmere. Only in the last few hundred yards of his journey had a sensation of something like anticipation built inside. A sensation that was in no way diminished by the sight of Frances Copeland perched in front of an easel, wearing a vast black mackintosh and a broad-brimmed black hat and with a large box of pencils on her lap.

Astonished, but fearing it might seem rude to appear so, Frances duly made a show of inspecting the repairs on his bicycle and nodding sagely. 'Looks great.'

'And I hope you've noticed that I bear a close resemblance to a Belisha beacon,' he said dryly, casting a disparaging gesture at his attire.

Frances laughed, noting in the same instant that he looked chilled and wet through. 'Seeing as you've come so far, would you like a cup of tea?'

'Oh no, thanks. I was just passing really, and besides, you're obviously hard at work.'

'I've barely begun. Look, three lines of a fence and some spiky grass. I thought I wanted to draw the hawthorn, but when I sat down I kept noticing a line of raindrops along the fence, the most perfect necklace of opals – except one would insist on dropping off whenever I raised my pencil . . .' she broke off, embarrassed. 'And the light's hopeless in any case.'

'Thomas Hardy wrote a wonderful line about raindrops . . . let me see, something about meadow rivulets overflowing and then "drops on gatebars hang in a row, and rooks in families homeward go" – I think that's it. Terribly underrated as a poet, he had such a brilliant eye for everyday things and this wickedly simple way of describing them.'

'I thought he just wrote gloomy books about people with not enough money making a mess of their love lives.'

Daniel burst out laughing. 'Oh yes, he did that too. Anyway,' he added, remembering himself, 'I'd really better be going.'

'Have a cup of tea first to warm up,' insisted Frances, overcome with motherly concern at the thought of him pedalling off into the dank afternoon. 'I made a cake this morning, which I shall only regret keeping to myself.'

'No marauding hordes at teatime then?' he asked, drawing on vague recollections of mantelpieces of family faces in picture frames.

She smiled, folding up the easel and looping the stool over her arm. 'I'm afraid not. My son's at university, my daughter lives in France and my husband died last year.'

'Oh, bloody hell. Sorry.'

He looked so awkward and crestfallen that Frances's immediate overriding concern was to put him at his ease. 'Please, don't feel bad. It was very hard at first, but it's OK now. When I tell people these days, they feel far worse on my behalf than I do myself.'

A few minutes later they were sitting at the kitchen table with steaming mugs of tea and slabs of carrot cake, topped with white icing and coconut.

'How's Signorelli getting along then?'

Daniel, his mouth full of cake, made a face and rolled his eyes at the ceiling. 'Little better than the England cricket team. All out for a hundred and thirty-four,' he explained hurriedly, seeing her blank expression. 'But I sorted a few things out in my head on the way here – so there's light at the end of the tunnel. I think perhaps it's a bit like your hawthorn and raindrops – I thought I knew which angle I wanted to take, but every time I set about trying to put it in words I get distracted by other ideas and find myself going down all sorts of avenues that hadn't occurred to me before I started.'

Frances watched him as he talked, aware that she was enjoying herself enormously and wondering if it was because of the rare phenomenon of having an entertaining conversation at the kitchen table or because of the sheer improbability of befriending someone she had almost killed. On the night of the collision he had been so monosyllabic and hostile that such an outcome would have seemed ludicrous. And when he had called round with the bill, she had been too taken aback to draw any firm impressions of his appearance or demeanour. He had an interesting face, she realised now, with intense brown eyes set between a high wide forehead and strong cheekbones. His hair, cropped very short and still stiff with damp, stuck out in different angles all over his scalp, as if he had spent all night burrowing under pillows. His manner of speaking was unhurried and assured, lingering on certain and sometimes unexpected words as if for the sheer pleasure of shaping his lips round the sound. Listening to him, it was easy to imagine a lecture hall, and an audience of eager students.

'What was that Hardy poem called? Perhaps I should go out and get hold of a copy, try and broaden my horizons or something.'

'I don't know about that.' He frowned. 'Anyway, I can't remember the title. I did my main degree in English, but it feels like centuries ago now. Oh, hang on,' he slapped the table, 'it's come back to me – "Weathers" – that was it.' He grinned, evidently pleased at this small feat of memory. 'Hardly the most imaginative title, if you think about it.'

'The only trouble is, I've never been much good with poetry,' Frances confessed. 'I like the idea of it, but if ever I try and read the stuff I'm usually baffled. People who boast about keeping anthologies of poems on their bedside tables make me feel sort of jealous and inadequate, like I'm missing out on something that I wouldn't be up to anyway.'

'You wouldn't find Hardy baffling,' he assured her earnestly. 'He also wrote some brilliant ones about missing his dead wife, the irony being that he only realised the extent of his love for her after she was gone. By all accounts, when she was alive he spent much of the time being pig-headed and ignoring her . . .' He stopped abruptly, horrified at his lack of tact.

'My husband was quite nice to me,' Frances said easily, steering the crumbs on her plate into a small pile. 'Too nice in many ways. After he'd gone I was like a helpless child, completely unused to standing on my own two feet. The smallest things were so hard—' She broke off and patted the lid of the cake tin with a short laugh. 'Even something so stupid as baking a cake, it's taken a while to learn that it's OK to do that for myself, that I don't need the pretext of other people for doing something that gives me pleasure.' She stopped again, expecting him to say something to change the subject. But he had folded his arms and was studying her with what felt like a genuinely sympathetic silence. 'Being alone has also made me look back a lot,' she continued, haltingly, 'I've found myself reassessing everything, wondering if perhaps I let Paul dictate the terms of my life too much, whether conforming to all his wishes was in fact a way of avoiding facing up to things I needed to develop in myself. I never even wanted to come and live in the country, you know, I loved London. But the children were small and full of energy and south London even in those distant days was just one long traffic jam. Though now, funnily enough, I wouldn't dream of living anywhere else. God, sorry, I'm rambling and you're probably desperate to get home.'

'No I'm not. In fact,' Daniel stretched slowly, tipping his chair so far onto its two back legs that Frances had to suppress a reflex to cry out in alarm, 'I feel rather sleepy. Too much warmth and pampering.' He smiled and rubbed his eyes with his knuckles till his eyelids looked raw and pink. Pink dots had emerged on his cheeks too, she noticed, contrasting curiously with the dark shadow across his jaw. He let his chair drop back onto all four legs and stood up, leaning heavily with his palms on the kitchen table.

'I'll run you home if you like, it must have taken hours to get here on the bike. And it's already getting dark.'

'I wouldn't dream of it. I've treated myself to brand new lights – front and back. And what with these delightful objects,' he picked up the vest and bands which he had thrown onto the seat next to him, 'I'm about as unmissable as a light-house.'

'Goodbye then,' she said when they'd got as far as the door, holding out her hand to cover a fleeting pulse of awkwardness. 'It's been such fun talking.'

'Yes it has.' He took her hand and shook it once, quite hard. 'Maybe we could do it again some time?'

'Maybe.' Frances laughed uncertainly.

'A happy collision after all, eh?' he quipped, bounding down the front step and running alongside the bike for several yards before flinging himself onto the seat.

Having closed the door, Frances leant back against it for a few seconds, luxuriating in the discovery that life could still surprise her. The sense that she had made proper amends for the awfulness of the accident was so uplifting that it remained with her long into the evening, making it hard for the first time in a while, to settle into sleep.

Chapter Nineteen

'But this is very good,' said Libby at once, holding the sketch up to the light and nodding with what appeared to be heart-felt appreciation.

'The framing is pretty basic, I'm afraid.'

'I don't think so at all – a simple wood is all it needs – such a delicate thing. Where is that anyway? It looks familiar.'

'The view from the bottom of the garden, down towards the river—'

'Of course, of course. And that roof in those trees would be the Brackman place. Which reminds me, how is the poor man?'

'I haven't been round lately – I wasn't sure I was doing any good,' Frances explained hastily, feeling a flicker of guilt at her own recent lack of solicitude with regard to her neighbour. 'He knows he can ring my doorbell whenever he wants.'

Libby gave a shudder of distance. 'You are very noble. I know I should feel pity, but I'm afraid he gives me the creeps. I gather that place of his is falling down – how he continues to live there I do not know.'

'It's his home, I suppose.'

'I want to put a price tag on this straight away,' continued Libby, returning her attention to the picture. 'I'm sure we could get at least thirty-five – forty maybe – goodness, I've no idea how one is supposed to carve up the profits in such situations.'

'If the price is thirty-five I'd be happy with twenty,' said Frances, who, foreseeing the embarrassment of money discussions, had given the matter some thought. 'In the unlikely event that it sells, that is,' she added hastily.

'Twenty's not nearly enough. Let's try it at thirty-five and I'll give you thirty. Is this the only one?'

'I'm working on some others, but they're not ready yet.'

'Bring them in as soon as they are.' She put an arm round Frances's shoulders and squeezed hard. 'You are doing so well, I can't believe it. Paul would have been so proud.'

'Thank you,' murmured Frances, feeling a little patronised, but knowing that, as ever, Libby spoke with the kindest intentions.

That day, instead of going straight to the coffee house during her lunch hour, Frances walked to the book shop at the bottom of the high street. It took several minutes to locate the poetry section which only occupied a couple of lower shelves. There was just one book of Hardy's entitled *Chosen Poems of Thomas Hardy*. She slipped it off the shelf and turned to the index. Having found the poem 'Weathers', she was on the point of standing up when her eye was caught by the title of a slim black book which had been left face up on top of the lowest shelf. *Joseph Brackman, Selected Poems*. Impressed, Frances knelt back down on the floor and picked it up for a closer look. Slipped between the first two pages was a tired looking piece of paper scrawled with the words, *Local Author*. The publication date was eight years previously under the name of a company of which Frances had never heard. The book was hardly bigger than an envelope, and couldn't have contained more than ten poems. At the till Frances couldn't resist tapping the cover and saying, 'I know him, he lives just down the road from me.'

'Really?' said the girl, giving the cover a second look before slipping it into the bag. 'That's nice.'

Over lunch Frances studied her purchases, keeping the covers down, as if there were something improper about a lone woman reading poems in a public place. Apart from the occasional mystifying line the Hardy ones seemed, as Daniel Groves had said, mostly very straightforward, full of everyday incidents and images. Joseph's in contrast were short, dense, impenetrable collections of words, containing no string of reason that Frances was able to identify. She was still puzzling over the first one when Libby burst into the coffee shop, coat-less and flapping both arms in excitement. Filled with a sudden uncertainty about what had prompted this new interest in literature, Frances hurriedly returned both books to her bag.

She need not have worried however, as Libby had other things on her mind. She began speaking several yards short of Frances's table, so loudly that there were looks of mild irritation from other customers and amusement from the women behind the counter, who knew her well. 'You're not going to believe this,' she exclaimed, grabbing hold of the back of the spare seat opposite Frances with both hands, 'I've just sold your picture. To a young couple – labrador and pushchair – seemed very nice – would have paid a lot more I'm sure. I simply had to come over and tell you. In fact it's been a brilliant hour – thank God I don't close for lunch any more. A whole gaggle of Spanish students came in looking for presents for relatives in Barcelona and then a dear man with no teeth – best rush of business in weeks. Could you bring a sandwich back for me, do you think? Anything will do – chicken or something – preferably with mayonnaise. And congratulations – I owe you thirty pounds.' And with that she breezed out again, leaving the door to slam so violently that there was a ripple of rattling crockery.

When Frances got home that evening, she looked at her other recent drawings with new eyes, suddenly eager for her two days out of the shop when she would be free to finish them properly. Seeing the Hoover and bucket of cleaning equipment on the landing she decided to finish the top of the house there and then, so she would not be tempted to waste precious hours doing so on Thursday and Friday. She worked quickly, swabbing at stains on the walls and aiming the snout of the Hoover attachment into all the corners and crevices she usually ignored. The top spare room took a little longer, since she had to negotiate Paul's wine racks, still there from the flood, as well as a spider metropolis which had been spun along the top of the curtain pelmet and across half the ceiling. The windows were dirty too, smeared with greasy finger marks which she had not noticed before. She was half-way through erasing them, her duster squeaking feverishly across the panes, when it suddenly occurred to her that the fingermarks were hers, left on the afternoon of the funeral, when she had stood looking down at the mourners, pressing her palms against the glass with Libby at her side. The flashback was so vivid that for a moment Frances had to steady herself against the window sill. She could almost taste the tea Libby had brought her, its sickly sweetness, how it had compounded the nausea pushing up inside. It was weeks since she had experienced anything so acute. Nor did it derive purely from a sense of loss, but from something now more complicated. Something to do with realising that she would never again miss Paul as she had, that after barely half a year she had moved on and become someone else. Someone who did not mind eating alone, someone who worked an enjoyable three-day week, who spent her spare time drawing and buying poetry books.

Several minutes passed before Frances felt sufficiently re-covered to confront Paul's study, looking now so dusty and neglected that the residue of her sadness was at once super-seded by a twist of guilt. What would Paul have made of this new version of his wife? she wondered, frowning to herself as she set about stacking away his old magazines and periodicals into an empty cardboard box. Glimpsing a curl of white hanging out of the back of the fax machine and remembering James Harcourt, her heart missed a beat, but it was only a few blank torn inches of paper. When her duster reached the desk and filing cabinet she had a final, desultory look in the pigeon holes and folders for the missing share certificate. But it was hard to muster any enthusiasm for the task. It did not seem to matter as it once had. Frances closed the study door behind her with a new sense of calm. There would always be loose ends, she mused, slowly making her way back downstairs, for that was the nature of things, all part of the mystery and mess that made human life so endearing.

Reading Hardy's poems later on in bed that night only reinforced such convictions. Some of the illuminating detail of the unruliness of everyday life was so good that Frances caught herself exclaiming out loud. After half an hour however, this happy communion was brought to an abrupt halt by the remorseful loving outpourings dedicated to the dead wife. Anybody could love a dead person, Frances reflected crossly, pulling the duvet round her ears and congratulating herself on having managed twenty years of solid affection for a husband while he had been alive.

Chapter Twenty

Nothing ventured, nothing gained, Daniel told himself, sliding the stick of French bread into his rucksack along with a wrapped wedge of Ardennes pâté and several other pots of delicacies from the deli section of his local supermarket. At the last minute, he remembered a knife and a corkscrew, slipping both into the side pocket where a bottle of French country red was already stowed, protected from accidents by several layers of old newspaper. It was Friday and he needed a break from his desk, the previous weekend's conclusion of the test match having driven him from the sitting room to the second bedroom which doubled as a study. His neck ached from four days of virtually uninterrupted work, a spell which had resulted not so much in written achievement as a keener awareness of the yawning gaps in his scholarship. Acquiring knowledge was like falling into a dark, widening pit, he reflected gloomily, packing his rucksack into the boot of his car and slamming the lid shut. The more one found out, the more one realised how much still needed to be known.

After days of interminable drizzle, to wake to a morning of blue skies and sunshine had felt like a gift. A single band of silky cloud was the only break in colour, reaching from one end of the horizon to the other like a ribbon round a wrapped present. To begin with Daniel drove fast, beating one hand on his thigh in time to a new tape, one of several to which he had treated himself the week before. Having chosen it because of a recent hit single, he wasn't yet sure how much he liked the other songs. It took time, Daniel found, before he was sure whether the familiarity of a tune made it irresistible or merely irksome. Only during the last couple of miles did he slow down to the prescribed speed limit, at the same time switching off the tape to aid his concentration. He took deep breaths too, his mounting nervousness alerting him to the fact that no matter how much he tried to convince himself otherwise, the step he was about to take felt significant. Huge, in fact.

When there was no answer at the door Daniel felt crushed. For some reason it had never occurred to him that she would not be there. Friday was one of her two days off. He knew because she had told him, hinting, so he had conveniently imagined, that such a day would be appropriate for a visit. On seeing that the garage door was closed however, and therefore possibly occupied by a car, he ventured round the side of the house to the garden. The lawn looked green and lush, like a smooth doormat for the expanse of muddy brown field beyond. He was about to turn back when he noticed a line of footprints – clear imprints flattening the wet grass – stretching from the back door of the house and down to the gate in the perimeter fence. He followed them at once, hope rising again, his trainers sinking slightly in the soft wet ground.

Frances, stomping into her drive after the discovery that a beautiful morning was no guarantee of a satisfactory session with her sketchbook, was not pleased to see a dirty grey car parked at the foot of her front door. It took a few moments for her to recognise it as belonging to Daniel Groves, where-upon her annoyance turned to curiosity.

'And what brings you here?' she called, after spotting her visitor leaning on the gate at the bottom of the garden.

'Dervayne Abbey.' His voice failed him and he had to say it twice. At the sound of her he had twisted round so fast he cricked his neck. The pain of it spread slowly, a burning, fluid sensation that seeped under his collarbone and down into his shoulder blades. 'I'm on my way there. Popped in on the off-chance you might want to come too.' He strode back across the garden to where she stood.

'Really?' Frances could not hide her surprise. 'But how kind. I haven't been to Dervayne for ages, years in fact.'

'It was closed for a while, I believe,' he continued, feeling more like his old self, 'declared unsafe – too many crumbling walls and so on.' He followed her back round to the front of the house. 'So, would you like to come?'

'Goodness, I don't know . . . I don't think I'd better. I've got nothing done this morning at all.' She put down her drawing equipment next to the front doorstep and began groping in her pocket for keys.

'It's such a nice day . . .' He hesitated, wondering if she was reluctant or merely undecided.

'That's true.' She slipped the key into its slot and turned suddenly, her face illuminated by a radiant smile. 'I'd love to come. Give me a minute and I'll be right back. Come in, if you like,' she added, hurrying into the kitchen clutching her pad in one hand and her muddy boots in the other.

'I'll be fine here, thanks,' he shouted, stamping the clods of mud off his trainers in what quickly became a little jig of celebration.

Looking back, Frances was unable to impose any coherent narrative on what happened. There was no obvious turning point, no pivotal moment when the outcome of the afternoon became, for her at least, either foreseeable or inevitable. Seeing the ruined monastery again gave her a jolt. She had forgotten its majestic, rugged profile, noble in decrepitude and somehow more mysterious. They and the cluster of other visitors walked in silence round the grassy knolls at the foot of the walls, humbled by the aura of reverence which seemed to shadow every stone. Scattered at their feet, like giant chipped teeth, were broken sections of wall and the occasional smooth slabbed relic from days of scrubbed refectory floors. The wind in the surrounding circle of bare trees seemed full of ancient whispered prayers and the rustle of vestments. As they explored, Frances grew, if anything, less aware of her surroundings, lost in contemplation not only of blurred images of thirteenth-century monastic life but also, more prosaically, of the occasion of her previous visit. A wet spring day shortly after their move from London. Daisy sulking for some forgotten reason, Felix insisting on trying to climb the ruins instead of look at them. Paul, who had insisted on the family outing in the first place, walking determinedly, commenting on every little detail, working so hard at extracting appreciation that for Frances at least, none was to be had.

It was curious to remember such disappointment and yet feel so differently a second time; almost like looking at two parallel worlds. Human mood dictated everything, she mused, following a little behind Daniel as he led the return to the car and switching her thoughts to her hopeless efforts with her sketchpad that morning. Without a certain feeling inside her head, she realised, she could not see what needed to be drawn, no matter how hard or how long she looked.

She was jolted from these contemplations by the sight of Daniel pulling a bulging rucksack from the boot of the car. 'I brought a few refreshments,' he said, shepherding her onto the back seat and then proceeding to lay out an elaborate picnic which had clearly been bought for two. Even then, her overriding reaction was one of amusement, especially when he unwrapped two wine glasses from a wadge of the previous day's *Guardian*.

'You'd have had a lot of eating and drinking to do if I'd said no, wouldn't you?' she teased, 'there's enough here to feed a small army.'

'I eat a lot,' he confessed, tearing off a hunk of bread and passing it to her together with a large stainless steel knife. 'No butter I'm afraid. Just pâté and houmus and a few other things which I thought looked interesting. Especially that.' He pointed to a styrofoam pot of pasta squirls and black olives.

They were sitting on either side of the picnic, their wine glasses balanced on the bridge between the two seats.

'We're going to muck up your car,' said Frances, her mouth full.

'It's mucked up already. It's a tip, I like it that way. Do you want some of this?' He held out the pot with the pasta and a teaspoon.

Frances took a mouthful and chewed thoughtfully. 'Delicious. Try it.' Through the misting window next to her she could see a small minibus of new arrivals, several in wheelchairs, others leaning on helpers for support.

'Your label's sticking out,' he said.

Disconcerted, she bent forwards, fumbling for the neck of her jumper. They had taken their coats off and folded them on the front seat.

'Here, let me do it.'

If there was a moment it was then. But upon them so quickly that there was no time to assess it or wonder about it or even savour it. All Frances could remember was that in tucking away the offending label some part of his hand touched the skin on her neck and the effect of it was to make her go quite still. For several moments neither of them moved. Then slowly she became aware of his palm pressing gently against the nape of her neck, while his fingers pushed up through the lowest strands of her hair. She stared ahead, until the smooth brown leather of the front passenger seat blurred to a muddy brown and she was aware of nothing but the sensations seeping through her like the spread of warmth.

'No,' she said, her throat dry.

But Daniel had somehow reached across to place his mouth where his hand had been. He murmured her name, burying his lips in her neck, behind her ears, against her hair.

'The food, mind the food,' she whispered.

'If you want me to stop, I'll need a better reason than that,' he muttered, using one hand to turn her face towards his.

Frances caught hold of his wrist. 'Please, you mustn't.'

'Why?' His eyes were so close to hers that she could see flecks of black in the brown.

'A thousand reasons.'

'There's only one reason that matters.'

'And that is?'

'That you don't want to.'

Frances felt the blood rush to her cheeks. Whether she wanted to kiss Daniel Groves was not in contention. In another, impossible life she would already have returned his caresses with an energy that he might even have found alarming.

'I am a forty-three-year-old widow,' she said quietly. 'I have two grown-up children . . .;

'I know.' He ran his index finger round the outline of her lips.

'I have stretch marks and broken veins. I have scores of grey hairs . . .'

'Where?' He feigned deep concern, slipping the hand on her cheek up through her hair. 'Here?' He ran his fingers through several strands, pulling them out and letting them drop back to her shoulder. 'Here?'

Frances closed her eyes, as if by blocking out the sight of him she might will strength from some invisible source inside herself.

'You are twenty years younger than me—'

'Seventeen, a measly seventeen. And what has that got to do with anything?'

'Everything. It has everything to do with everything. In addition to which you are now sitting on the houmus.'

'Fuck, and I thought I was being so smooth and careful.' He laughed, reluctantly pulling away.

Frances couldn't help laughing too at the state of his jeans. 'Where's the knife? I can use it to scrape the worst off.' It was a relief to have broken the moment, to have something to do other than resist him. Deftly, she worked the blade under the blobs of mess on his trousers, wiping each smearful onto an old bit of newspaper. She kept her head down, pretending to be absorbed in the task, pretending that the long tight curve of his front thigh muscle, faintly visible through the faded denim, meant nothing to her.

Daniel meanwhile began hastily returning their half-eaten picnic to the rucksack. The moment Frances had finished he snatched the knife from her hands and picked up both glasses of wine. 'Now, where were we?'

'We were nowhere.'

'If these windows steam up any more we'll be arrested on suspicion of indecent behaviour anyway. Might as well justify it in some way.'

'Don't be silly.' Frances sipped her wine in an attempt to bury her smile. 'It's time to go.'

'One kiss. Just to see how it feels. What harm could that do? Unless . . .' he was suddenly serious for a moment, 'Frances, if it is simply too soon, if it is because of Paul of course – I mean you have only to say—'

'No, it's not that.' She watched him take her empty glass from her hands, her fingers lingering for a moment on the stem as if offering some pitiful final attempt at resistance.

Outside, the handicapped group, defeated by the obstacle course of a tour round the ruins, were already slamming doors and stowing away equipment, too wrapped up in their own world to spare any curiosity for the blurred silhouettes in the mud-spattered grey car parked alongside.

Chapter Twenty-One

Joseph walked quickly, occasionally patting the breast pocket of his jacket to check the letter was safely stowed inside. March was still weeks away, he reassured himself, plenty of time for an appeal or refusal, or whatever one did in such circumstances.

The letter had arrived in the second post. Not one of their interim declarations about proceedings and rights this time, but an official notification, with the date for his removal heavily underlined in black. It had taken several minutes to absorb the contents, feeling as he did so all the blind panic of a child. The letter contained two mistakes, a missing 'r' from *February* in the date and the omission of the word *you* in the second line.

Further to our conversation last week I am writing to inform that a one-bedroomed flat in Falcon Crescent has become available . . .

To Joseph's troubled mind, the errors, as well as being somehow insulting, confirmed the presence of a malignant intention behind the veneer of polite formality. While aware that there existed systems for resisting such cruelty, he felt incapable of assessing them on his own. The mere thought of even researching how to embark on such a process filled him with dread and despair.

With each of the council's recent lumbering machinations on the subject of evicting him from the cottage, Joseph had clung to the logic that by remaining silent and uncomplaining he might eradicate the need for the issue to be pursued. It had never been of any consequence, either to him or his mother, that their surroundings constituted a serious health hazard; if the lights fused there were candles; buckets resided permanently under the worst of the roof leaks; and all the really bad patches of damp were behind the sofa and in the top bedroom, which only got used as a dumping ground anyway.

The sight of Frances's garden enjoying a healthy burst of spring growth, thanks to his own handiwork earlier in the year, was comforting. Although his refusal of money over Christmas had been genuinely uncalculating, the reminder of the favour now provided a welcome bolster to Joseph's courage. Since the death of his mother, nothing had been the same. He felt disorientated, suffused both with sadness and a redoubling of the crippling shyness which had afflicted him since childhood. While grateful for Frances's house-visits back in January, a part of him sensed that they had been performed out of a sense of duty, that they did not reflect the genuine desire for comradeship which had driven him to make similar advances a few months before.

The garden gate, warped by weeks of heavy rain, put up quite a struggle. Joseph hurried across the lawn, suddenly fearful that the presumption of arriving the back way might lessen Frances's inclination to offer help. He reached the corner of the house in time to see the object of his journey emerge from an unfamiliar grey car. He was on the point of signalling his presence when a tall dark young man got out of the other side. Instead of proceeding to her door, Frances hovered near the front wheels while the man locked up, writing an invisible message in the gravel with the toe of her shoe. When Joseph next looked they were moving towards the house together. He shrank back between the side of the house and the fat bay tree that grew under the dining-room window. They moved with the perfect choreographical alignment of two dancers, stepping slowly and in time, arms across each other's backs, heads turned slightly towards the other. At the foot of the doorstep they stopped and kissed, so deeply and passionately that Joseph, in the midst of the other emotions surging inside his breast, felt somehow impressed.

Even when the slamming of the front door had removed any immediate need for concealment, Joseph remained crouching amongst the lower branches of the bay, his head full of the sweet, minty smell of the leaves, his heart pounding. He had pinned his hopes on Frances and could think of nowhere else to turn. Somewhere deep inside this practical disappointment he was aware of another, less justifiable emotion; something like rejection, a sense of betrayal. He had been drawn to Frances because of her loneliness, the notion that they shared common emotional ground. Seeing her with a lover shattered such illusions in an instant. That it was such a young lover too, somehow doubled the hurt.

With a sharp dismissive cough, Joseph at last stood up, ejecting a gob of saliva from the back of his throat and spitting it fiercely to the ground. He was on his own after all, he realised bitterly, stomping back down the garden, vowing that even if he was seen and summoned he would continue to walk away. Having reached the garden gate with no break in the silence, he nonetheless could not resist a backward glance, a part of him still hoping to find Frances beckoning from a window. But all that moved was a jay, a flash of blue and rust swooping along the central ridge of the roof, screeching at some invisible enemy on the other side.

Instead of returning home, Joseph turned left along the riverbank and walked until he came to the bridge near the weeping willows. The manner of his mother's death still pained him deeply. No matter how hard he tried to romanticise it in his mind – imagining sometimes that she had slipped into the dark water's cold embrace of her own volition – ugly images of reality blocked the way. Particularly her face, discoloured and bloated, filled, so it seemed to Joseph, with all the failed effort of that last long struggle for breath. Then there was the question of his own culpability, his failed vigilance during the afternoon she disappeared, which sat like cement in his head, precluding even the remedy of his beloved poetry to describe and so ease the pain.

He stooped under the arch of the bridge and slithered to a sitting position on the edge of the bank, letting the soles of his rubber boots trail in the water. For a few minutes the guilt ebbed away. He was a little boy again in wellies that were too big, with a mother and a big tea waiting for him at home. Tears rolled down his cheeks, as they often seemed to these days. That it was unfashionable for a forty-seven-year-old man to miss his mother was a fact of which Joseph was only too well aware. A lifelong acquaintance with the alienating effects of his own eccentricity made it impossible not to know such things. Any doubts on the matter had been erased by the youth who had turned up a few days before to assess the cottage on the council's behalf. A shiny-haired, shiny-suited creature, brimming with daft, unfeeling comments about being able to start afresh and live like a 'proper' man. Joseph had trailed after him from room to room with deepening gloom, dwelling on the hopelessness of explaining to anyone that how he loved his mother went beyond personality; that she had been his protector, not just from the dark old days of his father, wedging herself like a fortress in the path of the blows, but in recent years as well, through the very dependency for which he had received so much pity. The only person who had ever given a hint of understanding such things was Frances, and now he had lost her too.

Joseph pushed his legs further over the edge of the bank, not flinching as the cold water spilled over the tops of his boots and its iciness soaked into his socks. Taking the council's letter from his pocket he screwed it up into a tight ball and hurled it into the centre of the river. For a few seconds it caught on a thick island of weeds, bobbing round the edge as if trying to clamber aboard. But then a strong thrust of a current, breaking the surface of the water like a rising fish, caught it with its tail and pulled it out of sight. Joseph squinted into the grey afternoon light, waiting until the blurred grey speck had resurfaced several yards further on before lying back on the bank. He slid his shoulders from side to side in the soft ground, stretching his arms at full reach above his head, relishing the feel of the mud tangling his hair and soaking into the back of his coat. After a few moments his fingers encountered something half buried in the mud. Lifting his feet from the water, he sat up expectantly, only to let out a sigh of disappointment on finding that his discovery was nothing more than a large black plastic bag. Joseph shook off the worst of the clods and peered inside, experiencing as he did so a sudden urge to plunge his head into the dark interior and pull the sides around his ears.

'What are you doing?'

'Jesus – you – I didn't see you.' He punched at the bag, beating the air back out of it till it was flat and harmless once more.

A part of Sally was quite unsurprised to see him. 'I found her there, amongst those reeds.' She pointed with her index finger. 'Then I phoned you.'

'I know. It was kind.'

'Do you miss her a lot?'

He rubbed the back of his head, absently pulling at the blobs of mud. 'Some things. I miss some things. Not the wet sheets. She used to wet her bed.'

Sally made a face and squatted down beside him, a little thrilled at her own lack of fear. Nothing got to her these days, not because she had grown brave, but because she had perfected an artful state of level-headed numbness. Not even the sight of his scar was shocking. It had faded to a dirty grey, she noticed, and sunk back into the skin of his forehead as if resolved upon burying itself from view.

'One of my brothers did that for years and years. Mum and Dad took him to a special doctor. Turned out to be a weak sphincter muscle. Even now he isn't allowed to drink anything after supper time.' She picked up a stick and traced a pattern in the ground. 'I come here quite a lot.' She hesitated, resisting the urge to mention Felix.

'Because of the Copeland boy?' he whispered, watching her face.

'How . . . ?' Sally began, before quickly recovering herself. 'Nah. That's all over. Sometimes I need to see the river without your mother in it, if you see what I mean and also . . . with such a big family I like to have a place to go. Space and all that.' She laughed uncertainly, her eyes flicking to the wall for mementos of their trysts and then remembering that she had ritualistically removed and destroyed all such evidence weeks before. Apart from the black bag. She picked up the corner nearest her and began pushing holes with her fingers through the thin plastic, her expression momentarily soured by the recollection of old hopes.

'You could come to my cottage if you wanted. Anytime.' Joseph spoke firmly, warming to the idea as it took shape, liking the sense it gave him of life in the surroundings he loved stretching ahead into some still unidentified future. 'Plenty of space there.'

'Could I?' Sally's eyes lit up.

'Come now, if you like.' It was only as he struggled upright that Joseph became aware of the discomfort round his feet. Sally watched curiously as he emptied each boot of several cupfuls of water and wrung out his socks.

They emerged side by side into the muted daylight. A thick band of mist had materialised from nowhere, an elegant swathe of white that erased the trunks of the trees, leaving their branches protruding like shipwrecks on a snowy sea. Sally pulled a half-crushed box of chocolate finger biscuits from her pocket. She took three herself before offering one to Joseph, who accepted out of the desire to appear companionable rather than because he was hungry. The girl looked plumper than he remembered, the features of her pretty face submerged in a roundness that he associated with female adolescents. She ate very quickly, he noticed, her pink lips closing round the entire half of one biscuit at a time, her tongue greedily searching for signs of any remnants.

'If you like sweet things, I've got jarsful at home.'

'Oh, don't tempt me,' she groaned. When she smiled he could make out smudges of chocolate on her front teeth.

'I wouldn't dream of it,' he quipped, aware of the importance of appearing normal, fearful that if he gave any inkling of his precarious mental state she might turn tail and run.

Chapter Twenty-Two

'Have you got any jam, by any chance?' Daniel spread generous portions of butter on his toast and popped two more pieces of bread into the toaster.

'Jam . . . let me see.' Frances opened her larder door and reached for the still unopened jar that had been left on her doorstep by Joseph Brackman months and a lifetime before. 'Yes, but I'm not sure what flavour.' She tipped the jar and squinted at the winy red contents, which looked ominously runny. 'Either a dark strawberry or a light blackcurrant. Consume at your own risk. It was given to me ages ago.'

'I'm so famished I'll eat anything.' Daniel took the jar from her and sat back down, for a few moments oblivious to everything but the pleasure of eating.

Watching him, Frances felt suddenly consumed by uncertainty and shyness. She wanted to touch him but did not dare. That they had made love seemed nothing short of incredible. She tried to cast her mind back to how it had happened, to each step that had led them to the first embrace, to the house, to the stairs, to the door of the bedroom. It was at her insistence that they had returned from Dervayne Abbey to Leybourne, part of her hoping that the familiar context would provide some yardstick of common sense, some obvious reason for her to call a halt to the tidal wave of insanity which had begun in the car.

But somehow the obvious reason never presented itself. The thought of using the more neutral territory of the spare room popped into her head and slid out again. If demons had to be faced, then she wanted to confront them head on. But no demons had appeared, either in her own mind or between the crisp white sheets of her double bed. The sight, over Daniel's shoulder, of Paul's photograph on her dressing table made her pause, but only for a moment. The smile in Paul's eyes was unchanged, fixed at some vague point on the opposite side of the room, an integral part of an existence which she still cherished, but from which she had moved on.

Soon Frances was focusing on the rather more pressing concern of what Daniel might think of her forty-three-year-old body, preserved by a combination of good fortune and a healthy lifestyle, but still looking as used and lived in as a favourite set of clothes. At each fresh revelation of the smooth hard physique of the man undressing her, Frances felt more and more inclined to keep her own silhouette under cover. If Daniel was drawing any such comparisons however, he gave no indication of them. The duvet was soon on the floor, removing every last possibility of modesty and leaving Frances no option but to concentrate on a pleasure that she had sometimes feared she might never know again. Binding, extraordinary pleasure, which had, for a while, suffused her with a wild confidence. It had taken time – half an hour at least – for the doubts to creep back in, for her to feel separate again, dumbfounded by her recklessness.

'Aren't you eating?' He looked at her own untouched piece of toast, surprised.

'Yes, I . . .' She picked up a knife. 'Daniel, I . . .'

He stopped, his mug of tea half-way to his mouth. 'You're not going to say you regret the whole thing and I should put on my trousers and leave quietly, are you? No, no, no, no.' He took the knife from her and began buttering her toast. 'I'm not having that. Either you have found everything that's happened every bit as amazing as I have or you're the most proficient faker in the . . .'

'Faker? Certainly not. Of course I—'

'Well, there you are then.' He cut her toast into two neat triangular halves and pushed the plate back across the table. Jubilance shone in his face, widening the pupils of his eyes till the surrounding brown was barely visible at all. With his hair still dishevelled and wearing only his T-shirt and under-pants, he looked even younger than his twenty-six years. But inside he felt old and very wise, more than a match for her fears. 'I feel I have known you forever,' he continued quietly. 'You are so familiar to me Frances, it's almost weird. Just now – upstairs – I felt as if I was discovering what I have, unknow-ingly, been looking for – waiting for – all my life. For years I've been stumbling, falling, towards . . . this.' He spread his arms wide, reached across the table and cupped her head gently in his hands. 'I know you are scared. Please don't be. So long as we believe in each other, nothing else matters.' He leant across the table and kissed her on the mouth, flooding her senses with certainty again. 'Though,' he frowned, 'I couldn't help wondering . . . did you . . . did you . . . think of Paul?'

She met his gaze squarely. 'No.'

'Phew.' He pretended to wipe his brow. 'Glad I got that one over with. Now then, who are this lot?' Taking the remains of his toast, he leapt up from his chair and began scrutinising a collage of family photographs hanging beside the fridge. 'That's got to be your daughter – Daisy is it? And that's Paul, of course . . .'

Frances went to stand next to him, deeply grateful for his ability to sound so natural, to make her feel that he embraced her as much in the context of her family as for herself.

'And this must be . . . hang on a minute . . .' He leant closer to an image of Felix, triumphantly displaying a fish, caught on an expedition with his father several summers before.

'That's Felix.'

'Yes, I thought so . . . funny . . .' Daniel cocked his head at the picture. 'He looks extraordinarily familiar . . .'

'Everyone always says he looks very like me.'

'Where did you say he was at university?'

'I didn't. But it's the same place as you,' she admitted quietly.

Daniel clapped his hands together in amazement. 'Really? But that explains it − I know him − well, not know exactly − but I've met him − gave him a lift when he was hitchhiking home for Christmas. Isn't that incredible?'

He looked elated, but Frances could feel nothing but dismay. The coincidence merely heightened the anxieties which had deterred her from mentioning the connection in the first place. Anxieties connected to the grim fact that in terms of age and situation Daniel was much closer to her son than her, that the real world was already crouched on her doorstep, waiting to pounce and turn everything sour.

'He even mentioned that his father . . . about Paul . . .'

'Did he?' She was genuinely surprised. 'How improbable.'

'But Frances, why didn't you tell me about Felix being at Sussex?' he pressed gently.

'I . . . I didn't think it relevant.' She began clearing the table, scraping crumbs into the bin and dropping the plates into the kitchen bowl. Living alone, she had got out of the habit of using the dishwasher, since it took days to fill sufficiently for a load. 'He's doing Politics and Economics, which is nothing to do with your department, and of course with you on holiday—'

'Sabbatical—' he corrected her, pretending to look offended.

'Whatever. Look, it never crossed my mind that I would get . . . close to you, that it would matter where the hell my son was studying for his degree.' She tried to carry on washing up, but Daniel came up behind her and slipped his arms round her waist.

'Tell me what you're thinking.'

'No.'

'Please.' He pressed his hands against her stomach, pulling her back so hard she could feel his hip bones pressing into her waist. 'We must have no secrets or we haven't a hope.'

Frances sighed, letting the back of her head rest on his shoulder, unable to resist the notion that they didn't have a hope anyway. 'I was thinking that my son is only eight years younger than you and that if he finds out his mother has been screwing a member of the history of art faculty he will, understandably explode with disgust and outrage and never talk to me again.'

'That's what I thought you were thinking.' Daniel kissed the top of her left ear. 'And I'm certain you're wrong. Let's break the news next time he's home – together. It'll be fine, you'll see.'

'And Daisy? What are your plans for her?' Frances turned to face him, the rollercoaster of her emotions nose-diving again. 'I'm going to stay with her in a couple of weeks, I could just drop into conversation over dinner, that my lover is the same age as hers. She'd like that, I'm sure.' She was laughing but inside she felt hopeless.

'Frances, what do you feel when you're with me? Like now. What do you feel now?'

'Honestly?'

'Honestly.'

'Terror. Disbelief. Happiness. In equal quantities.'

His face creased into a broad grin of relief. 'Good.'

'You call that good?'

'I call it fucking marvellous. Can I come to Paris too?'

She let out a small shriek. 'You're unbelievable. We barely know each other. In a couple of days you're bound to wake up to common sense and realise that it's hopeless and that I'm irritating and carrying a lifetime of baggage with which you have no desire to become acquainted. Can't we just tiptoe along quietly for a while and let it all go wrong without anyone else having to know about it?'

He shook his head, smiling. 'You're awful. I can't think

what I find so attractive. Apart from, let's see now,' he held up his fingers as if to enumerate her qualities out loud.

Frances clamped her hand over his mouth. 'I would love you to come to Paris, but . . . but I'll have to think about it.' She hesitated, frowning. 'Maybe if you go independently, so that I can see how things go with Daisy, decide on the spot whether getting together would work . . . is that too mean?'

He nodded vigorously, pretending to look appalled. 'It's mean, all right,' he gasped, when he managed to prise her fingers from his mouth, 'But I accept. Beggars can't be choosers. I'll stay in a cheap *pension* nearby, skulk around the place in dark glasses and a trilby, waiting for secret meetings with you on street corners.' He rubbed his hands together. 'God, how romantic.'

'And now I think you had better go.'

He looked crestfallen. 'You can't mean it?'

'I do.'

'For how many minutes?'

'For a few hours. Till tomorrow. Come tomorrow evening, for dinner.'

'Promise?'

'You'll still be here? You won't disappear abroad or get run over by a tractor?'

'Promise.' It took some effort to retain her composure, not to lunge for him as he traipsed to the front door. Too much had happened too quickly anyway. She needed time to digest it, to try and get some perspective on what she was doing and where it might lead.

Chapter Twenty-Three

———◇◇◇◇◇———

'Good weekend?' enquired Libby breezily, when Frances appeared half an hour late for work on Monday morning.

'Yes thanks, fine, very good.' Frances felt as if a glass wall had slipped down between her and the rest of the real world. Everything was still there as it always had been, but continuing in a way that felt somehow distant and inconsequential. The attempt to marshal her thoughts on Thursday night had turned out to be a short-lived process. After obediently driving away as instructed, Daniel had reappeared on her doorstep a couple of hours later, clutching a heavy blue saucepan and a bottle of red wine.

'I thought if I made supper then you couldn't possibly throw me out at once. It's pointless being away from you because all I do is think about you. Whereas when I am secure in the knowledge that you're actually reachable I can concentrate on all sorts of other things.'

'Well thanks for the compliment.' She had laughed, unable to contain her delight at the sight of him. On opening the door wider, light from the hall revealed a sports holdall sitting behind him on the lower step.

'Just a bit of work,' he explained hastily, managing to look meek and impudent at the same time. 'And, I'll admit it, a toothbrush – just in case. Be prepared, that's the key. Let's see how dinner goes, shall we? My cooking is quite an acquired taste. I can't resist weird additions that aren't in the recipe.'

'Like what?' Frances folded her arms and peered sus-piciously at the saucepan, as if the answer to her question would determine whether she allowed him into the house.

'In this one? Let me see . . . there's chicken, brandy, sun-dried tomatoes and . . . fresh basil. I think that was all. Oh yes and some Chinese mushrooms – I put those in most things. Can I come in now? I'm freezing my bollocks off out here. Tomorrow I thought we might turn the tables and spend the weekend at my place. Feel free to bring an easel and anything else you might miss during the course of forty-eight hours away from home.'

It was imprudent of course. Frances knew that even as she took charge of the saucepan of chicken and ushered Daniel and his holdall across the threshold of her home. In the three hours since his departure she had not managed to progress beyond a sense of disbelief. Even at the height of a modest teenage rebellion she had never behaved in a way so contrary to her own instincts for wisdom and self-preservation. A colleague of her father's had once offered her a fur coat and a key to a flat in Parson's Green, but at the last minute the glee in his glassy eye had made her change her mind. She had entrusted the burden of her virginity to a sixteen-year-old classmate instead, a disappointingly unerotic experience which months of practice had done little to improve. A handful of subsequent affairs had failed miserably to match up to the levels of ecstasy claimed by friends and writhing lovers on the big screen. Sexual pleasure had not arrived in earnest until Paul. To encounter it so immediately and strikingly with Daniel seemed to Frances to be a matter not so much for celebration as acute wariness. She could feel the thrill of it impairing her judgement, pulling her in head first and jeopardising all the emotional stability which had taken months to rebuild.

'No more pictures then?' barked Libby, driven by Frances's lack of response to repeat the question for the third time. Recognising a semi-somnambulant state reminiscent of the weeks immediately following Paul's death, she feared the worst.

'Pictures?' Frances glanced up from the box of birthday mugs which she had been pricing in a desultory fashion for a good half an hour. 'Oh God, sorry . . . no. I mean, not yet. Almost. Three are being framed.'

'Same size?'

'I think so . . . that is, yes, they are.'

'Are you all right?' Libby peered at her anxiously. 'You'd tell me if you were back on the sleeping pills wouldn't you? I mean there are bound to be ups and downs, for quite a long time to come yet . . .'

'I'm fine thanks Libby,' Frances interjected hastily. 'A little tired, that's all.'

Deciding that some cheering up was in order, Libby spent several minutes toying with how this might best be achieved, inwardly lamenting that providing support to someone in Frances's position got no easier with time. 'What about a girls' only trip to the West End this Saturday,' she burst out eventually. 'Most of the big London stores are still running amazing discounts. After the kind of Christmas the retail trade has suffered, God knows they need to,' she added feelingly. 'Alistair could man the fort for a day – he's been offering to for weeks. What do you say?'

'It sounds a great idea,' faltered Frances, thinking both that there was nothing particular she wished to buy and that Daniel was already brimming with plans for the approaching weekend. In London too, as it happened. He wanted to take her to Somerset House, where the Courtauld Gallery had apparently opened an exhibition of Renaissance paintings. Her heart twisted at the memory of his enthusiasm, not to mention the delightful prospect of an entire forty-eight hours in each other's company. She glanced across the shop at Libby, who had turned her back and was busy rummaging for something under the till. 'The only thing is . . .'

'Yup?' Libby's voice was muffled. After a few moments she

straightened, looking crimson-faced and faintly irritated. 'Have you any idea where those new rolls of till-paper have got to? I swear there was a whole box of the bloody things right here yesterday.'

'I might have put them in the store room. I'll have a look.' Though Frances knew precisely where the box was, she took her time, rehearsing ways of saying what she had to say and cursing her cowardice. A string of shoppers delayed the process still further. Then at last Libby herself presented the opportunity by producing two mugs of tea and readdressing the subject of shopping.

'I might treat myself to a new coat. I've had my sheepskin so long it looks positively diseased.'

'Libby . . . I . . . there could be a problem with Saturday.'

'Oh dear, why?'

Frances cleared her throat and gripped the handle of her mug. 'Do you remember saying that you would be happy if I met someone else? Well I have . . . at least I think I have.'

Libby put down her tea and flung both arms round Frances's shoulders. 'My dear I'm thrilled – that's just wonderful, wonderful, wonderful. Don't tell me, you're meeting him on Saturday and can't think of anything more abhorrent than shopping – I quite understand.' She sat back and slapped both thighs with her palms. 'I knew you would – meet someone, I just knew it. I mean, Christ, look at you, pretty as a teenager and about as kind and honest as it is possible to be. Is he widowed too?'

The question reminded Frances that there was more to be said. 'No, he's not. In fact, there is just one small potential problem.'

Libby looked grave. 'Don't tell me, he's married.'

Frances shook her head.

'Well what other problem can there be?' exclaimed Libby, the wind back in her sails once more. 'Is he a recovering alcoholic? Does he practise voodoo in his spare time? Come on woman, out with it.'

'He's twenty-six,' said Frances quietly.

'Bloody hell. Bloody hell, Frances, that is . . . well, a little
. . . amazing.' Libby's tone was not so much appalled as
impressed. 'I said you looked like a teenager, didn't I?' She
laughed uncertainly, aware of Frances watching while her
mind groped for appropriate responses. 'Well, good for you,
that's what I say. And why not? Have a fling. Quite right too.'

'It . . . it doesn't feel like a fling.'

'Ah.' She looked nonplussed. 'Well . . . of course that's all
right too. It's your life Frances, you must lead it how you
please,' she continued, the hesitation in her voice belying the
other, more truthful and less generous reactions passing
through her mind. 'And of course you and . . .'

'Daniel.'

'. . . and Daniel have plans for Saturday.'

'Yes, we do. In London, actually. We're going to Somerset
House. The Courtauld Gallery has just opened a new exhibition of paintings there apparently. Lots of Renaissance stuff
that's never been shown over here before – that's Daniel's field
– he's a lecturer at Sussex. History of art. He's on sabbatical
working on a paper on Luca Signorelli.'

'How interesting,' murmured Libby, unable to suppress the
observation that Frances was speaking in the racy breathless
manner of an infatuated schoolgirl. 'And how – if you don't
mind my asking – did you two meet?'

Frances giggled. 'Don't laugh, please. But he's the cyclist I
ran into on the night I was supposed to meet James Harcourt.'

Libby's eyes widened. 'Good Lord, that's remarkable.'

'We sort of kept in touch.'

'Evidently.'

'Look, I know you think I'm mad,' Frances rushed on, 'I
think I'm mad too. The whole thing is just absurd, so utterly
foolish that when I think of it I can't believe it's real. But when
we're together . . .'

Libby watched her curiously, wondering whether the duty
of a friend in such circumstances was to offer support or to

attempt to tug the afflicted party back into the realms of the real world. Opting for the former, safer of the two strategies, she found herself issuing an invitation. 'I'd love to meet him,' she declared, genuine curiosity flaring at the prospect, 'and I know Alistair would too. If he means this much to you it is surely important that you introduce him to your friends.'

'That's extremely kind,' replied Frances carefully, trying and failing to picture the four of them round the large kitchen table where she and Paul had spent so many relaxed and enjoyable evenings in the past.

'Of course you must consult Daniel,' went on Libby hastily. 'Why not one evening this weekend? A dinner on Sunday is always a good idea I find, takes one's mind off the horrors of the week ahead. Ask Daniel. Let me know.' She left the counter to attend to a customer, inwardly complimenting herself on having handled a potentially explosive situation with exemplary maturity and tact.

Filled with eagerness to break the news to Alistair, the rest of Libby's working day passed slowly. He would be as scandalised as her, of that she was certain. A twenty-six-year-old was barely out of his teens. She pictured a rather fey, bookish creature with spectacles, unsure but sincere. Slightly dumpy, maybe. A little boy lost, looking for a mothering bosom in which to bury his woes. Tempted though she was to seek illumination on the subject from Frances, Libby refrained, aware that it might destroy the impression of broad-minded nonchalance which had taken some effort to achieve. Elation came before a fall, Libby reminded herself. And when the crash arrived it would be a lot easier to tend to Frances's wounds if she had given no hint of her own cynicism during these crucial early stages. Frances had to be allowed to make her own way, to make her own mistakes, in order to be able to admit to them afterwards.

Chapter Twenty-Four

———◦◦◦◦———

The rest of the week passed quickly, the latter half illuminated by a premature burst of mild temperatures and sunshine. March would wreak its revenge, Frances told herself, trying to inject some sombreness to her mood when she awoke on Friday morning, but managing only to feel wildly happy. At her insistence, she had not seen Daniel since Tuesday, a bid for a spell of solitude which had been somewhat thwarted by the number of hours they had spent conversing on the telephone. After the longest exchanges, Frances would look at her watch in astonishment at how much time had slipped by, already struggling to recall what they had found to say.

Pulling on her dressing gown, she made a cup of tea which she took back upstairs to enjoy in the comfort of the small Queen Anne armchair parked next to her bedroom window. Outside, a bossy jay was shooing several smaller birds from the upper branches of a tree, until scared away itself by two squirrels in the throes of an energetic game of tag. Frances sipped her drink slowly, savouring both its warmth and the prospect of the approaching weekend excursion with Daniel. It was only when her imagination advanced as far as Sunday evening that her heart sank. Libby's sustained display of mild interest throughout that week had not fooled her for a second. Underneath this careful disguise Frances sensed a bubbling blend of disapproval and curiosity, which she had no idea how to combat and which only fuelled all her own insecurities about the new course her life was taking.

She remained equally unsure of Daniel's display of non-chalance at the notion of an intimate dinner with her oldest friends. Familiarising themselves with each other's social worlds was a necessary prerequisite to achieving anything lasting and worthwhile, he said, so many times and with such studied carelessness that Frances longed to let him off the hook by cancelling the whole thing. For the first time in their brief, intense acquaintance, she was vividly aware of the real extent of the youthful uncertainty which lurked inside, his terror of appearing unwise or uncomposed, of justifying all the reservations which she was so adept at expressing out loud.

Leaving her empty mug on the window sill, Frances retreated to the bathroom where a confrontation with her image in the basin mirror continued to chisel away at her high spirits. Before Daniel she had never bothered much about the weathering effects of time, in recent months because it had seemed a matter of supreme insignificance and before that because having Paul suffering similar humiliations alongside – usually well in advance of her – rather took the edge off them. Yet now, even performing the simple act of cleaning her teeth, she found it impossible not to keep pausing for critical scrutinies of her profile. The shape of her face was still good, thanks to a natural roundness in her cheeks, overlaying the formidable bone structure still in evidence in the features of her mother. Her eyes were all right too, framed with fine radial lines, but wide and bright enough to offer distraction from such mortifications for several years to come. Of her teeth she was less sure, she decided, spitting away the last of the toothpaste and stretching her lips to facilitate a closer inspection. Warning herself that anything could look ugly if stared at for long enough did not prevent Frances from continuing to peer at her reflection with mounting dismay, licking her tongue round the tips of her front teeth, where the off-white seemed suddenly to look almost translucent. Yet more gloominess was induced by the detection of a series of small, faint vertical arrows pointing into the upper edge of her lip, like punishing imprints from a lifetime of being pursed in disapproval. And bracket lines were emerging on either side of her mouth too, she observed despairingly, etched into being by the equally destructive act of smiling.

While knowing it to be unwise, she could not resist transferring these attentions to the full length mirror in the bedroom. The more she stared, the more her self-confidence ebbed away. Her neck suddenly looked weathered and scrawny, her breasts not full so much as pendulous, her stomach and thighs crawling with silvery stretch marks which she had once, laughably, imagined to be barely visible at all.

By the time Daniel called she had retreated back to bed, curling herself round both pillows for comfort.

'What's the matter?' he asked at once.

'I'm an old witch compared to you.'

He laughed out loud. 'There could be something in the witch theory, since I am, most definitely, spellbound—'

'I'm serious. I'm physically repellent. And it's going to get worse.'

'Is it? Are you sure?' he teased, pretending to sound horrified.

'Yes. It's called the Ageing Process. No known cure.'

He sighed. 'Frances, I thought we'd been through this one. When I look at you, I see an entity. I see what you *are*, inside and out. Which isn't to say I don't want to rip your clothes off – I do – all the time,' he confessed ruefully. 'And if you're going back to your old hobby horse of what about in ten years' time – as I've told you, I refuse to worry about anything further than a week into my future. I've been through the kick of trying to map out my life in advance – it brought nothing but disappointment. I mean, Christ, you could dump me for being too immature, couldn't you?'

'I could, but I don't want to.'

'Well, thank God for that.'

'And what about babies?'

'Babies? Jesus, Frances—'

'In a few years I'll be menopausal. Hot flushes, KY-jelly or intensive hormone replacement. It's supposed to be a real picnic.'

'I don't want babies,' he put in, sounding exasperated.

'You might.'

'Nothing is impossible, I suppose, either in my head – or the realms of science, for that matter. Older women are procreating all over the place. But, I assure you,' he continued hastily, 'my oafish nephews and nieces have put me off the subject big time. Now can we talk about something a little more relevant, like when we can meet up?'

'Sorry,' murmured Frances, feeling mollified and a little contrite. She punched the pillows out of the way and pushed the duvet back off her legs. 'You're coming over here tonight, aren't you?'

'If the invitation still stands.'

'I think it probably does,' she teased, wanting to erase the trace of hurt from his tone.

'I was thinking maybe lunch in a pub. Scampi in a basket, that sort of thing.'

'I thought we'd agreed that today you were writing and I was drawing?'

'There's all morning for that.'

'And I've got to wash my hair – I assume it won't bother you to know I'll be rinsing colour into it soon, to help disguise the grey.'

'You could turn your hair a shade of violent rhubarb for all I care. The first girl I was ever mad about had this stripy look, green and yellow, in plaits all over her head. Many intimate moments were ruined by one of them swiping me in the eye. Shall we say twelve thirty? I'll pick you up.'

Frances laughed, reassured, as she always was after actually talking to Daniel instead of worrying about him. She re-entered the bathroom with fresh conviction, washing her hair with barely a glance in the mirror and then unashamedly opting for a new, shortish skirt that flattered her trim waist and the shapely curves of her legs.

'Now make yourselves scarce, the lot of you,' barked Libby, batting Sally's fingers out of a bowl of freshly made fruit salad and trying to herd all four of her children from the kitchen. 'I don't want you ogling the poor man like he's some unique species at a zoo.'

'Why not? That's what you're going to do, isn't it?' quipped her youngest daughter, managing to seize several wedges of banana before scampering upstairs after her siblings.

'I most certainly am not,' Libby shrieked indignantly, while inwardly acknowledging that she probably was. Although a handful of acquaintances had split up or had affairs with unsuitable partners, nothing in the kaleidoscope of her social experience could quite match what was happening to Frances. Every time she thought of it she felt appalled and intrigued in equal measure. A hint of *schadenfreude* also laced these reactions, the awful but wickedly thrilling sensation of watching someone hurl themselves at disaster. Whether it was her duty to stand by or to try and prevent the disaster happening was something of which she still felt deeply uncertain. Trying to discuss the matter with Alistair and being stonewalled by his obstinate lack of enthusiasm reminded her of the dark days immediately after Paul's death. That afternoon he had even accused her of treating Frances Copeland's life like a soap opera, an allegation which had hurt all the more deeply for containing what Libby feared might be a grain of truth.

After two decades of marriage, hurting each other was as easy as being kind had once been, Libby reflected glumly, slicing lengthways down several leeks to check for specks of dirt between the layers. To make matters worse, seeing Frances all dreamy-eyed had triggered memories of distant days when the unnatural generosity of spirit which accompanies new love had prompted her to feign a fascination for football and Alistair to pretend he liked Mozart. Admitting to boredom with a loved one's favourite hobbies took time, she mused wryly, peeling off several outer layers of the leeks and tossing them into a nearby sieve. She was busy holding the sieve under a tap when Alistair came in. Wanting to show she was still aggrieved, she kept her head down, focusing on positioning the worst patches of grit under the jet of water. Alistair picked out a grape from the fruit salad and then a segment of apple, chewing each slowly.

'Look, what I said – the soap opera thing – I'm sorry. It was mean and untrue.' He came and stood behind her, putting his hands on her shoulders, kneading his thumbs into the tense sensitive bands of muscle sloping down from her neck. 'You have helped Frances immeasurably over the last few months. And as for this young man, I think we should breathe a sigh of relief that she's managed to find someone else to mother so soon. As you know, I believe Frances to be one of those poor female souls quite unsuited to the rigours of surviving alone. Mind you,' he paused chuckling to himself, 'Jack might be a bit disappointed.' He watched for the response, knowing the comment would ensnare his wife's interest in an instant.

'Jack? Why?'

'He's always liked Frances a lot – told me so at Christmas. One of few females with the capacity to tempt him out of bachelorhood, he said.' Alistair shook his head, amused at the memory.

Libby laughed too, entertained by the idea. 'Jack and Frances? I can't see it somehow.'

'Other people never can,' he remarked dryly. 'Which is precisely why we must make this creature to whom Frances has attached herself feel as welcome as we can, no matter how misguided the enterprise appears.'

'I know,' Libby tipped her head to one side, briefly pressing her cheek against one of his hands to show that peace had been restored, but unable to resist adding, 'that's why I asked them.'

Chapter Twenty-Five

'You might as well know I'm scared shitless,' Daniel remarked cheerfully, as they set out on the short drive from Frances's house to the Taverners' on Sunday evening. He took a hand off the steering wheel and placed it in her lap.

'I know you are,' Frances replied quietly, accepting his hand and pressing it between her palms.

'Should I pretend to like fishing? I once went on a school trip to a trout farm. I caught a tiddler and cried when I was told to throw it back.'

Frances giggled. 'He does other things beside fish, you know.'

'What's his name again?'

'Alistair.'

Daniel slapped the steering wheel. 'Fuck, of course it is. For some reason I keep thinking he's Roger.'

Frances laughed. 'Alistair is most definitely not a Roger. Nor would he thank you for thinking he was one. He's got a slight Scottish accent, which might help. And he looks like an Alistair.'

'What do Alistairs look like?'

'Jovial, slightly messy looking. A bit on the round side. Tall. Nice smile. Something of the absent-minded professor about him.'

'Of course they do, how could I have forgotten,' he teased,

pulling his hand off her lap in order to negotiate a particularly sharp bend without the bother of decelerating. Frances clenched her knees in an expression of alarm which she hoped was indiscernible. Trivial though it was, Daniel's driving reminded her more than most things of the difference in their ages; not because he was bad at it (on the contrary, he was rather good) but because there was no caution in him, no fear. Turning to the window she wondered vaguely when Paul had started obeying speed limits and traffic signs, at what point a pair of leather driving gloves had assumed the role of an acceptable Christmas present. But the thought drifted away before she could see it through, distracted by the approaching ordeal and the realisation that the happiness generated by an entire weekend in each other's company had induced a surprising inner calm.

Going to London with Daniel had felt like an adventure to a new and exotic country. Every familiar landmark burned with fresh significance. Flying up the M23, with the mesmeric pulse of one of his cassettes filling the car, Frances had closed her eyes, overcome not so much by happiness as a profound sense of unreality. After parking they spent some time shoulder to shoulder on Waterloo Bridge, idly studying the choppy grey surface of the Thames and watching the half-empty tourist boats cruise underneath. Every detail of the scene had seemed unnaturally vivid, from the gun metal glints in the water to the coarse, dark grain of Daniel's coat. Leaning on the cold stone, elbows touching, the wind beating in their faces, Frances had been suffused by an unprecedented surge of wellbeing, a sense of rightness about being there. Paul would not have paused on the bridge, she had realised, approaching the comparison cautiously, not wanting to be disloyal. That her husband had never been happy with the inbetween moments of life had been an integral facet of his personality; he was always rushing on to the next known or planned thing, sweeping her along in the slipstream of his energy.

Seeing the effect of the paintings on Daniel put the seal on

Frances's enchantment with the day and the new course of her life in general. He looked not just with knowledge, but with an irresistible enthusiasm, jotting notes in a pad and telling fascinating anecdotes about the scenes depicted or the people responsible for them. The level of her own responding interest had been genuine and unreserved, while inwardly she experienced an inordinate fondness for sensibilities that could embrace unintelligible electronic music as easily as the glories of the Italian Renaissance.

Afterwards, they had wandered into a cinema showing an obscure tragic French drama about a mute postman who wrote love poems to a young housewife. In spite of the awkward subtitles and the pebble-dash quality of the reel, Frances found herself gulping hard at the denouement. During the course of her quiet struggle with this embarrassment, she suddenly became aware that Daniel was similarly afflicted. They had both laughed at their hopeless sentimentality, taking it in turns to blow into a dusty, man-sized tissue which Frances unearthed from the bottom of her handbag. Tumbling out into the street, they then linked arms for a stroll round Covent Garden, eventually stepping inside a small attractively lit Thai restaurant on the edge of Soho. While they waited amongst a crowd of other post-theatre arrivals, Daniel brushed his mouth across her ear, whispering, 'I love you Frances. Sorry. No pressure intended. Just couldn't not say it a moment longer.'

Reeling, she took a step backwards, whereupon someone in the queue behind tapped her lightly on the shoulder.

'It is Mrs Copeland, isn't it? I thought so. How are you? You look extremely well, if I may say so.'

She turned to find herself shaking hands with Hugo Gerard and a petite brunette whom she recognised from the photo in his office.

'We're making use of my parents,' declared Hugo cheerily, 'down for a couple of weeks from Scotland, full of desire to become better acquainted with their grandchildren. Won't last long, I can tell you. We've just seen a slog of a play about nuclear physics – God the things critics recommend these days. Hoping the meal's going to be rather easier to digest. Mind you,' he scowled at the crowded tables, 'if we have to wait much longer we might go for a change of plan. Darling, I knew we should have booked on a Friday . . .'

It was several moments before Frances realised that she still had not introduced Daniel, not simply because Hugo had been talking so much, but because she could not immediately think how to. She was prompted to remedy the situation by a sudden terror that the Gerards might mistake him for Felix. 'This is my . . . a friend of mine. Daniel Groves. Hugo and Laetitia Gerard.' She stepped aside so that the three of them could shake hands. 'Hugo was – is my solicitor. He was very helpful after Paul died,' she added, instinct telling her that mentioning the subject might defuse some of the awkwardness of the situation. That there was no awkwardness to defuse took a few minutes to become apparent. Hugo engaged Daniel in easy conversation about the demise of English cricket, while Laetitia made winning confidences about the relief of escaping her in-laws. Just before they were finally shown to separate tables, she touched Frances's arm saying, 'I remember Hugo telling me about you. He said if anyone could pick up the pieces it was you. I'm so glad to see he was right.'

Frances floated towards their assigned table in a trance of pleasure and confidence, musing upon the happy revelation that the outside world was neither menacing nor vindictive, that all the problems resided in her head and were of her own making. 'I think I might love you too,' she murmured, leaning across the table as they sat down.

'I never doubted it,' he replied cockily, his steady eyes meeting hers, 'I just guessed it might be hard to say.'

Remembering the moment that Sunday evening, Frances reached out and brushed the back of her hand against Daniel's cheek. 'Libby and Alistair are nothing to be afraid of,' she insisted, wanting to share some of her newfound confidence and composure. 'Next turning on the left and we're there. The big white house on the corner, opposite the post box. And if all else fails, I promise you'll enjoy the food – she's a great cook.'

Thanks to the Taverners' eagerness to appear welcoming, the encounter began with an unpromising tangle on the doorstep, as arms and cheeks were simultaneously proffered in salutation. After they had finally managed to progress as far as the hall, Libby began pulling their coats off their backs, gushing nonsensical greetings in a voice which Frances gloomily judged to be at least an octave higher than her usual pitch. While Alistair, hovering to one side, looking amiable but tense, accepted the more mundane role of finding out what everyone would like to drink.

Passing the staircase en route to the sitting room, Frances's mounting sense of unease was heightened by several loud creaks from the landing and a flash of disappearing legs. It was going to be even worse than she had imagined. Possibly even tortuous. Left alone for a few minutes as Libby scuttled off to do something in the kitchen, she exchanged nervous and unhappy glances with Daniel.

'I wish it was all over,' he hissed, clasping his hands behind his back and bending forward to inspect a set of framed photographs arranged on top of the piano.

'They are nice, really,' Frances whispered through gritted teeth, 'they just don't know how to *be* with you.'

'That makes three of us,' he replied darkly, turning his attention from the photographs to a line of framed prints on the wall. 'Hey, this looks like one of yours,' he exclaimed, his expression brightening as he came to stop in front of a small framed sketch in a far corner. 'Are these their children?'

Frances made a face. 'Yes, in the days when I still thought I could draw humans. I'm so much better at inanimate things.' She went to look over his shoulder.

'Landscapes are hardly inanimate,' he murmured, slipping an arm round her back. 'Monet apparently had scores of canvasses of the same scene on the go at once, because his subjects changed so much. Once he got so frustrated he threw the whole lot in the river.'

She laughed. 'God, what a waste.'

'Don't worry, he fished them out again—'

They were interrupted by the sound of their hostess's new, unnatural trill heralding her approach through the doorway. Frances quickly broke free and returned to the sofa, not knowing whether to be appalled or sympathetic at Libby's blundering attempts to put them at their ease.

'Here we are, some low-fat carbohydrates to keep the wolf from the door.' Libby placed two overflowing bowls of crisps on the coffee table before hastily retrieving one and trotting over to Daniel. 'Oh goodness, but you haven't even got a drink yet,' she exclaimed, backing away just as he reached out a hand to the bowl. 'What can have happened to Alistair? What did you ask for? A beer wasn't it? We don't usually – I mean it's no bother at all – but being wine drinkers – apart from real ale of course – what beer we do have is kept in a spare fridge thing in the garage. I expect he's forgotten. Or he could be struggling with the handle – it needs a sharp wrench upwards before it will co-operate. Hence its banishment from the house. Though in my view you can never have too many fridges. Excuse me a moment.' She backed towards the sitting-room door, narrowly avoiding a collision with her husband entering behind, self-consciously bearing a tray laden with glasses and bottles.

'I was just admiring Frances's picture,' remarked Daniel, refusing several offers of a glass and swigging straight from his bottle of beer.

'I know, she has *such* talent. They sell like hot cakes in the shop.'

'Three, Libby,' put in Frances wearily, 'three in two months. Hardly hot cakes—'

'But that's because you can't produce them quick enough. Give me anything of Frances's and I'll be able to get a good price for it,' she declared, as if to make herself sound – so

Frances could not help thinking – like some kind of hard-edged entrepreneur instead of the owner of a small, struggling gift shop.

'I'm sure you could,' agreed Daniel kindly, raising his bottle in toast and drinking until barely three fingers of beer remained.

Frances had not lied about Libby's culinary talents, but that evening, perhaps because the silent interplay of unspoken emotions was so vivid, the food on their plates seemed bland and indigestible. Ramekins of chewy potted shrimps and brown toast were followed by rolled parcels of white fish, lanced through with cocktail sticks to prevent them unfurling. The leeks, floating in a casserole of white sauce, looked flaccid and as uninviting as the heap of small brown potatoes in the dish next to them, their splitting skins like hatching eggs. Daniel ate steadily but with none of his usual relish, bravely accepting seconds and taking large appreciative swigs from his wine glass between mouthfuls. He didn't even like white wine, Frances reflected hopelessly, putting out her hand to prevent Alistair topping up her glass on one of his frequent wine-waiter tours round the table.

They clung to the subject of Frances's drawing skills for some time, wringing it dry out of a mutual desperation for common ground. An attempt by Frances to move the conversation on to the delights on view at the Courtauld Gallery proved short-lived.

'I thought Somerset House contained nothing but filing cabinets – hatch, match and despatch –' declared Libby, laughing at her own joke and then adding pointedly, 'We never go to art galleries any more, do we darling? Or the theatre, or the opera – God I love opera,' she sighed theatrically. 'Do you like opera Daniel?'

'Not mad about it, to be honest,' he confessed.

Recalling the selection of tapes in the glove compartment of his car, Frances pressed her glass to her lips to hide a smile.

'People say it's something you grow into,' Daniel continued, his brown eyes glittering with mischief, 'so perhaps I'm just not old enough.'

There followed a heavy silence, before Alistair came to the rescue. 'Well, that certainly hasn't been true in my case. Warbling women and implausible storylines. Give me the cinema any day,' he added with a grimace, inadvertently introducing a subject which saw them through, albeit in somewhat laboured fashion, to the arrival of Libby's fruit salad. A bottle of sweet wine, of a colour not too dissimilar to Daniel's preprandial beer, was produced at the same time. Frances accepted a half glass, trying and failing to catch Daniel's eye to indicate that it would be acceptable for him to do the same.

At half past ten Libby, staggering a little as she eased herself up from her seat, said, 'Coffee everyone?'

'Coffee. Great stuff. Thanks Liz.' Daniel wagged both thumbs in the air to underline his enthusiasm for the idea.

There was a moment of intense silence. Libby was never Liz. Those who knew her well were privy to the fact that it was a matter of ancient pride that her name derived not from Elizabeth, but the infinitely more unusual Lysbeth. Seeing the tightening of her friend's jaw line and remembering the Roger conversation in the car, Frances experienced a small explosion of panic. 'It's never a good idea to be too late on a Sunday,' she blurted. 'Don't you think we should skip coffee this time Daniel?' She locked her gaze on his, noting with a twist of alarm, that his dark pupils were illuminated with what looked like the light of defiance.

'Time for bed in other words. Goody.' He rubbed his palms together gleefully. 'We shag every chance we get, don't we Frances?' He pushed back his chair and pulled on his jumper, discarded early on because of the furnace-heat of the room. 'A good evening, thank you. Not great, I wouldn't say, but it's early days isn't it?' He seized Alistair's hand and gave it several hard shakes before easing himself behind the chairs towards the sink, where Libby stood, a stack of dishes in her hand, her lower jaw hanging slightly open in a caricature of speechlessness.

Glancing at the plates and seeing that they precluded any immediate chance of a handshake, Daniel leant down and planted a firm kiss on each of her flushed cheeks. 'Thank you Liz, for cooking so much food and so on.'

Frances suspected suddenly that he was not as drunk as he was pretending, but merely using it as an excuse to be shocking. 'Alistair, Libby, thank you for having us,' she said quickly, speaking in clipped businesslike tones to cover her embarrassment. 'It's been quite a weekend – not much sleep –' she dried up, colouring at the implications of such an excuse when all she had meant was that their Thai meal had ensured they hadn't returned from London until the early hours of that morning. 'Thanks again and er . . . see you tomorrow.'

'I hope so,' remarked Libby with undisguised curtness and leaving Alistair to show them to the door.

Once outside, Frances held out her hands for the car keys. 'I'd better drive.' Hearing the thud of the front door behind them, sounding so final in the dark silent air, her heart sank to a new low.

'You're cross.'

'No I'm not. Get in the car.'

'Yes you are.'

'No Daniel, not cross, just . . . disappointed.'

'Ah, worse still.' He shook his head solemnly and then levered himself into the passenger seat. 'Anger I could take, but disappointment . . .' he sucked in his breath, 'that is hard. You don't need to rev, by the way.'

'I beg your pardon?'

'When you start the engine, don't rev on the foot pedal. Let it fire on its own.'

'Since you were incapable of staying sober enough to drive your own vehicle, the least you could do is refrain from criticising me.'

'You're cross now, anyway. Which I feel a lot better about frankly. And your hair's all falling out of the bun at the back – I like that too.' He reached out to touch her, but pulled back in mock terror at the sight of the glaring expression on her face. 'Fucking disgusting wine.'

'Why did you consume so much of it then?' she retorted icily.

'Because the situation was so fucking awful. Because they had pre-judged me anyway – especially her. He wasn't so bad. Nothing like low expectations for a challenge, I always find.'

'And me? Did you think about me?'

'Hm.' He yawned deeply. 'Most of the evening. I always think about you. Could you pull over a minute?' He began groping for the door handle.

'What now, for heaven's sake?'

'A piss. You pulled me out of there so quickly, I didn't have time to ask for the little boys' room.'

Frances swerved the car onto the verge and sat with the engine running, arms folded tightly across her chest, while Daniel disappeared between two bushes. A few moments later he surprised her by appearing at the window on the driver's side, having re-emerged from a different part of the undergrowth. He gestured at her to wind it down.

'I think I'll walk.'

She rolled her eyes impatiently. 'Don't be silly.'

'There's so much smoke coming out of your ears I think it would be safer. I know the way from here. And I can sober up. Have a good think.' He tapped his temple.

'Fine, if that's what you want,' she replied tightly. 'I'll leave the keys under the flowerpot, shall I? Unless you were planning to trek back to Farley?'

He shook his head gravely. 'Would take all night.'

Frances roared off, revving the engine with deliberate, audible ferocity. When she got to her drive she sat for several minutes in the dark silence, telling herself that it would be of no concern to her if Daniel collapsed in a ditch or was mown down by a speeding juggernaut. A few minutes later she was nonetheless driving carefully back the way she had come, straining her eyes in the dimness for a glimpse of his dark jacket. She had all but given up hope when she spotted his tall frame leaning on a five-bar gate set a few feet back from the road.

'It's at times like this I wished I smoked,' he remarked, half turning to acknowledge her approach. 'At such moments a man needs a pipe, don't you think, something to lend a philosophical air with which to contemplate the stars.' As he talked, he gently took her hand and slipped it into his jacket pocket. 'Sorry. I know I screwed up. Something clicked and I couldn't help myself.' They interlaced fingers, hers warm, his icy cold.

'Oh, sod the Taverners.'

'Do you think if I hung around for twenty years they might get to like me?'

'It wasn't that they didn't like you. They don't know you.'

'He wasn't so bad – when he could get a word in. But as for her –' he rolled his eyes – 'or was I imagining things?'

'No, you weren't,' she admitted. 'Libby was disgraceful. But so were you.' Frances giggled suddenly, remembering the look of horror on Libby's face during the course of Daniel's parting remarks. Daniel began to laugh too, until the pair of them were doubled up helplessly, clinging to the gate for support. Overhead a screen of grey drifted across the face of the moon, like a scarf muffling a smile.

Chapter Twenty-Six

After worrying about it half the night, Frances decided that the best – the only – tactic for coping with Libby was to confront the matter head on.

'Thank you again for dinner – I'm afraid Daniel found the whole experience somewhat intimidating,' she burst out, with the door jingle of the shop still tringing behind her.

'It was never our intention to frighten him,' Libby replied dryly, wanting to make light of the matter, but the edge in her voice betraying harder, deeper feelings with which she was still trying to come to terms. That her expectations of a twitchy academic with a mousy bush of hair and acne scars had been cruelly disappointed was not a matter she felt prepared to discuss with anyone, least of all Frances herself. The lean, striking looks of Daniel Groves had thrown her off balance from the start. He was like some George Clooney of the Home Counties; the kind of lover most middle-aged women would not even presume to include in their fantasies, let alone stumble across in real life. Glimpsing the two of them standing together at the far end of her sitting room, Frances, as radiant as a recently deflowered virgin, pressed into the curve of his arm as if her body had been moulded solely for that purpose, had given Libby quite a jolt. A part of her had wanted to protest out loud at the almost tangible sense of their shared intimacy, the horrible, excluding intensity of it.

'It was bound to be awkward at first,' ventured Frances. 'Especially with Daniel feeling so shy—'

'Yes, I suppose it was,' cut in Libby. 'Never mind. Think nothing of it. I'm sure he's a thoroughly nice . . . man.' Libby only managed to stop herself saying 'boy' at the last minute, acknowledging that her motive for using such a term would have been pure unkindness. In spite of the many flaws of their recent encounter, it was clear to her that Daniel Groves was perfectly adult, both in his intellect and his appearance. That he had drunk an enormous quantity of alcohol was not something which Libby felt in any position to judge too harshly either. The next morning Alistair felt so bad he had decided to take the day off, while she had filched two of his extra strength migraine painkillers before being able to face the mêlée of family breakfast. When the girls declared that their ailing father had given them permission to use his car for a shopping expedition into Hexford after school, instead of ranting about homework she gave the most cursory of mumbles about obeying the Highway Code.

As Libby's headache receded, images from the previous evening came back to her more clearly, sharpening her understanding of why she had felt so affronted and bringing little comfort in the process. Daniel's early silences and subsequent outspokenness may well have derived from shyness; but behind that Libby, in her fatigued and anxious state, felt sure there had lurked a desire to mock his hosts' middle-aged mundanity. As if he knew that mentioning sex like that would cut to the bone. As if he wanted to make her feel even worse about the fact that recently she and Alistair made love twice a month if they were lucky, and even then performing the act in a shameful blur of exhausted detachment. A part of her wished she had possessed the courage to scream that once she and Alistair had shagged every night too, but that things changed, that worries about money and children blocked paths to pleasure with all the deadening efficacy of the most potent anaesthesia. Staring after the pair of them as they left the kitchen, such thoughts had for a brief moment, crystallised into pure, debilitating envy. When Alistair returned from seeing them to the front door, she did not dare to look at him, out of shame, and a small fear that the sight of the familiar, deepening lines on his face might prompt not fondness, but powerless dissatisfaction. Soured by the guilt of such unedifying and uncharitable sentiments, she resisted a meaty post mortem of the evening's events and told him off for not helping her enough instead, for failing even to stagger towards the kettle with the cafetière. Whereupon Alistair had added to her state of aggravation by meekly apologising and proceeding not only to help stack the dishwasher but to commit the virtually unprecedented act of rinsing the plates under the tap before he did so. The subject of Frances and Daniel wasn't broached directly by either of them until they were crawling into bed, when Libby could not resist opening proceedings by saying smartly, 'Of course, it can't last.'

Alistair stretched, emitting a sleepy groan. 'Why ever not?' He turned on his side and pulled his pillow round his face. 'An impudent bastard, but somehow I couldn't help liking him. Not what I was expecting at all. Bloody good show for Frances, that's what I say – there's clearly more to the old girl than I thought.' He closed his eyes, adding dreamily, 'Rather them than me, mind you, no plain sailing . . .' As he spoke he groped across the bed for the familiar frame of his wife, fondly patting the round of her stomach when he found it and then looping his arm companionably through hers. 'Put the light out, love.' Libby obeyed, disengaging from his embrace and then lying on her back in the dark with her eyes open, listening to the familiar small sounds and movements that accompanied her husband's drift into sleep.

'Daniel is sorry too,' persisted Frances, seeing from the dazed expression on Libby's face that her earlier comments had barely got through. 'He's going to write to you about it.'

Libby waved her arms dismissively and began checking the till. 'There's really no need.'

'It's not just the sex,' said Frances quietly.

'Of course it isn't.' Libby slammed the till drawer shut. 'I never thought it was,' she lied. 'You're clearly very fond of each other. I'm very happy for you,' she continued, not sounding happy at all and disappearing into the stock room.

The explanation, when it dawned, was so obvious, that Sally dropped her mouth at her reflection, freezing in a moment of gormless horror. She was in the changing cubicle of one of her favourite boutiques in Hexford, with a pile of variously coloured trousers strewn around her feet and Beth waiting patiently outside. They were spending the last of their extremely generous Christmas money from Uncle Jack. Beth had bought two CDs and a set of blue eye shadows, arranged in a circle like the petals of a flower.

Everything was too tight, not just round the waist and hips but across the chest too. How could she have been so dumb, so naïve? Punching viciously at the new thickness round her hip bones, Sally performed a frantic mental calculation about her periods, never punctual at the best of times. The last one had been just before Christmas. Remembering her encounter with Felix in the attic she let out a moan of horror, grimacing at her reflection with fresh misery.

'Everything all right in there?' Beth's face appeared round one side of the curtain. 'Do you want me to find anything else?'

'A shirt,' said Sally quickly, putting her hands protectively across her chest and sucking in her stomach, wanting only to be rid of her. 'Anything dark and . . . er . . . baggy.'

Her elder sister raised an eyebrow. 'No trousers then?'

'No, I hate them all. I want a shirt, size twelve. Or maybe fourteen.'

Beth burst out laughing. 'Fourteen? Are you mad? You'll drown—'

'Please?'

Something about her sister's tone deterred Beth from

protesting any further. Clothes were personal things, as she well knew. There was only one friend whom she really trusted to say the right things in changing cubicles. Back behind the screen of the curtain Sally quickly pulled her school skirt back on, leaving the top button undone as she always did these days, and slumped down on the stool. When Beth returned with three loose-fitting, long-sleeved shirts, she took them in a daze, finally choosing a charcoal grey one with long flapping panels that hung almost to her knees.

With Beth – freshly through her driving test – negotiating the road with all the panache of a turtle, the journey home was tortuous. Sally kept her head turned to the window, staring at the dull greens and browns of the passing landscape with bleak eyes. After a few attempts at conversation Beth gave up, partly because it was rush hour and she needed to concentrate and partly because experience had taught her that her younger sister in a bad mood was unassailable.

Once home, Sally locked herself in her room. She would have to tell Felix of course. Dreadful though it was a part of her even relished the prospect. He had thought he could just drop her, that he could run off to his new life without a back-ward glance at all the suffering she had been forced to endure. Well now there would be some suffering for him too. She would have an abortion of course, but not without putting him through a few hoops of misery in the process. Like where such a thing could be done, how much it would cost. At the thought of money Sally's throat went dry. She had seven pounds fifty left in her bank account and twenty-two in the post office. She would need Felix's help on that score if nothing else.

Tearing a piece of paper roughly from a pad, she began to write quickly, not caring that the Biro was smudging one word into the next.

Felix,

Sorry to interrupt your fun. But what seems to have been our farewell screw amongst the mothballs has left me pregnant. Like a

sick joke, isn't it? Though I don't see Mum and Dad laughing somehow. I haven't yet decided whether to tell them. Like I haven't quite decided what to do about it either. Having a baby would get me out of GCSEs at least. I look forward to hearing your views.
    Sally.

That would make him stew, she thought viciously, sealing the letter and slipping it into her satchel. After motoring through her homework, she crept into the kitchen and treated herself to three pieces of stale shortbread from a Christmas tin sent by a Scottish aunt. She was eating for two, after all, Sally reminded herself, skipping back upstairs to put on her new shirt and feeling a wonderful sense of reprieve at the way it masked the flab round her midriff.

Chapter Twenty-Seven

The jigsawed terrain of south-east London streaked past the train window, playing fields and concrete, dotted with the occasional speck of colour: a pair of pink trousers flaying on a washing line, a yellow plastic slide, a purple fuzz of early crocuses. The sky was a sheet of white, flecked with pearly grey, sunless but bright. There was something noble, glamorous even about the journey, Frances decided, not just because of the train's magnificent speed, but because it was heading for the Continent, destined to zip under the Channel courtesy of engineering feats which she could hardly begin to comprehend. With every swagger of the carriage, her body swayed slightly across the seat-divide, reminding her of the improbable presence of Daniel, whose relentless pleading had finally worn the last of her resistance down. When she said it was too soon to think of introducing him to Daisy, he assured her that there were innumerable useful things he could do in Paris on Signorelli's behalf, and that any secret rendezvous with her would be icing on the proverbial cake.

'What I don't understand is how they kept back the water while they were digging,' Frances murmured, as they slid into the muffled darkness heralding the start of the tunnel.

Daniel glanced up from the Paris street map spread open on his lap. 'By digging very deep I suppose.'

'Very deep.' She gave an involuntary shudder at the invisible universe of icy wet darkness stretching over their heads, thinking in the same instant of poor Mrs Brackman and Joseph. Her neighbour had slipped back into his own world, she realised, recalling the peculiar flurry of their friendship and experiencing a now familiar flutter of guilt at having allowed it to lapse. 'I told Daisy not to meet me – said I'd take a taxi to the flat.'

'Yes, you said.'

'So we'll say goodbye at the station.'

'No need for that. We could share a taxi. Look, my hotel is only a stone's throw from Rue Lyonnaise.' He held up the map with a smile of triumph. 'You'll be able to pop in and see me whenever you want.'

'I thought you were going to spend your time beavering away in libraries and museums,' she remarked dryly.

'Well, *some* of my time. It doesn't stop you leaving messages at reception.' He pretended to read a note on the palm of his hand, 'Darling Daniel, near death from deprivation of love and passion, require urgent meeting – that sort of thing.'

Frances smiled, but continued to look doubtful. 'It all sounds fine in theory, but I suspect we won't end up seeing too much of each other.'

'Unless you change your mind and decide to declare my existence officially, of course. Your children have got to find out some time,' he added gently, folding up the map and stowing it in the side pocket of his leather holdall.

'Yes, I know they have.' Frances sighed. Daisy and Felix would be shocked enough at their mother acquiring a new partner, let alone one young enough to be their older brother. The thought prompted her to work out whether this was in fact the case. Forty-three years minus twenty-six. To have a child Daniel's age she would have been seventeen at the time of conception. Undesirable maybe, but highly possible.

'Don't worry about it now,' he urged, seeing the troubled

look on her face and wanting to erase it. 'I'm a great believer in things working out, in there being a sort of pattern to life that's only detectable afterwards.'

'In seizing any excuse to take no action at all, you mean,' she teased, linking her arm through his and letting her head fall onto his shoulder, where it stayed for the remainder of the journey.

As the crowd swept them towards the ticket barrier at the Gare du Nord, Frances could not help nervously scanning the forecourt for glimpses of Daisy's brightly bleached head, fearful that her daughter might have decided to meet the train after all. Getting as far as the taxi rank without being accosted was something of a relief, as was the unfolding view of Paris, dirty but defiant under the glare of afternoon spring sunshine. In spite of the cold, scores of brave souls were huddled round tables of pavement cafés, hunched over steaming drinks in overcoats and sunglasses.

Saying goodbye to Daniel on a street corner felt both absurd and sad. 'Come and see me soon,' he whispered, brushing his mouth across her cheek one last time.

On the second storey of an apartment block a few hundred yards further down the same street Daisy was putting the finishing touches to her make-up, standing with her hand-mirror facing the bedroom window so as to make the best of the light. A new, heavy foundation, bought the previous week, did a wonderful job of concealing the faint dirty yellow round her cheekbone, while the fading violet in the eye socket had taken a little more artistry with some of her heaviest eye shadows. Though her jaw still ached, the crack in her lip had healed remarkably quickly, to the point where it looked more like the remains of wind-chap than a wound. Seeing the end result, Daisy grimaced with satisfaction.

Having no idea of her mother's state of mind was making her nervous, she realised, doing a last tidy-up of the flat and reminding herself of the importance of appearing strong. She patted the dents out of the sofa cushions and emptied that

AMANDA BROOKFIELD

morning's cigarette butts from the largest of the ash-trays, a heavy pewter saucer which Claude had lifted from an English pub. Absently lighting a fresh cigarette, she went to stand at the sitting-room window overlooking the usual urban frenzy in the street below, which these days barely even receded at the weekends.

It was only after several moments of tracking an elegant fair-haired woman striding down the pavement on the opposite side of the road, that Daisy realised she was staring at her mother. Her hair had grown considerably since she had last seen her and bounced prettily over her shoulders. Instead of the sombre appearance Daisy had been expecting, she was wearing a knee-length green dress and a long honey-coloured coat that reached to the ankles of her leather boots. A velvet green scarf was flung casually round her neck and over one shoulder, where it flapped stylishly in the breeze. Her small brown suitcase looked smart and weightless, swinging in her right hand, as did her handbag, strung diagonally across her chest like a neat satchel. Daisy stepped back from the window, something inside her withdrawing at so unexpected – and somehow so daunting – a sight. Dropping her cigarette into a half-drunk mug of coffee, she pulled the cuffs of her thin grey jumper – shapeless from being tugged in a similar fashion innumerable times in the past – down over the palms of each hand and then crossed her arms, pressing them against the ridges of her ribs. The woman in the street looked like a stranger, she reflected miserably, letting go of a last, hitherto acknowledged, hope of confessing that Claude had been a wrong turn after all. For weeks she had been telling herself that the need to bury this truth stemmed from a charitable unwillingness to burden her mother's fragile mental state with fresh woes. Yet the notion of revealing her predicament to the unfamiliar, self-assured creature striding towards her front door felt just as impossible. Not even a chapped lip would do, Daisy decided frantically, rushing back into the bedroom and coating her lips in sheeny scarlet. She was still tidying up the edges with her fingernail when the doorbell rang.

'Oh Mum, great, you're here. Come on up.'

They hugged, Frances thinking that her daughter looked very skinny and French, while Daisy digested the fact that her impression from the window had been correct. Compared to the haunted, tremulous creature she had left after the funeral, her mother was virtually unrecognisable; glowing from her walk, her eyes shining, her movements brisk and confident.

'I saw you from the sitting room . . . walking . . . did the taxi tip you out at the wrong street?' she asked, leading the way into the kitchen and busying herself with filling the cafetière.

'No, no,' Frances replied quickly. 'I asked him to drop me a little early on purpose. Such a nice day, I wanted a walk. But how are you – are you well? This flat looks splendid – and so central too. I'm sorry it's taken such ages to see you. Are you well?' Frances repeated, trying and failing to catch her daughter's eye as she scuttled between cupboards.

'I'm fine. I'll heat some milk, shall I? Claude insists on us getting this really strong Turkish stuff – undiluted it's a bit of a shock to the system.' She opened the fridge and pulled out a tall carton of milk.

'And how is Claude?'

'Fine.' Daisy tipped some milk into a small saucepan and began stirring it, somewhat unnecessarily Frances thought, with a wooden spoon. 'Though I'm afraid you won't catch him this time. He's had to go away for a few days. New York again. Business is so good he says we might have to move there permanently in the summer.'

'Really? And how would you feel about that?'

Daisy hesitated. New York had been partly responsible for the remnants of bruising on her face, and the more vivid purple patches still visible on her back and the tops of her legs. He had used his feet as well as his fists this time; immaculate suede leather boots, with neat zips to the ankle. Curling her legs into her chest as she lay on the floor, readying herself for the impact, there had been a still mad moment in which she found herself noting the beauty of the leather, acknowledging something like admiration for a man who could own such things for so many months and not create one discernible scuff mark. She didn't want to go to New York. Her work at the gallery was going too well. And Marcel was being kind; not enough to justify any of Claude's latest bout of suspicions, but sufficient to plant the hope that there might be a way out after all, a bolt hole from the tense uncertainty which had regained its stranglehold over life in the flat. Claude's remorse, the calm after the storm, had been as intense as before, but this time Daisy did not – could not – trust it to last. The only way to find the courage to leave, she knew, would be if all Claude's accusations were true, if she had someone else to go to, someone strong and successful like Marcel. Without that she knew she would continue to be crushed by her lover's belief that everything she possessed and achieved was thanks to him, that on some level he had every right to drag her by the roots of her hair across the floor – or the Atlantic for that matter – if he chose.

'Oh, I think New York would be brilliant,' she gushed, 'everybody says it's just the most exciting place to live. The only thing I'm not sure about is leaving the gallery. It turns out I've got quite a talent for selling paintings.' She led the way into the sitting room. 'At least Marcel – that's the guy who runs it – tells me I have. Of course it's all thanks to Claude that I got the job in the first place. He really couldn't have set me up . . . better,' she faltered, gesturing at the high-ceilinged room and fine views to give weight to the sentiment, but seeing only the walls of her incarceration. 'But tell me about home,' she continued quickly. 'How is working with Libby going and what is Felix up to? I must say, Mum, you look incredibly . . .' she hesitated, '. . . you look very well.'

It suddenly occurred to Frances that behind the gloss of this observation lay a seed of criticism. Looking well was hardly something that Daisy would find flattering to the memory of her father.

'I still miss Dad,' she said quietly.

'I didn't mean . . .'

'I know you didn't. But I want you to know that I've learnt to keep the sadness at bay, in a part of my mind where I can go if I want to, but which does not flood my life as it did at the beginning. For a while I found things very hard, very hard indeed, but I've . . . moved on. I had to Daisy. It was either that or go mad. Working in Libby's shop was the start of it – she's even been selling a couple of my drawings . . .' Frances broke off, suddenly aware that alluding to such minor successes was hardly a tactful move given her daughter's own thwarted ambitions.

'Have you?' said Daisy carefully, 'that's fantastic.'

'And are you painting at the moment?'

She shook her head. 'Don't want to. I don't miss it either.' She stood up, as if to dismiss the subject, confirming Frances's fears that she had blundered on every front. 'I thought we could go for a stroll and then perhaps eat out, have an early supper somewhere. If that sounds all right to you?' she added uncertainly.

'It sounds wonderful. I'm in your hands. It's just nice to see you darling.'

'And you Mum,' Daisy replied, slipping into her bedroom to re-powder her face.

Chapter Twenty-Eight

Lying on his hotel bed, his head resting on the palms of his hands, Daniel felt rather at a loss. It was too late in the day to consider heading off in pursuit of culture and he was in no mood to tackle any of the various tomes still residing in the bottom of his holdall. The French were no good at luxury, he reflected gloomily, surveying the cramped ill-lit room and marvelling at the price he was being charged for it. For something to do, he flicked through the channels on the small television, set on a high shelf because there was no slot for it on the ground. There had been an avalanche at a resort in the French Alps, ten people killed and scores injured. French farmers were threatening to block the ports, again. A minister had been sacked for embezzlement. As with Italian, Daniel had little trouble comprehending the language, though his ability to speak it remained patchy at best. Turning the television off, he dropped the console onto the floor and closed his eyes in the vague hope of drifting off to sleep.

The thought of Frances just half a mile away was distracting. The way she had invaded his life still astonished him, confirming his view that the best things happened when they were least expected. While sympathetic to Frances's apprehension about the difference in their ages, Daniel could not bring himself to regard the situation in quite the same negative terms. Not just because of grand schemes about living for the moment, but because her maturity was an integral part of why he loved her, why he felt that, romantically, at least, the central quest of his life had found fulfilment. After years of failed relationships with much younger, insecure and volatile creatures, being with Frances was little short of a revelation. There was a calmness at the heart of her which he found beguiling, and which he had the sense to attribute in part to the solid qualities of the man to whom she had devoted the previous twenty years. Though she spoke little about Paul, Daniel could feel her thinking about him sometimes, whether with longing or matter-of-factness he never knew. Nor did he succumb to the temptation to ask, powerful though it often was. He had found that if he waited long enough the moments receded of their own accord, passing like clouds across her face, making the glow of her full concentration all the more vivid when it returned. The destructive influence of the living worried him far more. Laughing about the fiasco of the Taverners' dinner party had helped to put it behind them, but it had cast a shadow nonetheless, even after his infinitely re-written thank-you and apology had finally found its way to a post box. In spite of his protestations to the contrary, Daniel remained deeply anxious about being accepted by the key players in Frances's life, simply because he knew how much it mattered to her. The haphazard circle of acquaintances on his own side filled him with far fewer apprehensions; not only because Frances's manifold attractions were so irrefutably in evidence to him, but also because he had a reputation for going his own way. His parents might raise an eyebrow or two, but that had never stopped him from doing what he wanted in the past.

Aware that he was growing, if anything, more wide awake, Daniel opened his eyes and rummaged impatiently in his bag, hurling items onto the bed. A few minutes later, kitted out in trainers and an old track suit, he made his way down to recep-tion, his rubber soles squeaking on the polished linoleum floor. Outside the sun was already losing out to the pull of evening, returning buildings and streets to their true state of blackened decrepitude. Daniel shivered in the cut of the wind, pulling the zip of his top up to his chin and tucking his hands into his sleeves. Breaking into a jog, he set off down the street, dodging pedestrians and dogs, stiffly at first and then with more grace and enjoyment as he got into his stride. Passing what he calculated to be Daisy's block of flats, he noticed a light on in a second-storey window, but no sign of any movement from its occupants. Reluctantly, Daniel returned his attention to the obstacle course of the busy pavement ahead of him, kicking up his heels to give more of a bounce to his stride. If he remembered the map correctly there was a large park a few blocks ahead and to the right. And there might be the reward of a message from Frances awaiting his return, he comforted himself, sprinting across a red pedestrian light and getting violently hooted at by a woman in a white Mercedes.

'I know it looks like any other seedy Paris hotel, but it's got this brilliant restaurant in the basement – or perhaps I should say wine cellar. You eat surrounded by walls and walls of wine bottles – it's kind of spooky but nice. Lots of garlic, though, if you don't mind that.'

'No, I don't mind that.'

'Claude discovered it. His family knew the proprietor or something. Here we are.' Daisy pushed her way through the revolving doors of Daniel's hotel and led the way to a stairwell next to the reception desk. 'I booked. You don't get in otherwise, no matter what day of the week it is. Mum? Is everything all right?'

'Yes . . . I . . . it's just that we don't have to eat anywhere too grand or expensive . . .'

'Oh, but it's not expensive at all. When the Michelin lot get their hands on it no doubt things will change, but for now you really couldn't pay so little for such good food.' Daisy frowned, puzzled by her mother's evident reticence. 'But if you're not hungry, I guess we could just—'

'No, it sounds wonderful. Let's eat,' Frances urged, tensing at the swish of opening lift doors behind her. Following her daughter down the stairs she glanced nervously over her shoulder; but it was only an old lady with lilac grey hair clutching a small terrier between the broad lapels of her coat.

The atmosphere down in the restaurant was even more impressive than Daisy had described. Every wall was stacked from floor to ceiling with full wine racks, artfully illuminated to cast long shadows and exotic glints of green and red glass. Overhead, flame-shaped light bulbs, strings of onions and dried flowers hung from the beams, creating their own dramatic circus of shapes on the surroundings. They were shown to a table for two in a far corner, sufficiently tucked away from the main body of the room for Frances to think about relaxing and enjoying the company of her daughter.

It was the first time they had ever eaten out in such a fashion on their own, she realised, wondering in the same instant if this lay behind the obstinacy of the awkwardness between them. Seeing her no doubt brought back vivid memories of Paul, Frances reasoned, studying her daughter's expression, animated in conversation, and wondering what it was she found so unconvincing. Although too heavily made-up for Frances's own tastes, there was no doubt that Daisy had learnt how to accentuate the striking features of her face, somehow made all the more compelling by the frame of messily cropped hair. Daniel would find her attractive, she decided suddenly, stopping with a snail half-way to her mouth, her heart leap-frogging at the thought.

Although Frances did her best to raise opportunities to talk about Paul – wanting to probe the most obvious cause of the sadness, or uncertainty, or whatever it was she detected behind the glassy smile in her daughter's eyes – Daisy seemed far keener to talk about other things.

'Is Felix quite all right do you think? Only I haven't heard a thing from him all term. I know he's not the greatest

214

correspondent, but after Dad . . . after the funeral . . . we were . . . communicating more than we used to. Till Christmas anyway. I've written twice since then and got nothing back.'

'Too busy having a good time, I expect. I haven't heard a word either.'

'I hope so,' murmured Daisy, aware that her own secret sufferings had made her more alert to the possibility of un-happiness in other people.

'He didn't by any chance mention anything about Sally Taverner did he?' ventured Frances after a pause, 'only I gather he was having a bit of a thing with her during the Christmas holidays.'

'Sally Taverner?' The look of unabashed amazement on Daisy's face struck Frances as the first truly genuine outburst of emotion since her arrival. 'What sort of a *thing*?'

'I don't really know – Joseph Brackman claimed to have seen them together a few times, meeting in secret, poor loves. Anyway, my guess is that it's all fizzled out. Felix got horribly grumpy towards the end of the holidays and poor Sally had that dreadful business of finding Mrs Brackman and then getting so ill – remember, I told you on the phone?'

But Daisy was shaking her head. 'Sally and Felix,' she murmured, 'I just can't believe it somehow. I mean Sally, of all people – she's just a kid.'

Frances let out a short laugh. 'She certainly isn't. You should see her these days – almost as tall as Beth, filling out all over the place and being bloody-minded to everybody. Libby was really concerned about her at one point, but they seem to have sorted it out now. I never mentioned the Felix thing to her, by the way,' she added, 'because it was only hearsay and she's had quite enough on her plate – the shop seems at last to be emerging from the doldrums but it's going to be a long haul.'

'Libby's always been a bit of a worrier, I know it drives Beth mad.' Daisy grinned, relaxing partly because of a third glass of wine and partly from the simple pleasure of talking about home. 'It *is* good to see you, Mum. And I think it's brilliant that you're so . . .' she struggled for the right word, '. . . together about Dad. Anyone else would have cracked up.'

'Thank you darling, you're very kind,' murmured Frances, glad that she had managed most of her emotional disintegration in private. Looking back, she decided that the only truly visible sign of madness, had been agreeing to meet James Harcourt, kidding herself that he constituted some sort of rescue package designed by Paul from beyond the grave. Remembering the extent of her inner desperation and the unlikely, magical way in which Daniel had subsequently eased her out of it, Frances was briefly tempted to tell Daisy everything. But the moment passed, banished by the arrival of a dessert trolley laden with gâteaux and fruit tarts.

Too full to do justice to such a rich selection, they decided to settle the bill and go back to the flat for coffee. After a show of resistance, Daisy let her mother pay the bill. Money was one of the cruder reasons for her state of entrapment. Her salary from the gallery was pitiful. Everything else came from Claude, whose early *laissez faire* attitude had lately been superseded by erratic and intense interrogation each time a centime left the account.

Daniel never ate early anyway, Frances reflected cheerfully, seeing from a glance at her watch that it was still only half past eight. They emerged at the top of the stairs to find the hotel lobby deserted.

'I'm dying for a pee,' Daisy confessed, pausing at the main door and looking round for a sign to the toilets. She started to approach the reception desk to make enquiries but then changed her mind. 'Oh what the hell, I can wait till we get home.'

Though minor, the delay was sufficient to ensure the encounter Frances had been so dreading. Daniel, returning from a beer at a café on the corner of the block, began pushing through the revolving door just as Frances and Daisy were doing the same thing on the other side. Recognising him through the glass, Frances blanched and tried to mouth the word 'no'. Once outside she started to hurry away, but the door continued to revolve, spilling Daniel out into the street like a ball from a roulette wheel. The gleeful expression on his face warned Frances at once that he had assumed she was trying to see him and had not yet made any connection with the tall blonde-haired girl at her elbow.

'Daniel meet Daisy,' she almost shrieked, instinctively putting out a hand to keep him at arm's length while Daisy spun round to see what was going on. Daniel's expression changed in an instant, shrinking from exuberance to formal pleasure.

'Hello,' he said, reaching out his hand.

'A friend?' enquired Daisy, hopping from foot to foot.

'Yes, we . . .' both Daniel and Frances began speaking and then broke off at the same time.

'A few weeks ago your mother almost ran me down in her car – we've been firm friends ever since.'

Daisy looked puzzled but smiled. 'Sounds fascinating . . . er . . . look, would you like to come back for coffee with us or something? Only I'm rather . . .'

Frances glanced sharply at Daniel, but he was already nodding. 'That would be great. Do you live far?' he added innocently, sucking in his cheeks to show Frances that he sensed her disapproval and was going to ignore it.

'No, really close.' Daisy trotted off up the street, keeping slightly ahead but not sufficiently out of earshot for Frances to say any of the things she really wanted to.

Their only brief chance to talk was after getting inside the flat, when Daisy bolted off to relieve her discomfort and attend to coffee.

'I don't know what you think you're doing,' Frances hissed.

'I thought you were trying to see me,' Daniel murmured, his tone apologetic, but his eyes gleaming.

'We ate dinner in your hotel – Daisy had booked it. There was nothing I could do. I do wish you hadn't got yourself invited up here.'

'It would have looked rude to say no.'

'No it wouldn't.'

'Or odd then. It would have looked odd.'

Frances shook her head. 'Meeting acquaintances on holidays is a known horror. Nobody likes doing it. Accepted practice is for all parties to issue a few polite exchanges and then walk on.'

'Fuck accepted practice,' he growled, bending towards her and whispering, 'I couldn't resist you.'

At which point Daisy returned with their coffee, causing Frances to spring back to her corner of the sofa. 'I was just telling Daniel that his hotel has one of the best restaurants in the area – he had no idea—'

'You mean you're staying there and you didn't know?' exclaimed Daisy. 'Where on earth did you have supper?'

'I had a sandwich and a beer round the corner,' Daniel confessed meekly. 'Still, there's always tomorrow.'

'Be sure to book. Even hotel residents have to.' She poured coffee into three delicate porcelain cups that Frances did not recognise. 'So how long are you staying in Paris?'

'Just till Sunday afternoon.'

'Like Mum then,' replied Daisy easily, kicking off her shoes and tucking her long legs up into her armchair. 'She nearly ran you over, did you say? What a weird way to become friends.'

'I know, isn't it? But weird things are sometimes the best.'

'Aren't they?' She leaned forward eagerly. 'What do you do . . . Daniel, was it?'

'History of art. I'm a lecturer at Sussex university.'

'But that's where Felix is,' she exclaimed.

'So I gather.'

Frances sat watching them, taking small sips from her coffee which was lukewarm and flecked with granules that looked like chocolate and tasted of wood. After getting up from the sofa to help with the tray she had relocated herself to an armchair several feet away from Daniel. While the pair of them talked, leaping from subject to subject with charming illogicality and ease, she felt not only excluded but afraid. Every so often Daniel did make a point of trying to get her to participate more fully, but each time she kept her response to monosyllables, hoping to communicate enough discomfort or displeasure for him to see that it was time to withdraw. But when the dregs of their coffees were cold Daisy fetched a bottle of wine and a bowl of fruit, placing them on the table in front of Daniel's knees.

'Would you do the honours?' she asked, handing him a corkscrew, 'corks disintegrate at the sight of me.'

'Speaking for myself,' Frances protested, 'I'm not sure I really want another drink.'

'Oh go on, why not?' retorted her daughter, clapping in unnecessary congratulation as Daniel popped the cork from the bottle. 'You're on holiday, remember? Let your hair down, Mum.'

Frances sank back into her chair, inwardly recoiling at the tone of her daughter's voice, feeling suddenly like an ancient relative on a day's excursion from a nursing home.

'Hmm, nice wine,' remarked Daniel, taking an initial sip and trying to catch Frances's eye.

'Oh, I just go on the labels,' replied Daisy breezily, reaching for her cigarettes and the large pewter ashtray, which she balanced on the arm of her chair.

Frances watched the beam of her lover's smile illuminate her daughter's face. The more fluently they talked, the more she shrank into her chair. Her glass remained untouched on the table. Deep in the nape of her neck she could feel a headache stirring.

'Cigarette?'

Daniel shook his head. He turned to look at Frances. 'Are you all right?'

She smiled tightly. 'A little tired. In fact,' she stood up slowly, 'if you don't mind, I think I'll turn in for the night.'

Daniel was on his feet in an instant. 'It's really very late – I must be going—'

'Finish your wine at least,' commanded Daisy. 'Mum won't mind, will you Mum?'

'Not at all,' replied Frances dryly, her eyes barely leaving the floor as she muttered a farewell and slipped from the room. Behind her she heard Daisy saying, 'So who is it you're writing this thing about?' Then she closed the door, shutting out the scene, feeling like an actress leaving a play in which her role had been snatched away.

Chapter Twenty-Nine

Frances woke early the next morning, roused by the window panes rattling in protest at the Saturday traffic already streaming through the street below. At first disoriented by her surroundings, it took a few moments for the unsatisfactory events of the previous evening to flood her consciousness, ruling out either peace of mind or a return to the blissful oblivion of sleep which had finally claimed her in the early hours of the morning. After retreating to bed, she had lain awake in the dark for what felt like hours, straining through all the unfamiliar noises to discern the door-slam that would signify Daniel's departure from the flat.

Having accepted that she was in no frame of mind for a lie-in, Frances pulled on a jumper over her nightie for warmth and crept along the hall. All was silent as she passed the door of Daisy's bedroom. The sitting room looked grimy in the ivory light of early morning. The remains of their small party were still scattered about the room, three coffee cups ringed with brown stains, a heap of cigarette stubs, an apple core, cushions in disarray. Her own full wine glass remained at the opposite end of the table from the two empty ones, a bitter reminder to Frances both of the fact and justification of her sense of exclusion. And the wine bottle was clearly empty, she noted grimly, starting, out of habit to tidy up and then hurling a cushion across the sofa instead. It bounced once and landed silently on the floor next to Daisy's abandoned shoes.

Sexual jealousy – particularly with regard to her own daughter – was a novel and entirely unwelcome experience. Though it was reasonable to assume that during the course of two decades Paul must have felt the occasional twinge of attraction for other women or other lives, he had never once given Frances grounds for suspecting as much. Neither, for her part, had she. A crush on the doctor who had been so kind during their first summer in the country, when Daisy broke her collar bone falling off a fence and Felix had so many ear infections they thought his hearing might be impaired for life, was not something Frances had ever felt the need to act upon or confess to. That the doctor liked her had been as evident as the impossibility of anything coming of the situation. When, a few months later, he and his family moved away, Frances had breathed a sigh of relief, glad to be able to readjust her focus to her husband without the inconvenient distraction of so futile an infatuation.

Retreating to her bedroom, Frances began tugging on her clothes, thinking with some longing of the sometimes dull, but reliable solidity of her marriage. What she shared with Daniel felt like a tornado in comparison. Having tied the buckles of her boots, she flopped back onto the bed, suddenly exhausted by the see-sawing of her emotions and the new despicable envy burning in her heart.

Leaving a note to say that she had gone in search of fresh pastries for breakfast, Frances took Daisy's keys from the hall table and let herself out of the flat. She would walk and think she decided, setting off with a determined stride in the opposite direction to Daniel's hotel. After only a few yards however, she spun round to retrace her steps, her handbag swinging wildly round her hips. A few minutes later she was at the hotel reception asking a young man with pimples sprinkled on his cheeks for Daniel's room number, too fired up to care what conclusions he might draw. Then she was outside the room, banging her fist on the door. It swung open so suddenly she almost punched him in the face.

He was clutching a towel round his waist, his face and hair crumpled from sleep.

At the sight of him Frances could feel her anger dissolving into longing.

'I was so hoping you'd come,' he exclaimed, forgetting the towel and pulling her into his arms. 'Last night I nearly . . .'

'About last night,' she began, struggling to extricate herself from his embrace. 'How dare you – I was so – I felt so – flirting like that—'

He broke off at once, retrieving the towel with as much dignity as he could muster and knotting it tightly round his waist. 'Flirting?' He scowled. 'I was not. I was being friendly. I want your daughter to like me – is that such a crime?'

'Like you?' Frances's tone was sneering. 'Staying up like that all cosy on the sofa after I'd gone to bed—'

'She gave me little choice, if your recall. And we weren't cosy on the sofa. And Daisy finished off the bottle virtually single-handed. And she did practically all of the talking. It might interest you to know that she doesn't seem very happy—'

'Oh, so now I'm going to get a detailed character analysis of my own daughter, am I?'

'Jesus, Frances, I thought you'd come here to see me.' Slumping down on the bed he squinted at his wristwatch. 'Fuck, it's only seven o'clock. Far too early to be attacked by anyone, let alone you.' He dropped his head into his hands and rubbed his face. 'I'm sorry about last night,' he muttered, 'hijacking your evening and so on, but when things scare me I've always had this habit of running at them instead of away from them. Clumsy, no doubt, but that's my style.'

Frances looked for somewhere to retreat and regroup, but the room was so small and cramped that the best she could do was lean against the wall, and fold her arms. 'I thought you fancied her,' she whispered, trying to cling onto her anger but aware only of sounding absurd – and so pitiful she blushed from the shame of it.

Daniel chuckled, shaking his head. 'I'm in a real no-win situation here. If I say Daisy is not attractive you'll jump down my throat and if I say—'

Without meaning to and much to her horror Frances burst into tears, overcome by the realisation that she had lost her judgement entirely; that such was the intensity of her feelings towards the man on the bed that she could no longer trust herself to know anything relating to him with the remotest degree of wisdom or impartiality.

'Come here.' He reached out his hand, drawing her to sit next to him. 'Daisy is lovely. Too thin, too mixed up, too . . . basically, she's not you.' He put his arm round her, squeezing her shoulders hard. 'I'm sorry if I upset you last night. When she asked me back I just couldn't resist it. And then the situation just sort of evolved – you saw for yourself. I think she liked me – I hope she liked me – like I said, she did most of the talking. I left as soon as I could. About eleven o'clock I think.'

'Sorry,' Frances whispered. 'I didn't get much sleep.' She stood up and blew her nose on a few segments of starchy toilet roll. 'Better go. I'm supposed to be buying breakfast. Daisy doesn't know I've gone.'

'Nor will she for a while, no doubt,' he replied, an impish grin spreading across his face. He took Frances by the hand and pulled her back onto the bed. 'I'd give her another two hours at least.'

'Two hours?' murmured Frances, trying to focus on the conversation rather than on Daniel's fingers which had started working their way down her shirt buttons.

'At least,' he whispered, shifting in the narrow bed so that there was room for her alongside.

★

Letting herself back into the flat and finding Daisy still fast asleep, Frances felt as guiltily jubilant as a truant schoolgirl. After bustling quietly round the sitting room, clearing up the debris and opening windows to remove some of the stale smell of tobacco, she managed to negotiate both the microwave and the cafetière in order to prepare herself breakfast. Licking warm croissant crumbs off her fingers and seeing that it was nearly half past ten, she decided to surprise her daughter with a similar feast.

Knocking briefly, she entered the bedroom, pushing the door open with her shoulder because of the tray, laden not only with warm croissant and coffee but also a small glass of freshly squeezed orange juice.

'Come on sleepyhead,' she called softly, sliding the tray amongst the jumble of toiletries on the dressing table and smiling to herself at the general disarray of the room, glad that it was no longer her role to remark on it. The curtains, which were heavy and far too long for the window, took some wrestling to open, even with the aid of the pullies on either side.

'Daisy – wake up now.'

The heap of bedclothes moved, causing another stirring of Frances's heart. She sat on the bed and stroked the section of head visible above the edge of the duvet. 'Sleep well?'

Thick with the after-effects of wine and the four analgesics she had swallowed at five o'clock that morning, Daisy groaned and turned onto her back, still registering nothing beyond a reluctance to open her eyes. If her short hair had not been so flattened against the pillow Frances might not have noticed the trace of yellow and violet curling round her right eye. As it was she had several seconds in which both to observe it and to register that it was not leftover make-up as she had first supposed, but the remnants of physical damage.

'Daisy?' She patted her shoulder. 'Wake up, I've brought you breakfast. What happened to your face?'

Although Daisy kept her eyes closed, the question fired her

into immediate and intense consciousness. In the same instant she managed a quick appraisal of her options. Her body was under the covers. Only her face needed defending.

'Walked into the edge of the cupboard in the bathroom,' she said carelessly, manufacturing a deep yawn that became real half-way through. 'Half asleep one morning – bloody stupid.'

'Why didn't you tell me about it?'

Daisy sat up, rubbing the sleep from her eyes. 'Mum, it was ages ago.' She shrugged her shoulders impatiently. 'There was nothing to tell. It doesn't hurt at all and is hardly noticeable. Did you say something about breakfast?'

Frances fetched the tray.

'Daniel whatshisname was nice.'

'Yes, isn't he?' Frances straightened the section of the duvet nearest her. 'Funny who you bump into – I hope you didn't mind him coming back like that.'

Daisy shook her head, her mouth full of croissant. 'We could meet up with him again if you like.'

'No,' put in Frances hurriedly, 'I don't think so – I mean, it's nice just being the two of us. What I'd really like, if you could bear it, would be to play at being a tourist. I've never been up the Eiffel Tower, or taken a boat down the Seine, or—'

Daisy let out a good-humoured groan. 'OK, OK, I get the picture. And thanks for this Mum,' she gestured at the tray on her knees, 'it's lovely to be spoilt sometimes.'

'Nice for me too.' Frances paused at the door, thinking how vulnerable and young her daughter looked, propped with her sore face amongst the pillows, and fearing suddenly that she might have been neglecting her.

Chapter Thirty

A brown puddle – whether of tea or coffee Sally wasn't sure – lapped round one side of the foil ashtray. Inside the ashtray was the yellow cork of a cigarette butt, tipped with pink. Sally pinched her lips round the end of her own cigarette and inhaled deeply. An ill-directed plume of smoke caught her left eye, blurring the edges of Felix, standing in the queue with a tray, studiously not looking at her. Even when he met her at the school gates, he had kept his head down, beckoning her to follow him down the street with ugly haste. Clumping after him in her now not so new weighty-soled shoes, her school bag heavy and her violin banging uncomfortably against her thigh, Sally had felt undignified and indignant. Only when they were several streets clear of the school and the immediate possibility of familiar faces, did he slow and wait for her to catch up.

'How are you?'

'Fucking marvellous, how do you think? Could you carry this please?' She thrust her violin at him and swung her satchel to a more comfortable position. 'I'm supposed to be in Combe Road having a music lesson. I'll be in deep shit for missing it.'

'Can't you call from a box – say you're ill or something?'

Sally shrugged. 'Don't know the number. Where are we going?'

'To talk. Somewhere we won't be seen.'

'So you got my letter then. I was beginning to wonder.'

'Yeah.' He took a deep breath. 'I got your letter. Not the greatest of news. Not the friendliest of communications either.'

'Oh, excuse me.' Behind the shield of the scathing tone she shrivelled with unhappiness. 'How am I supposed to feel? You pissing off like that – after what I'd been through – and now this—'

'I tried to see you,' he snapped. 'I was refused admittance, if I recall correctly.'

'I was ill. And anyway I knew already you didn't love me,' Sally wailed, forgetting all her resolve to remain cool, too weary suddenly to care.

The silence from Felix felt dark and unbridgeable. He led the way – walking so quickly she had trouble keeping up – down several more unfamiliar streets and then ducked into a poky café that smelt of onions.

At least he looked as bad as she felt, Sally observed now, studying Felix as he delved in his pocket for money to pay the girl at the till and noticing for the first time the stoop in his broad shoulders and the greyness in his cheeks. When he set the tray down she saw that there was a cluster of angry pink spots on his forehead, half screened by the lanky shelf of his fringe.

'Look Sally – of course, I'm really sorry about the . . .' He broke off, unable to see through the ordeal of completing the sentence. 'I mean, I know it must be awful for you.' He unloaded the bottle of water she had asked for and a cup of muddy tea for himself. 'But Christ, you were the one who said it was safe.' The complaint burst out of him on a wave of rage, erasing the feeble mask of empathetic composure which he knew was expected of males in such circumstances.

'I thought it *was* safe,' she whispered.

'And you don't even look – I mean I'd never have guessed—' Although his expectations had been ill-defined to say the least, Felix was quite unprepared for the subtle changes in Sally's appearance. She did look larger, but somehow more attractive too, fuller and more curvy, as if she had been too thin before. 'I mean, you've done the proper tests and so on have you?'

'Of course,' Sally retorted, even though she hadn't, deterred by a combination of grim certainty and sheer terror. She yanked up her school jersey. 'Take a look for yourself.'

Felix, together with several curious diners at neighbouring tables, glanced at Sally's midriff, identifying nothing very much amongst the crumpled folds of her school shirt and skirt. 'Stop it for God's sake,' he growled, busying himself with sachets of sugar until their audience had lost interest. 'In your letter – what you said about it being a way to avoid GCSEs – you were just joking weren't you?'

Hearing the fear in his tone, Sally felt the tiniest tremor of power. She was on the point of ignoring it, of admitting that no matter how hard she tried she could not envisage herself in the role of willing teenage mother, that not one single stab of a maternal instinct had yet pierced the unattractive horror of her new circumstances, when the girl behind the counter called out a number and Felix leapt to his feet, returning with a full plate of fried food. 'How can you eat?' she said hoarsely.

'Because I'm starving.' He helped himself to several dollops of ketchup, the plastic bottle squelching rudely between his palms. Sally grimaced in disgust, not out of antenatal nausea so much as a deep sense of personal outrage that the father of her unborn child could think of his stomach in such harrowing circumstances. Two fried eggs were draped over a large piece of fried bread, next to a thick blackened sausage and several fatty rashers of bacon. She sipped her mineral water – chosen more because it seemed appropriate than because she liked the stuff – feeling suddenly very distant and fantastically cruel.

'I'm not sure I believe in abortion, Felix.'

He stopped, swallowing slowly, his Adam's apple sliding down his throat like stone. 'If it's about money, Sally, I've got enough . . . Dad left me some and I . . .'

'And how much is enough?' she snapped.

He put down his knife and fork. 'Look, I know this is hard, that you must be feeling really shocked – but fuck it, so am I – ever since I got your letter I haven't slept—'

'Poor you,' she sneered, aware that the deeper she waded into the cruelty the easier it became.

'I came as soon as I could,' he muttered. 'And I don't see any point in going through a charade about either of us having any options. It would be mad for you to have a kid. It would ruin your life as well as mine.' He cut off a corner of fried bread, loading it with a ragged portion of egg and a wedge of bacon. 'If you went ahead . . . well . . . I'm not sure I could ever forgive you.' He stared at her defiantly, chewing hard.

'Forgive me?' Sally knew that her bravery was hanging by a thread. She had wanted to hurt him, but she had also longed to be comforted by him, to find some space for a shred of the intimacy which they had once taken for granted.

He reached into his jacket and extracted a long fat white envelope. 'There's some money here.' He lowered his voice. 'Three hundred pounds. I can get more if necessary. There are some good clinics in Brighton apparently – I've written down the phone numbers.' He began fishing inside another pocket but Sally had already stood up.

'You've thought of everything, haven't you?' She picked up her satchel and violin. 'Don't let your tea get cold.' And with that she made as grand an exit as she could manage, shouldering her way between the tight jaws of the café door. A minute later she hopped onto a bus heading back into town, though to which part exactly she neither knew nor cared.

It was only after a good ten minutes of senseless running that Felix accepted that Sally had somehow given him the slip and gone home. He could feel his meal churning unpleasantly in his stomach, forcing up burps that felt close to being sick. In a final act of desperation he bellowed out her name, only to swallow the final syllable and quickly glance round for fear that someone would think him mad.

By now it was gone five o'clock and getting dark. Street lights were flickering into life, their haloes of yellow light illuminating the moisture particles thickening the dank air. Felix made his way to a bus stop advertising the right numbers for Leybourne and propped himself against the inner wall of the small shelter parked alongside. He had already been home once that afternoon, only to find the car missing and the house empty. Remembering that these days his mother had a job and could not be expected to return much before six, he had conducted a desultory key-hunt under several flowerpots before dumping his bags at the back of the garage. His own set of keys had gone missing together with his leather jacket and forty pounds in cash during the course of a particularly unintelligible maths lecture the week before.

He must have just missed a bus Felix realised, as the queue beside him grew, snaking out of the shelter and for several yards down the street. Immediately next to him stood a pale stick of a girl with a pushchair. The baby had fallen asleep, a plastic bottle half filled with purple juice dangling out of one corner of its mouth by the teat. The girl's thin lips worked alternately at smoking and chewing gum, while one foot absently rolled the wheel of the stroller. She looked bored and tired, Felix observed, watching from under half-closed lids and shuddering at the thought of such a fate befalling him or Sally. At the approach of a bus, the girl scooped the child in her arms and began grappling to dismantle the stroller. The baby, dismayed at being roused, writhed and howled in protest.

'Could you give us a hand?'

Blushing at the realisation he had been staring, Felix responded at once, seizing the pushchair, which she had cleverly collapsed into something equivalent in size to a large umbrella, and one of her shopping bags. He stood back to let her go first, feeling like a fraud, especially when she smiled in gratitude. Having stowed the bag and buggy behind her seat, he escaped upstairs, taking the steep steps two at a time in his rush to get away.

He had messed up big time, Felix reflected bleakly, staring out of the window into the damp night and thinking back over the afternoon. He had handled it all wrong, been so determined not to appear weak that he had only succeeded in being foul. Worst of all, the sight of Sally had made all the old feelings flare up again, erasing in an instant the messy end to the Christmas holidays and the pretence that he hadn't minded being exiled in a vacuum of silence since the start of term.

The bus stop in Leybourne was ten minutes' walk from home. Felix kept to the verge, heading into the face of the oncoming traffic, squinting at the glare of headlights and teasing himself with the idea of stepping into their path. While aware that he was confronting perhaps the grimmest turning-point in his life, a curious sense of detachment had descended. A detachment born of the conviction that Sally would see sense in the end and that the moment to panic in earnest had not yet arrived.

By cutting across the field round the back of the house Felix saved himself several minutes. The drizzle had stopped and the clouds, still visible in the darkening sky, were tinged with impressive streaks of pink. A smoky corkscrew zigzagged up from the Brackmans' chimney, poking out from amongst the distant clump of trees. Felix took deep breaths as he walked, wanting to retain his new and fragile sense of calm. At the garden gate he paused, looking up towards the house. A big square of light was projected onto the lawn from the sitting-room window. He approached slowly, curious to glimpse his mother unawares but conscious that a face appearing suddenly at a window would be alarming. He edged forwards, his heart surging with sudden generosity at the magnitude of her problems compared to his, of the trauma of having to relearn the art of facing life alone.

Fired with such thoughts, a first glimpse of the scene in his own sitting room caused Felix to pull back in shock. The familiar figure on the sofa looked neither suffering nor solitary. Sprawled next to her was a dark-haired man whose face Felix couldn't see. Although they were engaged in the blameless pastime of watching television, the sense of intimacy in their poses was palpable. The man had taken his shoes off and was resting his feet on the coffee table. While his mother was sitting cross-legged, as she sometimes did, nursing a glass of wine.

Felix backed away from the window, letting out a string of expletives under his breath, his heart racing in confusion. Though it occurred to him to run away, it was dark and late and there was nowhere to go. He walked briskly to the garage instead, retrieved his bags from where he had stowed them earlier in the day, and staggered to the front door. He should be glad for her, he scolded himself, pushing hard on the door-bell, the weight of all his problems now compounded by the sensation of being an unwelcome visitor to his own home.

Chapter Thirty-One

'Who the hell can that be?' groaned Frances, glancing at her watch.

'Shall I go?'

'No, I'd better.' She put down her wine and unfurled her legs. It was the Thursday following their return from Paris, an excursion which, for all its hiccoughs and limitations, had ultimately tightened the cord of intimacy between them. After Frances's early morning visit to his hotel room, they had not met until Daniel crept out from behind a station news-stand at the Gare du Nord and clamped both palms over her eyes. Having their return seats upgraded to first-class due to the happy circumstances of overbooking, put the seal on their delight at being reunited. They spent the journey making plans for the approaching week, each eager to make up for having let the other down. Although still somewhat ill at ease over her daughter's state of mind, Frances was careful to avoid the subject of Daisy. In retrospect, it was painfully clear to her that she had over-reacted badly about Daniel's behaviour in the flat and she had no wish to remind him of the episode beyond the necessity of apologising. Which she did, so many times that he ended up making her promise never to mention the matter again.

One of the most immediate results of this renewed commitment to each other was a lunch fixture with Daniel's parents.

They had set off in Frances's car that morning, leaving early because she was nervous and thus prolonging the ordeal by arriving only minutes after Mrs Groves had placed her stuffed chicken in the oven. They were much older than Frances had been expecting, with inscrutable expressions that betrayed no obvious reservations about their son's choice of partner. After a while the degree of this reticence struck her as almost rudely incurious. Having braced herself for an ordeal comparable to their soirée at the Taverners, the experience was so painless and bland as to be fractionally boring. For the entire three-hour period that they were in the house, the conversation see-sawed between the progress of a recent international golf tournament and their opinions of an unsightly reception tower erected by a local mobile phone company. Afterwards, although the original intention had been for Frances to drop Daniel back at his house, their new reluctance to spend time apart prompted them to retreat straight back to Leybourne instead.

At the sight of her son on the doorstep Frances experienced a reflex of pleasure followed closely by alarm. Not only because of the presence of Daniel in the room behind her, but because of the expression on Felix's pale face. 'Darling – what a surprise – I – you should have told me you were coming –' She broke off to kiss his cheek and then caught sight of the heap of bags behind him. 'Has something happened?'

'You could say that.' Felix glanced quickly over her shoulder for any sign of the man he had seen through the window, calculating, with a spurt of uncharacteristic slyness, that the presence of a third party might deflect some of the initial shockwaves of his bad news. 'You might as well know, Mum –' he broke off to drag all his luggage across the threshold, 'I've quit college for good. I'm not going back,' he added, slinging in the last of his bags and kicking the door shut with a deafening slam of finality.

'You've what?' Frances could not conceal her dismay. 'Whatever for?'

'Hello Felix.'

The sight of Daniel Groves in the doorway of the sitting room stunned Felix into silence. Not simply because he recognised him as the driver of the grey Ford from whom he had hitched a lift in December, but because he was the very person he had spent a considerable portion of the previous week debating whether to contact. In the end he had been deterred both by doubts about seeking help from a virtual stranger, and by Sally's letter, which had tipped the balance on his need to get home. 'You?' he said at last.

'So you remember,' said Daniel, stepping in front of Frances and extending his hand. 'Good to see you again.'

'Did you know Mum then – when we – at Christmas?'

Daniel laughed easily. 'No, no. We've only become acquainted during the last few months. She tried to mow me down on my bicycle and is still trying to apologise.'

'Daniel I think perhaps you'd better go,' Frances murmured.

He held up his hands in mock surrender. 'Don't worry, I'm on my way. You two have obviously got lots to talk about. I couldn't help hearing what you said, about leaving the university,' he added, pulling his jacket off the bannisters and slinging it casually over one shoulder. 'And I'm very sorry to hear it.'

'Yeah, well,' muttered Felix, subdued both by the curious irony of the situation and a sudden vivid image of this man having sex with his mother. Remembering the sticky lipped woman in the café and all the things he had once dreamed of doing with her, he dropped his eyes and took a step sideways so Daniel could get to the door.

'I'm going to have to call a taxi,' Daniel reminded Frances, frowning apologetically.

'Of course, you haven't got your car.' She laughed nervously, turning to Felix to explain. 'This morning we went on an . . . excursion together. I picked Daniel up from his house – I was going to drop him back, but I think perhaps in the circumstances . . .'

'Go ahead,' interrupted Felix, suddenly relishing the idea of a breathing space to himself, 'I'll be fine.'

'I suppose I still could. Are you sure you don't mind Felix? It won't take long. We'll talk when I get back. Darling, are you certain you're all right?' She tried to touch him, but he dodged her hand with an impatient shrug.

'I'm fine,' he growled, kicking a bag out of his way. 'No need to hurry, I'm not going anywhere, am I?' After they had gone he parked himself in front of the television with a gin and tonic and a bag of peanuts, blanking out his troubles with the aid of a European football match.

By the time Frances returned he was on his third gin and feeling very much more sanguine about his immediate predicaments and life in general.

'Now, what is all this about?' she burst out at once, switching off the television and standing in front of the screen with her arms folded in expectation. A certain belligerence was called for, she had decided, in spite of – or maybe even because of – Daniel's well-intentioned, but ultimately riling advice about how to deal with the situation during the course of his ride home. It had triggered uncomfortable reminders of Paris, of the implication behind his unsolicited opinions on Daisy, rubbing her nose in the fact that he was far closer than she ever could be to the preoccupations of her own children.

'This?' Felix made a big show of craning his neck to see the TV screen. 'This *was* Real Madrid versus Man United. Nil nil, but a good match. I was hoping to see the end.'

'Felix, no games please. To have taken such a drastic step as walking out mid term you must have had some pretty good reasons. I believe I have a right to hear them.'

He levered himself upright with a scowl of reluctance. 'It wasn't working out. I hated the course. I hated being a student. It just didn't feel right.'

'Why didn't you say something before? I might have been able to help. That's what parents are for, isn't it?'

'Is it?'

'I beg your pardon?'

He shrugged. 'Doesn't matter.'

'It does matter. What are you saying?'

'That you haven't exactly been *around* much recently. I know it's not your fault, what with Dad and so on – you've had to look out for yourself and stuff. I just haven't felt I could talk to you about anything. It's like you're on another planet. And now with . . .' he had to force the words out, '. . . Daniel Groves and you together –' he was blushing furiously, but pressed on, 'I mean it is obvious you're kind of tied up with each other.'

'Oh dear.' All Frances's vague hopes of maintaining the pretence of mere friendship melted in an instant. She uncrossed her arms and put her head into her hands. 'I – we – were going to tell you – when the time was right . . .'

'Sure you were. Does Daisy know?'

'No . . . I . . .'

'But you've just been to Paris, haven't you? No right time to tell her either?' he sneered.

'Felix, I can understand how you must feel – about Daniel usurping Dad's place – but it's not like that . . . it's so different, there's no comparison – nothing could take the place of what I shared with your father.' She hesitated, letting this sink in before adding quietly, 'He would have hated you giving up on university.'

'That's right, take his fucking part, like you always did,' Felix shouted, slamming one palm hard down on the arm of his chair. 'You always took his side against me – why stop the habit of a lifetime now?'

The shock of his anger punched the breath from her. For a moment she could not speak. 'I . . . I did not take his side . . . I . . . I just . . . I tried not to interfere.'

Felix laughed bitterly. 'Like I said, you never took my part.'

'I hated crossing him,' Frances whispered, sinking to her knees on the carpet, 'it never did any good.'

Felix let out another short laugh. 'Oh yes, I know all about that.' He stood up, so quickly that black specks danced before his eyes. 'He was always on my back, always criticising, putting me down—'

'The pair of you were going through a bad patch – it hadn't always been like that – it would have got better, if there had been time . . .'

Felix snorted. 'I can't share your conviction I'm afraid. I've tried to miss him, to feel the *right* things, but I can't.' He swirled a pebble of an ice cube round his empty glass before tipping it to his mouth. The coldness made his teeth ache. 'If Dad had been alive,' he muttered, 'I wouldn't have had the guts to leave, I'd have endured three years of misery for him. Is that good or bad?'

Frances was kneeling on the carpet by the coffee table, fiddling with the tassles on the rug and staring at the patterns on the carpet till the colours ran. 'I don't know, Felix, I don't know. Bad, probably. What do you want to do?'

He shrugged. 'I've got some things to sort out first . . .' He broke off, clenching his teeth until the image of Sally had receded, 'then . . . travel maybe. I always wanted a year off, if you recall. Dad—'

'Yes, I remember. He didn't want you to. He thought it was more important to qualify yourself for a good job. With unemployment and so on. He worried for your future. He thought time out would be an indulgence.' Frances delivered these sentences in a monotone, remembering Paul's arguments as if he had spoken them only seconds before, remembering too her silence and feeling ashamed of it. 'But he did love you, Felix. I know you don't – you can't – believe that right now. But he did. He was trying to do what was for the best, he was scared to let go control for fear you might come to some harm . . . in a way you could say he cared too much.'

'I'll bear that in mind,' replied Felix darkly, getting to his feet.

Frances stood up too, feeling suddenly small and impotent beside the lanky frame of her son. He was as tall as Daniel, but much skinnier, still with boy's flesh on a man's outline. 'You're right,' she said quietly, 'I wasn't brave with Dad. I never challenged him if I could help it. It was my way of being happy.'

Felix dropped his head and walked out of the room. Going up the stairs he gripped the bannisters, pulling his body after his feet, as if each step required monumental effort. Frances stood watching him until he disappeared round the corner of the first landing, appalled as much by the fresh perspective their conversation had cast on her own past cowardices, as the mounting realisation that she appeared to have mislaid the art of being a mother.

Chapter Thirty-Two

━━━◆◇◆━━━

Joseph was wheeling his trolley out of Tesco when he spotted Sally emerging from the chemist opposite. The shopping mall was considerably emptier than when he had entered it an hour before, most of the noisy families having retreated home for tea. She had her hair scraped back into a bedraggled stub of a ponytail and was carrying a violin case as well as a large ruck-sack style satchel. He quickly steered his trolley across the gangway of grey speckled linoleum, waving to catch her attention.

'Blimey, you've bought a lot of stuff,' she remarked at once, momentarily distracted from her own woes by the layers of shopping bags stacked inside his trolley. 'Are you expecting visitors?'

'I don't like shopping so I do it infrequently and on a large scale,' Joseph replied, which was true, but not quite the reason for his extravagance that evening. 'It means I don't have to bother with the real world for at least another month,' he continued, wondering to himself how long these stocks would last, and whether his recent decision to dig his heels in would lead to peace or the ignominy of policemen and bulldozers. With the date set for his eviction now just forty-eight hours away, desperation had hardened into resolve. He would tie himself to the beams in the kitchen if necessary. He had even found chains and a rusty padlock for that very purpose.

'God, I'd give anything to leave the real world,' Sally murmured, remembering herself and hurriedly stuffing the small paper bag she had purchased from the chemist inside her blazer pocket.

'Come and have tea with me then,' blurted Joseph. 'I can offer you more than sweets this time,' he added, gesturing at the shopping. 'I've got a taxi picking me up in –' he looked at his watch – 'eight minutes exactly. Just one more thing to get from the electrical shop on the corner and then my mission is complete.'

The thought of not having to go home, of being granted a reprieve not just from the hothouse of her family, but from all the unresolved mess inside her own head was immediately irresistible. 'All right then, I will,' Sally agreed, falling into step beside him with a determined smile. When they reached the hardware store, she paused to scowl at the window display of power drills and paintbrushes. 'What do you need in here?'

'Just some wire. My electrics are on the blink. The council have given up on me so I have to see to such things myself.'

'Oh, right,' said Sally, not really listening. 'I'll guard the trolley shall I?'

'That would be kind. I won't be long.'

A few minutes later they were speeding towards Leybourne in the back of a taxi, Joseph's shopping crammed into the boot and Sally's bags wedged on the seat between them.

'Mind if I smoke?' enquired the driver, lighting up once they had negotiated the traffic jam onto the ring road and were heading out into the countryside.

'Only if I can have one too,' quipped Sally. The man laughed and tossed her a cigarette and a box of matches. Sally inhaled deeply, tipping her head back against the seat, dizzied both by the nicotine and the sense of her own daring. Soon her parents would start worrying, she realised, feeling the cruelty start to flood out of her and clinging onto it like a life-line, knowing that without it there was only shame and self-recrimination and despair.

Joseph wound down his window a couple of inches, eyeing the girl through the screen of smoke and wondering – as on the occasion of his previous invitation – what he was playing at. The hem of her school skirt had ridden up several inches over her knees, revealing a towering rectangle of pale flesh where her tights had laddered. There was a blob of dried pink nail varnish on the end nearest the knee, he noticed, his heart quickening at the pin-pointing of so fine a detail. He blinked and looked quickly away, humming under his breath, marvelling for by no means the first time in recent weeks at the vagaries of his unhappiness, how it had begun to trigger the most unexpected impulses.

It took several trips to ferry the shopping from the edge of the road down the wooded path to the cottage, which crouched, black and unwelcoming, in the dark. Joseph produced a small torch from his coat pocket which he used not only to marry the key to the lock, but also to lead the way into the kitchen. 'Hang on and I'll light the candles.'

'You mean . . . aren't there any lights?' Sally shrank back. She had envisaged the warmth and conviviality of her last visit; chocolates and mugs of coffee and watching soaps on the telly.

'That's why I had to buy the wire,' explained Joseph, a trace of impatience in his tone. 'It won't take long.' He moved round the kitchen as he talked, stepping over the sea of splurging shopping bags and striking matches at various candles precariously arranged in saucers and mugs around the room. By the time he had finished, the kitchen, so homely and higgledy-piggledy in daylight, had the eerie look of a ramshackle chapel.

'Perhaps this wasn't such a good idea,' began Sally.

'Nonsense.' Joseph felt a flutter of panic. It suddenly felt imperative that the girl should stay. 'In a minute I'll light the fire. First I'll put the kettle on. Look, the gas still works.' He struck a match at the hob, illuminating a ring of blue flame. 'Unless you would prefer to try some of my mother's home-made wine? I've still got bottles of the stuff.'

'Tea would be great thanks. And could I phone home? So they won't worry—'

'By all means. And perhaps, when the kettle boils you could see to the tea? You'll find a new box of Typhoo somewhere in that one I think –' he kicked at one of the bags on the floor – 'I'll go and see to the electrics. The box is down in the basement, I won't be long.'

Reassured by his cosy tone, Sally unearthed the old black telephone and dialled home. Thanks to various extra curricular activities of her siblings, she was greeted by the answer machine, into which she relayed a vague apologetic message about stopping on the way home for tea with a friend. Her conscience clear on this small score, she then fished out the paper bag from her blazer pocket and studied the pregnancy testing kit she had bought at the chemist. *POSITUROR*, it said, *for peace of mind*. Inside was a booklet of instructions and two white plastic sticks with small framed squares of what looked like white blotting paper on one end. With no sign of Joseph and the old copper kettle showing little inclination to absorb heat, Sally took one of the sticks and a candle and groped her way into the broom cupboard of a toilet by the back door. It was as cold as an ice-box and smelt of urine and damp. The door was so warped that it did not shut properly. Being one hundred per cent certain, even of the worst news, would bring peace of mind of sorts, Sally told herself, hoicking up her skirt and squatting awkwardly over the loo seat, anxious not to let any of the icy, cracked wood make contact with her skin. After the deed was done, she held the dry end of the stick between her teeth while she pulled up her pants and tights. It could take up to a minute, the instructions said, before the white square turned pink. Sally stood in the eerie flickering light, her teeth chattering with cold, one eye on the white square and one on the second hand of her watch. After counting ninety seconds with no visible change in the colour, she seized the candle and hurried back into the kitchen to check the pictures in the leaflet, expecting to find that she had misread it and pink meant negative after all.

A moment later the kettle began emitting an ear-piercing whistle, the fridge whirred into life and all the lights came on. It took Sally several dizzying seconds to get to the hob. As she did so Joseph appeared in the doorway behind her, triumphantly brandishing a handful of chewed wire.

'Do you know, I think I might have some of that wine after all,' she said hoarsely, 'if it's still on offer, that is.'

'By all means. I'll join you. We'll need food as well. It's rather strong. How does baked beans on toast sound?'

'Great. Baked beans on toast sounds great.' Waves of incredulous relief were still coursing through her. Fatter, without a doubt, but apparently not pregnant. Mars Bars not babies. She had been given her life back. The giddiness in her head mushroomed till she thought she might faint – a euphoric giddiness that felt quite unrelated to the goblet of wine which Joseph had set before her. The liquid, sweet and yellow and moreish, quickly dulled her appetite. When Joseph handed her her food, she merely picked at single beans and toast crusts, absently draining her glass as fast as he could fill it.

It was only when Joseph asked her to play the violin that Sally realised she was drunk. Aware that a sober version of herself would have cringed in horror at being called upon to make a public exhibition of herself, she eagerly seized her instrument from its velveteen nest and embarked on a whirlwind rendition of her entire repertoire. As she played, she twirled round the kitchen table, side-stepping the still unpacked shopping, her shirt tails flying, fresh wadges of hair breaking free from her ponytail.

Joseph clapped and whistled till dark circles of sweat pressed through his shirt. The girl was mesmerising. He could feel a poem pushing at the edges of consciousness, the first in months. A poem connected to the ladder in her thigh and the rise and fall of her plump breasts as she cavorted round the room. A poem about the precipice of need, about the darkness where only the bravest fell.

'I must go home.' She stopped, breathless, breaking the spell.

'How old are you?'

'Nearly sixteen.' She seized her glass and drank greedily, emptying it and then wiping her lips dry with the back of her hand.

'Old enough to do what you want, then?'

'Oh yes.' The room was spinning.

'And what do you want, Sally?' The legs of his chair squealed on the stone-tiled floor as he stood up, steadying himself on the table, his eyes squinting to calm his vision.

'Right now?' She dropped her violin into its case. A giggle began to ripple through her, turning into a deep yawn. Her eyes watered from the effort of giving in to it. 'To sleep, I want to sleep . . .'

'Here?'

'Anywhere.' She slumped down in a chair, dropping her head and arms onto the table.

'Anywhere is fine,' said Joseph. He took a step closer and stroked the bent head, running his fingers back through her hair until the small blue band holding the last twig of her pony-tail slipped out and fell to the floor.

Chapter Thirty-Three

Drained by the emotional exertions of the evening, Frances decided to tidy up the kitchen and have an early night. She worked methodically, grim-faced, wiping down surfaces, returning things to their allotted places, wishing the elements of her life could be so neatly filed away. The showdown with Felix had caused all her anxieties about Daniel to resurface. He was leaving for Cambridge early the next morning and would not be back until late the following night – a once dreaded separation which Frances now found herself regarding as an important breathing space. Closing her eyes, she felt a momentary surge of the old longing for Paul, for a second chance to be stronger and better, to iron out all the imperfections which were so relentlessly obvious with hindsight.

The tring of the telephone made her start. Her first instinctive thought was of Daniel. But it was Libby, her breathy, clipped tones alerting Frances at once to the fact that the troubles of the day had yet to complete their unravelling.

'Frances – sorry to call so late – only it's Sally – she's not come home.'

'Oh no, not again.'

'We're out of our minds with worry. She was supposed to have a violin lesson – she goes to Miss Laurent in Combe Road – but apparently she never turned up. I'm frantic on a Thursday as you know, the girls have to see to themselves because of late closing and me having to get Pete from youth orchestra. I didn't get home till seven. There was a message from her on the machine saying she was having tea with a friend, so I didn't worry for a bit. It was only when Alistair got back at eight I realised how late it was so I rang round and it turns out no one has seen her. I've tried everybody in her class. I phoned Miss Laurent who said she had assumed Sally had forgotten – it wouldn't be the first time – the poor child's been bullying us to let her give up . . .' Libby's voice dissolved into unintelligible sobs.

'Jesus, Libby, I'm so sorry. Have you phoned the police?'

'Yes, we've done all that – though you can't help getting the impression they've seen it all before – fifteen-year-old girl in a sulk with her parents—'

'But I thought things had been much better lately?'

'So did I . . .' There was more sobbing.

'Look, would you like me to come over? Just for a bit of support?' pressed Frances, longing suddenly to prove that she could be worthy and helpful, to do something to validate a friendship which in recent weeks had felt in danger of crumbling to nothing. Since the fateful Sunday night dinner the pair of them had maintained a manner of amicable civility, working side by side in the shop with all the show of companionship but none of the feeling.

But Libby had already recovered her composure. 'No need for that.'

'Are you sure? It would be no trouble.'

'Very kind, but no. Alistair is being the proverbial brick, dishing out brandy and regaling me with tales of all our dear daughter's scrapes in the past. The reason I phoned was because . . . it's probably nothing, but I did just want to ask you one thing.'

'What? Ask away.'

'One of Sally's schoolfriends, a girl called Jennifer Lacy, has just phoned back to say that she thinks she might have seen Sally walking off with Felix after school. I know it's mad, with

Felix in the middle of term and so on, but I thought I would just double check with you whether . . .' Her voice tailed off, sounding fearful of its own desperation.

'Felix?' Frances felt her mouth go dry. 'Well . . . curiously enough he did turn up on the doorstep earlier on this evening – right out of the blue.'

There was a stunned silence on the other end of the telephone.

'He hasn't said anything about seeing Sally,' continued Frances hastily, 'though, it's probably only fair to tell you that I think there might have been something going on between the pair of them at one time.'

'Something going on?' Although no more than a whisper Libby's voice contained all the shock and anger which Frances had dreaded. 'Why in God's name didn't you tell me?'

'It was ages ago, round Christmas time, just a bit of gossip – Joseph Brackman mentioned he had seen them – I thought you had enough on your plate – and I was sure that if there had been anything it was all over—'

'Where is Felix now?'

'Upstairs—'

'Go and ask him. Go and ask him this minute if he was with her, if he knows anything. Jesus Christ, Frances – I can't believe this – how could you not have told me something like that – how could you – after all these years – to think that you—'

'I didn't mean—'

'The fact is you're just not the same these days, not since Paul and . . .' At the last moment Libby could not bring herself to mention Daniel. 'You've changed Frances. I don't know you any more.'

'I don't know myself,' replied Frances hoarsely. 'I'll speak to Felix and call you back.'

But Felix, roused by the telephone, had heard enough of the conversation to make a hasty exit through the front door. It was only delaying tactics, he knew, but he had had enough of showdowns for one day. When Frances raised her hand to knock on his bedroom door she found herself facing the back of an old envelope instead, stuck in place with a strip of Sellotape.

Gone out for some fresh air – don't wait up, Felix.

She wrenched the envelope off the door, peeling away a thick strip of paint with it. Libby was right, she thought miserably, screwing the paper into a tight ball. She wasn't the same. She was different, worse, weaker, uncoping, negligent. And Daniel Groves was at the heart of it. She had lost the plot entirely, blinded, flattered by the revelatory fact that a man half her age was capable of finding her attractive. If it wasn't so sad it would have been funny.

After a brief phone call explaining and apologising for the situation to Libby, she pulled a pad out of the kitchen table drawer and seized a Biro from the pot on top of the fridge.

> *Daniel,*
>
> *Don't tell me letters are for cowards. I am a coward, I know that. But I have to be because if I see you I'll cave in, muddle my attraction for you with all the other bigger, more important things.*
>
> *Since Paul died I have been struggling to find myself, to see how I could carry on. Falling in love with you was, I thought, a wonderful, vital part of that process. But I was wrong. I have neglected my friends and family, who still need me very much. I have been selfish and mad and everybody is suffering in consequence. I don't want to see you any more. It was always going to end one day. I see no reason to postpone the pain.*
>
> *I will always remember you with fondness and gratitude,*
> *Frances.*
>
> *Please, please do not try to get in touch. It will only make this harder for both of us.*

Knowing that her resolve might have faltered by the morning, and nursing vague hopes of stumbling across Felix, Frances sealed the letter in an envelope and slipped out of the house. Although it wasn't actually raining, the night air felt heavy and damp. As she walked down the lane towards the post box she found herself looking upwards, straining her eyes for a glimpse of a star through the black gauze of sky. Picturing Sally, curled up in the corner of a bus shelter, or worse, she shuddered, dreading what role Felix might possibly have played in driving the poor girl to such states of extremity. She had lost her judgement over everything, Frances reflected wretchedly, thinking back to the many suggestions that all was not well in her son's life and how adept she had been at ignoring them. She thought too of Daisy, feeling fresh waves of shame at her absurd jealousy in Paris and wishing she had made more progress towards understanding the trace of forlornness hiding in even the widest of her daughter's smiles.

Before dropping the letter into the post box, she nonetheless could not resist giving a long last look at Daniel's name, bidding him farewell in her heart, wondering if he would read the tenderness in the careful loops of her handwriting. Even with her hand deep in the mouth of the letter box, she held onto the envelope for a few last unnecessary seconds, prolonging the moment of parting.

It was only on retracing her steps back up the lane that Frances became aware of the smell of smoke drifting on the heavy air. As she walked it grew stronger, riding up with her towards the house on a breeze that seemed to herald a change in the clemency of the weather. By the time she reached her drive, the smell was so strong that she cut round to the back garden, curious to see which of her distant neighbours had felt compelled to light a bonfire at ten o'clock on a Thursday night.

Instead of the shadowy view she had expected however, the profiles of the landscape were black and vivid, illuminated by a central torch of light amongst the clump of trees beyond the river. The scene was so unexpectedly dramatic and splendid, that for a few moments Frances stared in awe, even as it dawned on her that the flames licking over the tops of the trees could only originate from the railway cottage. As the horror of the implications of this sank in, so did a sickening sense of inevitability, as if the slow disintegration of the day – of the fragile, flawed reconstruction of her life since Paul – had been hurtling towards that very moment. In the next instant she heard Felix, shouting to raise the alarm as he raced across the field up to the garden gate, his voice cracking with panic and excitement.

Chapter Thirty-Four

———◦◦◦◦———

When Sally regained consciousness she was surprised to find Felix bending over her, his face sheeny with sweat, his hair sticking in strips to his forehead. His brown eyes looked smudgy with tears. Or maybe she was the one crying. It was hard to be sure.

'There is no baby. False alarm,' she said, her voice sounding all raspy, like it was coming from someone else. Her throat felt peeled raw and her gums sticky. Then the frame containing Felix was replaced by several unfamiliar faces and she felt strong arms slide under her legs and back. She smiled, pleased to be lifted out of the long wet grass where she had lain for what felt like hours, struggling with the confusion of being uncomfortably chilled yet bathed in a blast furnace heat that made her eyes sting. The next moment she was horizontal, a blanket bristling against her chin, being posted through the doors of a white van. Dimly aware that she was in the midst of a crisis, Sally sensed too that she had somehow arrived into hands that would take care of her, that the necessity of a full conscious reckoning of what was taking place had not yet arrived. A mask was placed over her mouth, injecting her lungs with sweet air and her head with disconnected recollections: the reedy screech of her violin, Joseph's breathy whispering, the feel of his stubbled chin against her ear, not being pregnant. Having arrived back at this last thought Sally allowed her mind to hover there, luxuriating in the relief of it.

Daniel stayed far later than he intended, dining in college with an old friend and then talking for several hours before embarking on the journey home. The break, though brief, felt invigorating, both because it had provided much needed confidence for the tack he was taking on Signorelli and because a day's deprivation of Frances had sharpened his eagerness to return to her. He spent the last part of the drive daring himself to call in at Leybourne. Only the thought of Felix prevented him. Not because he imagined for a second that the boy hadn't worked out what was going on – he was evidently far too intelligent for that – but because the lad was clearly going through a hard time and having his mother's lover bursting into the house in the small hours probably would not help matters. Besides which, Frances would go mad, Daniel mused, smiling to himself in quiet confidence at his abilities to soothe any such outbursts of insanity into nonexistence.

In spite of his late night, Daniel woke early the next morning, roused by the early March sunshine cutting through his thin curtains and a keen sense of purpose. Pulling on a sweatshirt, he padded downstairs in bare feet and a dressing gown in search of the kettle and the post, which he had kicked to one side on his late return the previous night. A few fresh letters had already been deposited on the doormat, together with that week's copy of the *Hexford Gazette*. Yawning deeply, Daniel gathered the whole lot up and retreated to the kitchen.

He was squeezing his teabag against the side of his mug with a spoon when his attention was caught by a headline at the bottom of the front page of the paper.

LOCAL HERO IN LEYBOURNE
COTTAGE FIRE TRAGEDY

Have-a-go hero, student Felix Copeland, pulled fifteen-year-old Sally Taverner to safety from the flames of a burning house on the outskirts of Leybourne village late last night. The main occupant of the property, forty-eight-year-old Joseph Brackman, was not so lucky and died in the inferno. Although arson has been ruled out, experts are still trying to establish what caused the blaze. A representative from the Council said that the property was known to be in need of rewiring and modernisation and that Mr Brackman had been on the point of being rehoused. Last night Sally Taverner's parents were at their daughter's bedside, where doctors report her to be in a serious but stable condition. Speculation that their daughter was with Mr Brackman because she had run away from home was angrily denied. 'We're just thankful she's safe and sound,' said gift-shop owner, Libby Taverner, 'and deeply sorry that Mr Brackman was not so lucky.'

Shaking his head in wonder that so much drama could have been packed into such a short absence, Daniel tipped back his chair to reach for the telephone, pinned to the wall next to the fridge. As he did so he caught sight of Frances's writing amongst the still unopened pile of letters next to his mug of tea. He let his chair rock back onto all four legs with a clatter that seemed to echo round the kitchen. Several seconds passed before he could bring himself to open the envelope, his fingers already trembling with foreboding.

When the telephone rang, Frances, who had been up since five and was sitting alone at her own kitchen table, remained motionless. After four rings her answering machine whirred into life. '*This is Frances, please leave me a message—*'

'Frances, for God's sake, what is this? Pick up the phone. I know you're there. Pick up the fucking phone.' There followed two, perhaps three seconds of silence. 'OK, listen to this then. Yes, I do think you are a coward, perhaps the biggest coward I've ever met in my life. How can you think of ending everything with a . . . note? After all that we've been through, all that we've shared. I know not all of it has been easy, but I've tried my best. But clearly that means nothing to you. No, you want to brush all that to one side, like it never happened, and go back to your . . . your . . . safe, narrow, blinkered, timid –' there was another short, exasperated silence. 'Keeping life at bay is no way to live it, you know Frances. Someone once said – and I can't for the fuck of it think who – that if people weren't careful, life was what happened while they waited for their dreams to come true. Well, that's not my style. I'm not going to hang around waiting for stuff to happen – I – oh fuck, never mind.'

After the machine had clicked off, Frances stayed in her chair, staring hard at the patterns in the wood grain of her kitchen table, her fists clenched in her lap. In front of her was the same newspaper which had confronted Daniel. She closed her eyes, remembering again the fire, the chaos of sirens and heat and noise, Felix's wild euphoria, the shock of seeing Sally, curled in the long wet grass fringes of the garden like a wounded animal. Frances clung onto the images, wanting to sear them forever across her mind, knowing that they were her only sandbags against the monotonous pulse of sadness now beating inside. They would always be a reminder of how fragile life was, how perilously close she had come to forgetting herself and losing all that she truly valued. Although Felix had not for a moment been in physical danger, and Sally turned out to be suffering from shock more than actual injury, it felt to Frances as if they had both had a narrow escape. As if they all had. Meeting the Taverners in the foyer of St Stephen's hospital, they had clung to each other like survivors of a shipwreck, hugging and sobbing apologies and forgiveness, all of them sensing that the tragedy was a God-given clean slate for starting again.

While a comprehensive chronology of events had yet to

emerge, it appeared that Sally had indeed met Felix after school, but only briefly. She had then responded to an impromptu invitation to tea from Joseph Brackman, following up on a friendship which seemed to have sprung into being as a result of the events surrounding the death of his mother. Although the local paper's heroic claims were correct in that Felix had dragged Sally across the garden to a safer distance from the leaping flames, Sally herself remained adamant that Joseph had carried her out of the house. Which meant he must have gone back into the cottage afterwards. Like a captain going down with his ship. Or a man giving up, wading through the falling debris to his own fate. Frances shuddered, reaching for her tea only to find that it was cold. That Joseph appeared to have found some companionship during what turned out to be the final weeks of his life was for Frances the only consolation in the entire sorry business. The previous night, in some vague bid to atone for her own abandonment of the man, she had even found herself brushing the dust off the slim volume of poetry which had been consigned for many weeks now to the bottom of a stack of books under her bed. If she had hoped for revelatory answers to her neighbour's psyche, however, there were none to be had. The poems were as incomprehensible as ever. She had fallen asleep soon after opening the book, waking in the early hours to find it lodged under her hip, its flimsy spine torn and the pages badly creased.

After a final glance at the newspaper, Frances folded the article out of sight, shaking her head at its half truths and exaggerations, wondering what the whole story was and whether it mattered. That Felix had been made out to be a knight in shining armour would be no bad thing, either for his wilting self-esteem, or for fostering the warm relations now prevailing between themselves and the Taverners. He had spent nearly all the previous day at the hospital, fired up with concern for Sally and the patent relief of having their liaison out in the open. In the meantime, Frances had made herself useful by manning the shop for Libby, glad to have a busy Friday as distraction not only from the aftershock of the fire, but also from the temptation to hijack every passing postal van in a bid to retract her letter to Daniel.

Abandoning her cold tea, Frances went upstairs to get dressed. After tiptoeing past Felix's open door she could not resist retracing her steps and peering inside. All that was visible was one large white foot protruding under the duvet and a portion of ruffled sandy hair between the pillows. Just like old times, she thought to herself, but realising in the same instant that it was nothing of the kind. The sight of all the memorabilia of his childhood – once prized pop posters hanging by threads of stale Blu-Tack, dog-eared war comics, airfix models, plastic sporting trophies – suddenly made her inordinately sad. Even his hi-fi system, so treasured and well-used just a year before, looked neglected and outgrown. He had entered another phase of his life. They all had, she reflected sadly, retreating from the room.

While getting dressed she thought about her stoicism over Daniel's phone call and managed a small stab of self-congratulation. It might take a while, but she would get over it. Like mourning a death, it would simply take time and the ability to let go. Struck by the irony of this last analogy, Frances gave the reflection in her dressing-table mirror a grim smile, drawing harsh consolation from the pink fatigue in her eyes and the haggard set of her mouth. She was doing the right thing, she reminded herself, not just because she would have more time for her old – her real – life, but because in ten years she would be fifty-three and Daniel thirty-six. Better to have the pain now than later. Better to have her cruelty than his, to be the author of the split rather than its victim.

She combed her hair back into a ponytail, scraping the teeth viciously against her scalp and fastening it so tightly that she could feel the hairs framing her face straining at the roots. After staring at her make-up bag she zipped it shut and closed it away in her dressing-table drawer, not wanting to soften the tight, austere look of her reflection, seeing it as a beacon of her new resolve.

Chapter Thirty-Five

———⟫◦◦◦⟪———

Felix had never been very good with hospitals. The smell of disinfectant and floor polish turned his stomach. When Daisy had broken her collar bone, he had inadvertently diverted the spotlight of attention to himself by being sick all over a chair and his mother's shoes; a reflex of protest which had been repeated so often during the course of consultations over his ears, that Frances used to warn new doctors of the possibility as soon as they entered the room.

Visiting Sally however, was different from the start. Pushing his way through the heavy entrance doors of the hospital late on Saturday morning, a copy of the *Hexford Gazette* tucked under one arm, Felix's whole demeanour exuded confidence. Arriving in the ambulance had made him feel part of what had happened. The doctors and nurses had been gentle and informative, their happy prognosis easing the terror of the inevitable meeting with the Taverners which followed soon afterwards. Not even the smell of the place bothered him any more, he mused, casually thrusting his hands into the pockets of his chinos and rolling on the soles of his trainers as he followed the now familiar route to Sally's ward. Just down the corridor from the main entrance was a small shop run by a lady with three double chins and a wheezy laugh. Recognising Felix from the day before, she gave him a little wave.

'Getting better is she, your friend?'

'Oh, much, thanks.'

'A terrible thing, that fire. They say it was the council's fault – prehistoric wiring. They should have moved that poor man years ago. It's criminal, what these people get away with.'

Felix chose a packet of chocolate-covered raisins and a magazine with a waif of a model on its cover, wearing nothing but a vine leaf, blue lipstick and spangled eyeshadow.

'She'll be out soon then?' the woman asked, handing him his change.

'Tomorrow they say. Her lungs got a bit buggered.'

'I should think they did, poor love,' tutted the woman sympathetically.

Sally was lying on her side with her eyes closed. Her hair was all spiky and there were dots of pink in her cheeks. Felix stopped short of the bed, catching his breath, overcome by the urge to rip the bedcovers off and make love till the nurses called the security guards. He sat on the empty chair next to her and crossed his legs instead, looking round for somewhere to put his gifts. Her bedside table was laden with flowers and books and bottles of water.

'Hey,' said Sally opening her eyes.

'I thought you looked beautiful then, with your eyes closed.'

She giggled. 'I'd better get a guide dog then.'

'Read this first. Fame at last.' He handed her the newspaper and watched her expression change. 'They've twisted it all round, I'm afraid, not mentioned what you said about Joseph.'

'Stupid buggers.' Sally scowled impatiently and then grinned. 'Have-a-go-hero, eh? They'll be offering you a knighthood next.'

'Fuck off,' he replied happily, snatching the paper back and rattling the box of raisins. 'I bought you presents. These and this.' He began reading a headline on the magazine. 'Ten ways to achieving the perfect orgasm—'

'Shut up.' Sally pretended to pull the sheets over her head in embarrassment.

'How's your throat? Your voice sounds better. Not so husky.'

'Shame. I liked husky.'

He pulled the chair closer and seized the hand nearest him. 'Sally, I'm so sorry about . . . everything.'

She wrestled free and began peeling off the wrapping on the packet of raisins. 'We've been through all this. You don't have to say any more. I was an idiot too. It's all right now, that's what matters.'

'No, it isn't.' He snatched the box from her and took both of her hands, pressing them between his palms. 'I want to tell you. I've been a bastard, I know. I was just so fucking scared at the thought of you being pregnant, I sort of couldn't be nice about it. And before all that, at Christmas I . . . well I was unhappy because of hating my course so much and not knowing what to do about it, and I suppose I wasn't over Dad – I'm still not probably – and . . . there was this woman.' He broke off, his face burning.

'Now he tells me,' murmured Sally, taking in a deep breath and letting it out slowly.

'No,' he continued urgently, seeing what she was thinking, 'it wasn't like that – nothing happened. When I was hitching she gave me a ride home, after that guy I told you about the one who was going out with Mum—'

'Go on.' Sally's eyes were unblinking and dark.

'This woman, she was quite old, late forties, tarty and . . . up for it . . . I think. And . . .'

'And?'

'Well, nothing. I – we – did nothing. But afterwards –' he gripped her fingers hard – 'I kept wishing that I had and that made me feel guilty because since we started I'd never wanted anyone else.'

Sally let out a whoop of laughter. 'So you're, like, confessing to a fantasy? Oh Jesus. I have them all the time. If you knew what I've done to Robbie Williams in my head.' She collapsed into giggles.

'I won't tell you next time,' said Felix, pretending to sulk. 'What things anyway – with Robbie Williams?'

'My business,' replied Sally primly, her expression clouding at the sight of an approaching doctor, surrounded by a cluster of medical students. Felix was banished to the cafeteria where he ate a pot noodle and a bag of salt-and-vinegar crisps. He was on the point of going back up to the ward when Libby Taverner appeared through the doorway on the far side of the room. She saw him at once and came hurrying over.

'The doctor's still with her – doing a few last checks – but it's all good news, I think.' She set her handbag down on the table together with a pair of old woollen gloves and a black hat. 'Sally has told me about the pregnancy scare, by the way.'

Felix bit his lip, feeling his ears turn crimson, inwardly cursing Sally and waiting for recriminations to be heaped on his head.

'I've booked an appointment with family planning. I didn't go on the pill till I was twenty but I'm well aware that things happen earlier these days. Beth, for some curious reason, hasn't discovered the joys of sex, yet, but no doubt she will in her own good time. I do think it's made it harder for Sally, having such an unnaturally angelic older sister leading the way. I'm going to get some tea, do you want anything?'

'Er . . . coffee – great thanks,' muttered Felix, his ears still aflame.

'And she's agreed to see a counsellor,' continued Libby, matter-of-factly, setting down the cups and saucers. 'Alistair and I think it will help – to have someone who's nothing to do with the family to talk to. Sal does tie herself in knots about things,' she broke off with an uncertain laugh, 'but then I'm sure you of all people know about that. The thing is, Felix, I think it's important that you're on board so to speak – about the counsellor – if she thinks for one minute that you're making light of it, thinking it's a waste of time, she'll probably give up.'

Felix murmured assurances, unsure whether he was being

insulted or flattered, but taking heart from the directness of her tone. 'I'll do all that I can, I promise and I'm sorry for . . . if I've . . .'

'We've said all our sorries,' said Libby smartly, 'no point in looking back. Now that you've packed in university have you any ideas what you want to do instead?'

Felix swallowed, feeling suddenly like a suitor being grilled by a prospective parent-in-law. 'Travel . . . I want to travel. I was thinking maybe I'd wait and set off in the summer, then Sally could come with me for a couple of months.'

'Did you indeed?' remarked Libby, who had already heard as much from Frances on the telephone that morning. 'Presumably you're going to require funds for this adventure?'

'Yes, I was going to sign on at the job centre.'

'What I would like to suggest is that you work in the shop for a while instead. Frances – your mother has decided to give up. She's going to concentrate on her drawing. We've had a long chat this morning. And I think she's quite right. I've always said she was sitting on a great talent.' Libby paused to swig her tea, watching Felix carefully over the rim of her cup and musing upon the awkward pride of teenagers. She was certain Sally had only agreed to the counsellor thing because the young nurse with studs in her nostrils had helped break the idea, giving it a credence that she and Alistair never could.

'That's very kind Mrs Taverner,' said Felix slowly. 'I would like that a lot.'

'For heaven's sake, call me Libby, please. And it's not kind, it's practical. Business, for some unfathomable reason, seems to have picked up. You'll be working hard – and if things carry on as they are it won't be for just three days a week either – though we'll begin like that.' She drained the last of her tea. 'I'll see you Monday then, shall I?' She smiled, pitying all his youthful uncertainty and thinking suddenly of Frances's young friend and what a world of changes occurred between the ages of eighteen and twenty-six.

Chapter Thirty-Six

White ash dusted the surrounding trees and grassland like apple blossom. In the heart of the blackened skeleton of the cottage, the grey rubble was still smoking. Only a scattering of objects was identifiable, an old glass sweet jar, a charred broom handle, the remains of a toilet, saved by the haphazard intensity of the fire and the eventual success of the hoses in stamping it out. Unfolding her stool, Frances set to work, her pencil making short strong movements across the page. By the end of two hours she had the makings of three pictures; not the pretty, faint sketches which she had done to date, but dark, stark impressions, full of a smouldering intensity that went far beyond the wisps of smoke curling up from amongst the ruins. Frances frowned at her handiwork, aware that she was harnessing some of her sadness over Daniel and wondering whether this was something of which she should feel proud or distrustful.

Gathering up her things, she set off home, going the short route via the fields down which she and Felix had run two days and a lifetime before. She walked slowly, feeling stiff from sitting for so long, the weight of the stool and her drawing box numbing her fingers. The day was bright and mild. The dense cloud of the morning had shifted off-stage, leaving a broken jet stream of white along a backdrop of hazy blue. The daffodils, sprouting in clusters along the grassy bank lining the edge of the field and river, were already looking weary, their faded yellow heads swinging low under the burden of their own weight. Spring was in full flow, Frances realised, pausing to look around, drawing reassurance from the familiar landscape, unchanged in spite of the human dramas recently enacted upon it. Tired suddenly of the tight tugging of her ponytail, she pulled out the clasp and shook her hair free, relishing the tingle of fresh air on her scalp. She would be all right, she realised, her heart flooding with a wonderful and wholly unexpected surge of self-belief as she turned to continue her walk up the narrow muddy path.

She rounded the final bend in the path to see Daisy sitting on the garden fence, her hair sticking up in glossy white tufts, her bony knees showing through the slits in her jeans. She was wearing an enormous black jumper and one ear-ring the size of a small bird. Frances stopped and smiled, somehow un-surprised that her daughter should be perched at the end of the garden, shining and smiling like a skinny angel.

'I got your message – about Felix and the fire and every-thing – and I just thought I should be here. I flew over this morning. Is he all right? Is Sally? Are you?' She hopped off the fence and ran towards her mother.

'We're all fine,' Frances reassured her, putting down her things so they could exchange a proper hug. 'It was awful, but everything is all right now. Apart from poor Joseph of course. Everybody feels terrible about him –' She broke off and took a step back. 'I'm so pleased you're here, darling – and Felix will be too. I think he's still at the hospital with Sally – I lent him the car.'

'Was that wise?'

'Almost certainly not.' They both laughed.

'You've been drawing. Can I look?'

Frances stood awkwardly while her daughter examined her morning's output, screwing up her eyes because of the glare of the sun on the large white pages.'It looks like a battlefield,' Daisy said at length, 'a brilliant battlefield.' She carefully closed the folder, biting her bottom lip. 'Mum, I've left Claude. And I think I might have fallen in love with someone else – someone completely unexpected – though in some ways I feel I've known him all my life—'

Frances could feel the colour drain from her face. She gripped the stool with white knuckles, waiting to hear that all her terrors about the evening in Paris had been justified after all. It took a few moments to register that Daisy was talking not about Daniel but the man called Marcel who employed her at the gallery. 'It's grown slowly, sneaked up on me, so gradually that I'm not yet completely sure. Love is hard isn't it? I mean, knowing when it is and what it is.' She paused, frowning. 'It's weird, but I think the turning-point was you coming to stay – it kind of helped me realise how bad things were. And I had that long talk with your friend, that Daniel guy, which helped too. Afterwards it sort of came home to me that the only person with the power to change anything for the better was me.' She stopped again, digging deep inside herself for the courage to tell the whole story. 'The truth is, Claude was getting kind of violent and I was scared what he would do if I tried to leave—'

'Violent?'

They had got as far as the garden gate. Frances leant on it, staring at Daisy in horrified disbelief. 'Why – for God's sake why didn't you say something before?'

'I was scared of you too,' Daisy confessed in a small voice, 'first of how sad you were over Dad and then of how . . . sorted . . . you had suddenly become. I didn't know how you had got from one state of mind to the other. I guess I felt sort of left out of the loop.' She threw up her hands helplessly, causing Frances's drawings to ripple along the edges of the folder like the pages of an enormous book.

'Oh darling, I'm so sorry. So that horrible bruise on your face . . .' Frances reached out and pressed her palm to Daisy's cheek. 'I could see you were sad, I thought it was over Dad.' The feel of the soft, girlish skin, without make-up, she noticed suddenly, twisted the knot of guilt inside. 'God, I've been so hopeless. Absolutely bloody hopeless.' The tears were out before she could stop them.

Daisy flung both arms round her shoulders. 'Oh Mum, you haven't. It's not your fault, that's the last thing it is. It was me – my mess – something I had to work through myself. And it was tied up with Dad. Not just missing him, but because of how he used to spoil me, giving in to me over things he would never have dreamed of with Felix. Inside I think a part of me was still trying to be a little girl . . . and that . . . sort of made it harder to stand up to Claude.' She dropped her arms, shaking her head ruefully. 'In Paris, I knew you were trying to get me to talk, but I also knew I had to sort it out on my own.' She wiped her eyes with her sleeve and sniffed. 'Besides, you don't tell me everything about you do you? I mean, we all have a few secrets.' She smiled weakly, relieved to see that her mother had stopped crying.

'Yes, I suppose we do,' murmured Frances, managing to return the smile, but inwardly still reeling from the shame of having seen Claude's handiwork at first hand and not recognised it. Another near disaster indvertently caused by her self-absorption over Daniel Groves, she reflected bitterly, feeling a fresh burst of conviction that splitting from him had been the only way to bring her to her senses.

'Marcel wanted me to move in with him right away,' continued Daisy, taking charge of the fold-up stool as well as the folder of sketches, 'but I said I needed a break, a pause between the paragraphs of my life –' She broke off, laughing. 'I'm going to work full time which means I'll be able to rent a small place on my own. I found somewhere last week, just a five-minute walk from the gallery. The most bizarre thing was that when I finally plucked up the courage to tell Claude he watched me pack my bags like a lamb, on his knees most of the time, begging me not to leave. I had Marcel on standby outside, just in case, but there was no need. It was like showing him my inner strength totally put paid to his. Weird.' She shook her head.

'You poor darling,' murmured Frances.

'I'm not poor at all,' retorted Daisy, leading the way into the kitchen and taking charge of the kettle and coffee pot. 'I feel better about myself than I ever have. I'd like to stay for three weeks if that's all right. Marcel claims he can't manage the gallery without me, but he'll be fine. Do him good to miss me a little,' she added sounding pleased.

'Stay as long as you need.'

'And now I want to hear all about Felix,' she began, only to be interrupted by the sound of the doorbell.

'That'll be him now. He's lost his keys.'

'Typical Felix,' mumbled Daisy, smiling to herself as she opened the cupboard to get out another mug.

Frances hurried into the hall, feeling a sudden rush of satisfaction at the prospect of having the three of them back round the kitchen table, regrouping properly at last.

Chapter Thirty-Seven

There was a surprising turnout for Joseph's funeral, organised jointly by Libby and Frances once the various authorities had completed their investigations into the fire. Two weeks of deliberations resulted in a verdict of accidental death, a conclusion based on the evidence of Joseph's Heath Robinson wiring efforts with the fuse box in the cellar. The service was very simple, the twenty-third psalm, a few stirring hymns and – thanks to some last minute inspiration from Frances – a reading from Joseph's slim anthology of poems. After considerable debate as to who should undertake such a challenge, Felix surprised everybody by volunteering his services, preparing for the ordeal with lengthy private rehearsals in front of Sally and his bedroom mirror.

It was the first time Frances had been inside the church since Paul's funeral. Though she made a point of sitting on the opposite side of the aisle in a different row, there was an inevitable poignancy to the occasion, intensified by the stirring voluntary of St Martin's new organist, a choral scholar from Cambridge whose recent appointment at the Taverner girls' school had caused a flood of applications for GCSE and A level music. When Felix slid from the pew to take his place behind the lectern, Frances instinctively braced herself, not just mentally but physically too, tucking her legs tightly under the seat and clinging to the handles of her bag with both hands.

Seeing her son standing before the congregation, pausing at the heavy silence of the church, she had the strongest impression of a wheel turning full circle, the sense that life was not a linear process at all but a series of repeating patterns.

Felix had chosen a poem called 'The Deep', a particularly dense concoction of adjectives of which even the most skilful actor would have had trouble making any sense. Seeing how earnestly he tried, Frances was surprised and a little appalled to find herself repressing not sorrow, but the most unforgivable urge to laugh out loud. Only the severest inward reprimanding and a lot of hard staring at stained-glass windows allowed her to maintain her composure; a process unaided by the realisation that Daisy, madly chewing her lips in the seat next to her, was combating similar urges of insubordination.

Outside in the sunshine, standing amongst the semicircle of mourners as the pot of ashes was buried up against the church wall, France's mood reverted to a more co-operative sense of solemnity. As the final prayers were still being said, she tiptoed down the gravel path and threaded her way through the heaving green sea of tombstones. The bulbs she had planted on Paul's now grassy plot a few months before were pushing up nicely, many of the buds already unfurling to reveal glimpses of the velveteen gold and purple inside. Probably the most fitting tribute she had managed yet, mused Frances, smiling wryly to herself at the sight of this small horticultural triumph and pondering the fact that if Paul hadn't seized quite so many initiatives in their married life there might have been room for her to show a little more resourcefulness of her own.

'We only knew bits of each other,' she said quietly, not to the grave, but to the air in general, which seemed to hum with purity and promise. 'But it was enough and we did our best.' As she turned away she spotted Felix and Sally, hand in hand, heading, by a more circuitous route in the same direction. Not wanting to intrude, she hurried to catch up with the tail end of mourners wending their way back down the path towards the main gate. As she did so, a glimpse of metallic grey caught her eye through the thicket separating the graveyard from the road. The date and time of the service had been announced in the local paper; it wouldn't be beyond the bounds of possibility for Daniel to have seen it and decided to come. Though why he should was hard to imagine, Frances reminded herself, nonetheless craning her neck through the tangle of branches for a better view of the road. Apart from the spitting phone message responding to her letter, he had acceded to her plea for silence with impressive co-operation. In the intervening weeks, Frances had made the unhappy discovery that applying herself to the mislaid art of mothering her children had proved neither as time-consuming nor as efficacious in forestalling other emotions as she had hoped. As a result she had not only continued drawing with frenzied determination, but also embarked on a picture-framing course in Hexford and water-colour lessons with an eccentric acquaintance of Alistair's. As if such diversions were not enough, she had that week resurrected Alistair's drawing plans for converting the upper storey of the garage, not to guest quarters as had originally been intended, but into a studio for herself, together with a small adjoining bathroom. The money, already set aside, would be the same Alistair assured her and the layout much more simple. Both the Taverners had been wonderfully supportive about the idea, which like the funeral, had called for many telephone calls and sorties into each other's houses.

'All right?' enquired Libby, who had been watching with some curiosity as Frances disengaged herself from the hedge.

'Fine – caught my skirt,' muttered Frances, hurrying up to her. The car had been an old grey Jaguar with a dented boot. After a brief announcement about the split, the subject of Daniel had been declared strictly out of bounds, both because she knew it would help her to move forward and because enduring Libby's I-knew-it-would-end-in-tears wisdom on the matter was more than she could bear. Libby had readily acquiesced, but not before a startling announcement-cum-apology that any manifestations of unfriendliness on her part towards Daniel had almost certainly derived from jealousy. 'The middle-aged cow in me took over for a while, sparked into being by the realisation that if Alistair popped his clogs I'd never find anything so handsome to take his place, let alone one that's youthful and intelligent into the bargain. Not the most worthy of emotions, I'm afraid. Took a while to admit them to myself, let alone Alistair—'

'You told Alistair that?' Frances had exclaimed, appalled.

Libby smiled ruefully. 'Yes and all he did was laugh, which was very smart of him, because it made it not matter and me love him all at the same time. He's rather cunning like that,' she had added proudly. 'And it helped that he thought Daniel was rather charming—'

'Yes, well, it's all in the past now,' Frances had interrupted, unwilling to hear any more of her ex-lover's praises sung at a time when she was trying so earnestly to forget them.

'I thought it went very well,' said Libby now, referring to the funeral.

'So did I.'

'And Felix was a star. He'll go far that boy, though I'm not yet sure in what direction.'

Frances laughed. 'I hope so.'

'Beth and Daisy are off to find a Sunday afternoon movie. Do you want to come back for a bite with us?'

Frances opened her mouth to refuse but then changed her mind. Making a conscious effort to fill her time had once more become something of a burden. 'Thanks that would be lovely. If you don't mind me popping home first to get the plans. I've had a thought about the loo.'

Libby groaned good-humouredly. 'Funnily enough, so has Alistair. That should make for scintillating conversation. What about those two?' She gestured at Felix and Sally, now sprawling on the grass next to Paul's grave.

'Looks like they've got other plans. Let's leave them to it.'

'God, all that pain and aggravation of Young Love,' declared Libby with a sigh, 'I wouldn't go back to it for the world.'

Frances laughed quickly in response, not quite able to agree out loud.

Felix broke off the most fully bloomed of the crocuses and stuck it behind Sally's ear. 'Dad won't mind. He could be a pain, but he won't mind one flower.'

'All parents can be pains,' she groaned, rolling over onto her back and blinking at the sky. 'Like Mum with this therapist I'm seeing. She pretends like she's not interested – because she knows she's not supposed to be – but she's always dropping these heavy digs about what we talk about and stuff.'

'What *do* you talk about?'

Sally threw the clump of grass stems she had been picking at his head. 'You're just as bad.'

'Do you talk about me?'

'Amongst other things.'

'Like?'

'Like, the fact that I think Joseph Brackman might have been trying to get inside my knickers.'

'Jesus, you're joking.' Felix sat up, shaking the grass from his hair and eyebrows.

'It doesn't matter,' said Sally mildly. 'All I can remember doing was giggling and then he fell asleep. And then he saved my life. Which is a pretty fair return if you think about it.'

'The fucking pervert.'

'I don't think so, Felix.' Sally sat up and put her face close to his. 'He was very sad and a little mad. He'd had a crap life. He had no friends. I think he knew his poetry was rubbish too, but he like, pretended it was special because it was all he had to believe in. That book – the one you read from – he had it published himself, he told me, five hundred copies, it took all his savings. If that isn't sad I don't know what is. So don't go telling anyone will you, 'cos he's dead anyway and I'd go fucking mad if you did.' For a moment her eyes glittered with a resolve that Felix was learning to respect.

'OK.'

'Would you like me to leave you alone for a bit, so you can be with your dad or something?' Sally had stood up and was twirling the crocus Felix had picked for her between finger and thumb.

'Nah.' He leapt nimbly to his feet. 'The old bugger's not here anyway. And if I ever start thinking he is, I want you to promise to shoot me.' He brushed the grass off his trousers. 'Like I told you, I don't feel so messed up about him these days. I think Mum was probably right – getting on would have come back to us in the end, a bit anyway. I mean, everybody goes through phases with each other, don't they?' he added, peering at Sally from under his fringe, hanging more persistently in his eyes as it always did when it was freshly washed. 'Sometimes without knowing why.'

'I guess.' Sally held out her hand and then snatched it away as he tried to take it, skipping off between the gravestones, her long black skirt whirling round her ankles.

Chapter Thirty-Eight

<hr>

'While you were shopping a man called James Harcourt phoned.'

Frances, whose loading and unloading of supermarket produce had managed to coincide with two torrential downpours, hurried out of her bedroom with a hand towel across her head and a wet sock in each hand.

'Why ever didn't you say so sooner?'

Daisy, kneeling next to an open suitcase, surrounded by piles of freshly laundered clothes, looked up in surprise. 'Because I didn't know it was urgent.'

'It isn't.'

'Oh. So that's all right then.'

'Yes. What did he say?'

'Just asked you to call. Left a phone number. I wrote it on the back of an envelope on your bedside table . . .' She would have carried on, but Frances had already retreated, closing the door behind her. Daisy shook her head, tutting to herself as a mother might at the inadequate communication skills of a teenage child.

Frances took a few moments to compose herself before picking up the receiver. She closed her eyes, trying to recall the attractive voice, the tone of mature assurance which had given her the nerve to hurl herself into the unknown three months before. With hindsight she felt all the more keenly the rudeness of having failed to deliver a proper explanation for her behaviour.

The phone was picked up at once, the voice initially sounding so formal and brusque that she wondered for a moment if she had dialled the wrong number.

'It's Frances Copeland, returning your call . . . I . . . I just wanted to apologise properly for what happened, for not having got in touch before . . . I mean after . . .'

'Frances.' There followed a sigh of what sounded like relief. 'I am so very glad to hear from you.'

'I had this accident,' she burst out, 'on the way to meet you' – an image of Daniel bobbed obstinately inside her head, where it hovered like an unwanted guest. 'Not a serious one as it turned out, but I simply could not get there and then . . . I did try to ring you a couple of times, but – I'm so sorry – goodness knows what you thought of me.'

'It doesn't matter. I was disappointed, of course. I wasn't sure what to think at first. And then I got called away on business – to sort a small problem that turned out to be a hornets' nest.'

'Oh dear, poor you,' Frances murmured, vaguely recollecting a profession to do with running hotels.

'Fortunately the problem was in San Francisco, which is one of my most favourite cities. But I thought of you often,' he added, in a tone of voice which made her blush in spite of being quite alone.

'But I only rang to make a belated apology, I—'

'Oh no, don't back out now we've got this far. Let's get together as soon as we can. We've nothing to lose, surely. You promised to meet me once – unless of course, in the meantime, you've met . . .' he coughed.

'No, no, I'm still on my own,' Frances assured him hastily, the image of Daniel ducking out of her mind at last.

'How about tonight then?' he pressed. 'We could try the Dancing Bear again, unless you've any strong objections.'

'No, I suppose not,' she whispered, terrified, but a little enticed as well.

It wasn't until Frances put the phone down that it occurred to her that succumbing to such an invitation on Daisy's last night at home was not only rash but also in keeping with the very brand of selfishness which she had so recently vowed to avoid. She was toying with the daunting idea of retracting her acceptance, when Daisy herself knocked quietly and came in.

'Oh darling, I've gone and done a silly thing – agreed to go out tonight, of all nights.'

'It doesn't matter.' Daisy slung one leg over her mother's dressing-table stool and leant forward to inspect her eyebrows. 'I wanted an early night anyway. And Felix is bound to be with Sally. Who is this James Harcourt anyway?'

For a moment Frances struggled to think of a suitable reply. 'If you must know, he's a blind date that never happened. A moment of madness a few months back.'

Daisy let out a low whistle.

'It is, as they say, a long story,' added Frances wryly, 'but he does sound extremely nice and having let him down last time . . .'

Daisy now busy at work with a pair of small tweezers she had found in the dressing-table drawer, frowned, whether at the conversation or the pain she was inflicting on herself, it was hard to be sure.

'But now, what about you?' urged Frances, eager to change the subject. 'Do you have money, passport—'

'Mum, I'm completely sorted. It's only Paris, remember? If you can get me to the airport by ten thirty tomorrow, that would be great.' Daisy returned the tweezers to the drawer and spun round on the stool. 'So Daniel Groves is out of the picture completely then?'

'Daniel?' Frances shook out a pair of dry socks and sat down with her back to Daisy to put them on. 'I suppose Felix has been talking to you, has he?'

'No, these days Felix talks to no one but Sally. It was Daniel who told me actually,' she confessed after a brief pause. 'That night in Paris. Swore me to secrecy – said you would go mad if you found out he'd told me without your agreement.'

'Oh he did, did he? And quite bloody right.' A sock snagged on the sharp edge of one toenail. 'I don't expect you to begin to understand—'

'Thanks a bunch,' retorted Daisy archly. 'For your information, I thought I understood rather well. I also thought he was very nice, a good laugh, clever—'

'And young enough to be your brother,' snapped Frances hurling both socks in the air and spinning round to face her daughter. 'You might as well say it, because it's what you're thinking. And with an age gap like that I can see nothing but problems ahead. So I had the sense to pull out. Do you understand that too?'

Daisy nodded. 'Oh yes,' she said quietly, crossing to the door and tugging it open. 'As it happens, it's a subject on which I could be said to have more understanding than most. Marcel is forty-two.' She cast a defiant look at her mother. 'And it doesn't stop me adoring him.'

By six o'clock that evening Frances was back in her bedroom addressing the problem of what to wear for James Harcourt. To opt for the blue trouser suit which she had selected on their previous attempt at a rendezvous would feel too unimaginative and even faintly sinister, she decided, longingly eyeing the casual outfits draped around her chair and battling with the vague sense that such an occasion demanded something more dramatic. After various prolonged tussles in front of the mirror, pulling so many articles back and forth over her head that her freshly coiffeured hair degenerated to a frantic mess of static electricity, she settled upon a mustard wool skirt suit with gold buttons, which Paul had bought her a few years before. A little staid, but close-fitting and definitely classy, she decided, performing a last turn before the mirror, her high-heeled shoes creaking from lack of use. The adornment of a pair of large gold earrings had just completed the picture when Felix appeared in the doorway behind her.

'Daisy says you've got a date,' he said, breaking off to roll his eyes at her appearance. 'Wow. Smart or what. Hope he's worth it.' He threw himself across her bed, grinning mischievously.

'So I'll do, will I?' remarked Frances dryly, aiming a light cloud of hair spray in the direction of the French bun into which she had coiled her hair and pressing her lips together to spread the colour of her lipstick.

'Yeah, I guess.' He frowned, punching all four of the pillows into a back rest and crossing his arms on his chest. 'Look Mum – I wanted to tell you – I think I might have changed my mind about university.'

Frances, inwardly congratulating herself that a sustained and at times taxing policy of non-intervention on the subject should have reaped so spectacular a reward, managed to contain her response to raised eyebrows and a cool smile. 'Have you now?'

'I'm going to take the rest of the year off and reapply to read Politics and History. Daniel says—'

'Daniel?'

'Yeah, he's been brilliant. We've talked about it a lot and—'

'You've seen Daniel?'

Felix's face creased with sudden concern. 'You don't mind, do you?' He had been altogether too preoccupied by the flourishing state of his own private life to give much thought to his mother's. The fact that she had embarked on and then terminated a relationship with a man who was not only agreeable but many years her junior had been judged by him and Sally – in the brief time they had devoted to discussing the matter – as an achievement worthy of considerable respect. 'He came into the shop this week – stayed for quite a while – had me and Libby in stitches—'

'What about?'

Felix broke off, both puzzled and somewhat annoyed at so many interruptions to the flow of what he was trying to say. 'Can't remember now. Anyway he invited me out for a drink and sort of helped me through my options. He says there's no guarantee, but still a good chance of getting on the course. He's going to put in a word. I'm still going to travel – Sal's got a Saturday job in a shoe shop to help save. We'd both really like to go to India but then neither of us are that keen on curry and Sal says she's got a godfather in Canada and we've got those friends in Toronto or somewhere, haven't we? Mum, are you listening?'

'Yes, of course.' Frances sat on the bed, her skirt making a soft shushing sound as it rode up her new tights. 'I really am very pleased that you've decided to try to go back to Sussex. I think it's very brave. And Dad would have liked it too,' she added quietly.

'Yeah, I know.' Felix picked at some dirt under his thumb-nail. 'Everything felt wrong for ages, but now it's all going right again. Funny how stuff works out in the end, isn't it?'

'Some things are just meant to happen, I suppose,' Frances agreed, thinking with a lurch of terror about James Harcourt and wondering whether she could possibly be about to embark on a journey towards something more significant than a one-off encounter.

A few minutes later she was driving slowly on the now familiar cross-country route towards the Dancing Bear, studiously looking away at any signposts to Farley. It had been a typical April day, patches of brilliant sunshine interlaced with squally downpours. With the turning back of the clocks the weekend before, the extra hour of daylight still felt like a gift. Thanks to the rain and the force of the evening sunshine, there was a silvery sheen to the surface of the wet road and a bejewelled look to the fields and trees. Glimpses in the rear-view mirror of a confident, attractively made-up woman whom she hardly recognised, provided a welcome bolster to

Frances's courage. There was a creature she wouldn't mind getting to know, she told herself, feeling suddenly very positive about the encounter ahead of her and letting the ever-present awareness of Daniel slip to the back of her mind. His evident determination to remain on the fringes of her life was a setback, but by no means an insurmountable one. Hard though it was to reproach him for helping Felix, she felt sure that part of his motive was to hurt her, to parade his own independence in the expectation that she could manage nothing so strong in return. Well she could, Frances told herself, gripping the steering wheel and making a firm arc across the intersection where Daniel Groves had catapulted into her life twelve weeks before.

To remove the possibility of making anything like a grand entrance, Frances entered the pub by a side door, getting to the main bar where they had agreed to meet through an obstacle course of pool tables, phone booths and cigarette machines. She saw the rose in his lapel at once, a red one, its petals only half unfurled, surrounded by a pretty sprig of white. That she had forgotten to fill her own buttonhole granted her the luxury of a little time in which to admire the profile, stronger and more handsome than she had dared imagine, lightly tanned, graced with a thick, beautifully groomed head of steely-grey hair.

Relieved and terrified in equal measure, she somehow propelled herself across the room, sticking out her hand in greeting long before it was necessary and clearing her throat several times in preparation for the ordeal of articulating her own name.

Chapter Thirty-Nine

'You will come and visit, won't you?'

'Promise.'

'Perhaps with Felix, that would be a laugh.'

'If Libby ever gives him any time off.'

They were standing in front of the barrier marking the entry though to the departure lounge. Behind Daisy a herd of Japanese tourists was swarming round the security camera's conveyor belt, unloading bags and purse-belts and sets of keys.

'About Marcel—'

'Don't give me the substitute father-figure crap, will you Mum, because if you met him you'd see that it wasn't like that at all.'

Frances smiled.'Believe me, I had thought about it. But no, I was simply going to say that what you feel is all that matters. From what you've told me he sounds delightful. I can't wait to meet him, I really can't.' She gave her daughter a firm hug, breaking off with a laugh to confess, 'You know, ridiculous as it now sounds, I used to worry about the age gap between me and Dad sometimes, thinking that when we reached our dotage even seven years could make a hell of a difference. But of course in the end we didn't get that far so it was irrelevant. Nobody can be sure of anything. Which means you should take happiness where you can.' She smiled, her eyes glassy with an emotion that reached well beyond the poignancy of airports and farewells.

'Thanks Mum,' Daisy grinned. 'So how did it go with this James Harcourt person then? You haven't really said.'

'Fine, it went fine.'

Daisy bent over to gather the handles of her bulging holdall, grunting with the effort of slinging it over her shoulder. 'Good. I thought he sounded nice on the phone.'

'Yes, very nice.'

They were interrupted by the announcement that Daisy's flight was ready for boarding.

'I'll ring when I get there if you like – give you my new phone number.'

'Yes, do that.'

Frances stood watching until the last speck of her daughter's denim jacket was lost from sight in the mêlée of passengers and security guards. By which time the tears were pouring freely down her cheeks. Aware of pitying glances, she hastily retreated to a ladies' toilet to compose herself before seeking solace in a cup of coffee.

She had not lied. The evening had gone well. James Harcourt was everything and more that he had advertised; attractive, kind, intelligent, sensitive. The weathered look of his face suited him, contributing to the impression of a man easy in his own skin. His wife had died of ovarian cancer six years before. He had two sons, one an anaesthetist in London, the other a journalist working in the Far East. That he was well off was in no doubt. He was part of a consortium that ran several luxury hotels, scattered in exotic sites round the world, an occupation that had apparently kept him too busy and itinerant to embark on the lasting relationship for which he longed. It was quite clear that whoever filled such a slot would be thrust into the fortunate position of accompanying him round the world, enjoying five-star meals and being beautified in health spas.

When nerves allowed, Frances had glimpsed a rich sense of humour and the sort of authoritative confidence that had drawn her to Paul. In fact, she reflected, furiously stirring a sachet of brown sugar into her coffee with a white plastic stick, if Paul's spiritual self really had been trying to appoint a natural successor he could not have done a better a job. James too, seemed in little doubt that their destinies had been meant to coincide. As soon as their plates had been cleared away, he had moved the candle and vase of flowers between their wine glasses and gently taken hold of her hand.

'God, I'm glad we did this,' he said, his voice velvety, his eyes pulling her into their rich blue stare.

Frances opened her mouth to say she was glad too, only to realise that making such a statement would suggest sentiments that were quite untrue. A tick-list of attributes was not enough. Looking across the table at the sincere, kind, hopeful, handsome face of her companion she could muster only the mildest interest. Nothing stirred inside, not the remotest fizzle of chemistry or desire, no sense that any yearning of his could ever reflect even the smallest pulse of hers.

The airport coffee was scalding and bitter. Frances sipped gingerly and doggedly, merely for something to do while inwardly she raged at the complicated way in which Daniel Groves had made her life intolerable and her powerlessness to do anything about it.

'Finished with this then?' enquired a young girl in a green uniform traipsing round the tables with a black rubbish sack.

'No . . . oh yes, go on then.' Frances pushed her styrofoam cup, still half-full of coffee across the table.

'Smile, it may never happen,' quipped the girl, taking the cup and tossing it, liquid and all, into her bag.

Frances smiled weakly and set off on the trek back to the short-stay car park. Next to her car an Asian family were piling out of a Discovery vehicle, stacking bags and suitcases across the space behind her rear bumper. They gestured apologetically as she got into the driver's seat, misreading the ill-humour etched into her face as being directed at them.

'No hurry,' she mouthed, slipping the key into the ignition and closing her eyes for the wait. You have a good life, she told the dancing yellow spots before her eyes. You have loved and loving children only making marginal messes of their lives. You have friends and plans and a rosy future. A wealthy hotel proprietor has offered to take you to grand establishments in exotic places. You have a home, money and self-esteem.

When she opened her eyes again the Asian family had gone, leaving a clear passage for her to exit from her space. What she could see of her level of the car park was deserted apart from a lone male figure pushing a trolley towards the lifts. On the trolley was one small suitcase and a large black coat, its sleeves trailing carelessly round the wheels.

Frances sat up, blinking furiously, for a moment seriously imagining that she was experiencing some form of hallucination. The figure was a few yards from the lift doors. A reflex of delight made her heart skip before she remembered herself. Then an extraordinary wave of what felt like anger broke inside, so forcefully that before she could contain herself she was striding towards him, her heels clacking on the concrete floor. On seeing her approach, Daniel merely turned and pressed the lift button.

'Where are you going?' she demanded, which was not what she had planned to say at all.

'Montpelier. Not that it's any business of yours.'

'I've been seeing Daisy off—'

'I know, Felix told me. I was worried I'd bump into you. Christ, is this fucking thing working or not?'

'You seem very angry,' she said quietly, all the wind taken out of her own sails by his evident sullenness and the sudden terror that, instead of missing her, he had, on the contrary, been coping rather well.

'Me? Angry?' He turned to her, pressing his hand against his chest in a show of sarcastic surprise. 'Now why would that be, I wonder?'

'Do you want to go somewhere we could talk prop—?'

'No, I do not. I am going to Montpelier where an acquaintance has offered me a flat for the next three months, where I

can apply myself to my work without any of the petty distrac-
tions of provincial England.' The lift arrived and slid open. As
he pushed his trolley in, one of the wheels caught on the side.
'And where I hope to have an affair with a sultry Frenchwoman, preferably one who's not so terrified of disaster that
she makes it a self-fulfilling certainty and whose loyalties are
the deep-rooted variety.' With these words, Daniel at last
successfully manoeuvred the trolley into the lift. He turned to
await his departure with a stern face and folded arms. What
would have made a wonderfully dramatic exit was however
thwarted by further displays of waywardness from the lift
doors, which, perhaps over-taxed from the recent exertion of
trying to close their jaws round Daniel and his belongings, now
chose to remain obstinately open.

'What's that supposed to mean?'

'Never mind,' he replied grimly, slapping with increasing
desperation at the panel of buttons.

'Anyway you're in the wrong car park,' she snapped, just as
the lift doors finally sealed Daniel's stony face from view.
'Long-term is the other side,' she shouted, turning on her heel
and almost colliding with a bemused looking businessman who
had been hoping to catch the lift before its departure. Giving
the man a defiant what-do-you-think-you're-staring-at glare,
Frances stomped away, managing not to glance backwards
until she reached her car. She was just in time to see the doors
slide open to greet their new passenger, revealing nothing
inside except four walls of silver spray graffiti.

Chapter Forty

———— ❧❧❧ ————

Back home there was a message on her answering machine. Not Daniel in an airport booth, as she initially, wildly hoped, but Hugo Gerard, asking her to call him as soon as possible.

'Nothing to worry about,' he assured her, hearing the breathiness in her voice, 'just to say that the truant's turned up at last.'

'The truant?'

'The missing share certificate – it had somehow got separated and misfiled. I'll pop it in the post, shall I?'

'Oh . . . yes please . . . thank you.'

'There was one other thing – a bit of a long shot. Four tickets to a film première have come our way – some well-to-do, charity-organising friend of Laetitia's. The fact is, we were wondering whether you and Daniel would like to come with us? I'm afraid it's the day after tomorrow, so we need to know soonish.'

'Hugo – how kind – I – thank, you but no. We . . . that is, Daniel and I are not together any more.'

'Oh dear, oh dear. How dreadfully clumsy of me. I am sorry.'

'Please don't be.'

'He seemed such a nice chap too.'

'He was. He is . . . it's complicated . . .'

'Complicated eh? Always a bad sign.' There was a gruff

laugh. 'Still, no loose ends at this end now, anyway.'

Frances put down the phone with a heavy heart. With Daisy gone and Felix at work, the house felt very empty suddenly. She shivered, as an echo of the crazed loneliness of the previous autumn fluttered inside, reminding her that such demons could be tamed but never entirely vanquished.

Feeling too gloomy to draw, she applied herself to the long-postponed challenge of finding the keys to the garden shed together with a manual for the lawnmower. The clean contours left by Joseph over Christmas had long since been lost to a frenzy of spring growth. Weeds were running riot round the flower beds, while the lawn had become a lush metropolis of dandelions and daisies. Daunted by the sheer size of both the lawnmower and the booklet detailing its features, she seized a garden fork and set to work on the biggest of the flower beds, beginning at the back where bindweed had knotted itself round the stems of the roses and a wind-blown cluster of tulips. The recent spell of clement weather had left the soil dry and compact. With each dig Frances had to jump on the metal shoulders of the fork to persuade it to sink into the ground. Soon she had thrown off her anorak and rolled the sleeves of her shirt to her elbows. The roots of the bindweed formed a maze of white stalks under the ground, so deep that she had to probe with her bare hands to find the source of them, sometimes two feet down. The deeper she went the more moist and malleable the soil became. It was a painfully slow, curiously satisfying job, but arduous enough, after forty minutes or so to make the prospect of motoring up and down the lawn seem positively recreational.

Happily, most of the manual turned out to contain information irrelevant to the business of cutting grass. A mere two pages, containing very clear diagrams, covered the necessities. Full canisters of oil and petrol had been left tidily beside the machine, together with a small handwritten reminder saying, 'NB: Easy on the choke!' Recognising Paul's writing, Frances smiled to herself, welcoming the accompanying ripple of affection like an old friend.

In spite of having followed all instructions to the letter, she could not resist letting out a whoop of triumph as the engine rumbled into life. After a cautious start she was soon beetling up and down the lawn, enjoying the breeze in her hot face and the simple pleasure of having mastered a new challenge.

Daniel, appearing unnoticed at the side of the house, paused to admire the spectacle before him: the gentle green slope of the garden, the woman in mud-spattered jeans and wellingtons, ploughing shimmering furrows in the grass, her sunny hair and shirt tails flying, a look of intense, eager concentration on her face. He leant his cheek against the cold stone of the wall, wishing suddenly that he could stretch the moment into an eternity, with everything between them still to play for, with none of the possibility of the rejection he so feared.

He began speaking as soon as she switched off the engine. 'You missed a bit just here,' he said, pointing to a patch of grass near his feet. 'And your lines swerve to the left, but only slightly.' He tipped his head, squinting at the lawn. 'Otherwise, not bad at all.'

'Why aren't you in Montpelier?' Frances retorted, dismounting from the lawnmower with as much dignity as she could muster, inwardly pleased at the archness of her tone, the way it masked her delight.

'There are so many answers to that question, that I hardly know where to start.'

'Go on.' She unscrewed the oil compartment and made a big show of studying the dipstick.

'Well, there was the problem of the car park. Very kind of you to draw my attention to it. Can't think what got into me, going to the wrong one. Then there was the small matter of a ticket, which I had planned on buying at the airport. What with full flights and impossible connections it was going to take me two days to get there. So then I got that sort of fate-is-conspiring-against-me feeling, making me wonder whether I really wanted to go to Montpelier at all.'

'I see.' Frances screwed the oil cap back in place and turned to face him. 'So you thought you'd bother me instead, is that it?'

'Yes, I think that's about it. I know you told me not to, but I've never been very good at doing what I'm told. I also wanted to tell you that I was pretty cut up to hear that you'd found a replacement for me so bloody soon. This Harcroft person, he sounds odious. Felix told me all about it.'

'Ah.' Frances turned away to hide a smile, relieved to have found so simple a reason behind his accusation of disloyalty at the airport.

'What do you mean, "ah"?'

'I mean, Felix doesn't know what he's talking about. I was just rekindling an old flame. A very wealthy flame too, fantastically eligible and utterly charming.' Behind her she was aware of Daniel leaving the sanctuary of the house wall and beginning to make his way across the lawn. 'So finding a sultry Frenchwoman is temporarily off the agenda then, is it?'

'Temporarily.' He walked slowly, sliding his feet through the mounds of freshly cut grass as if needing to feel each step of the way. When he got within a couple of yards of her, he stopped. 'I decided that if you hadn't had a residue of affection for me you wouldn't have shouted at me in the car park. And then I thought that perhaps you could see this Hargreaves person every other Saturday and let me have you in between. Because,' he rammed his hands in his pockets, clenching his fists out of sight, 'forcing myself to keep away from you has not been that much fun.'

'Every other Saturday? That does sound like a very fair offer indeed,' replied Frances thoughtfully. 'There's just one small problem.' She frowned. 'This other man – he's called James Harcourt by the way – I've tried to like him, I really have.' She shook her head to emphasise her exasperation. 'It's really extremely irritating, since he is everything a woman in my position could wish for. A respectable age, intelligent, good-looking—'

'Yeah, you said all that.'

'But the maddening thing is you kept getting in the way. In my head, I mean.'

'And is that so bad?' he whispered, releasing his hands.

'Unspeakable.' She dropped her eyes to the ground, where she watched a small ladybird alight on a single blade of grass that had somehow escaped the blades of the lawnmower.

'Because it's bound to go wrong?'

'Something like that, yes.'

'So let's make it go wrong anyway?'

'Put that way it doesn't sound the most watertight argument in the world.'

'It's about as watertight as deciding never to leave the house in case you get run over by a bus,' he retorted, taking a last step towards her with the intention of pulling her into his arms. The moment was however, rudely broken by a squeal from the direction of the house. They both turned to see Felix and Sally rounding the corner nearest the drive on an old bicycle. Sally was perched on a rusty metal rack behind the main seat, her legs flying, both hands gripping Felix's bony hips.

'Bloody hell,' exclaimed Felix, before a dig in the ribs from his passenger prompted him to swallow his surprise. 'Just wanted to ask – Sally's broken up and Libby's given me the afternoon off and I was wondering if I could borrow the car?'

'Take it,' Frances called back hoarsely, feeling for Daniel's hand and lacing her fingers in his. They stood in silence for a few minutes, listening to the sound of slamming doors and the revving of the car engine. 'I still think it's hopeless, obviously—'

'Obviously.'

'But I'm not going to talk about it any more. Just quietly let it happen.'

'Sounds good to me.'

'For some curious reason the children seem to like you. And from what I can gather you've even been buttering Libby up.'

Daniel widened his eyes in a show of innocence. 'All I did was pop into the shop a couple of times—'

'So Felix said. And I wanted to thank you with regard to him particularly—'

'No need. All I've done is point him in a new direction. And I like Libby too,' he added, 'now that she's stopped eyeing me like some kind of enraged beast.'

Frances giggled.

'She was also kind enough to sell me one of your pictures – the only way I could think of feeling close to you. Smouldering trees and scorched earth – I love it.'

'Silly, I'd have given you one. You had only to ask.' Frances turned to look down towards the countryside rolling away from the bottom edge of the garden. Daniel stepped behind her, slipping his arms loosely round the circle of her waist.

In the distance, the clump of trees encasing the remains of the Brackmans' cottage was already showing gashes of green amongst the tangle of grey and black, closing round the scene as if to bury it. Like fresh skin closing over a wound, mused Frances, the image shimmering before her eyes, bringing a rush of lucidity, a momentary conviction that she could see into the heart of things, understand how pain and love could be accommodated, how hope flowed through the human world as surely as blood to the heart. Remembering Daniel standing behind her, she shuffled backwards, wanting to press away the last inches of space between them.